Secrets after Dark

Secrets after Dark

Marie Higgins

WALNUT SPRINGS PRESS

Walnut Springs Press, LLC
110 South 800 West
Brigham City, Utah 84302
http://walnutspringspress.blogspot.com

Text copyright © 2012 by Marie Higgins
Cover design copyright © 2012 by Walnut Springs Press
Interior design copyright © 2012 by Walnut Springs Press

ISBN: 978-1-59992-805-0

Also by Marie Higgins

Winning Mr. Wrong
Heart of a Hero
Hearts through Time

This book is dedicated to Deborah Hymon, Ginger Simpson, and Melissa Blue. Without these ladies, this story wouldn't have been finished.

Acknowledgements

As always, I want to thank my family for supporting me, even when some of my stories seem so far-fetched and my dreams are unrealistic. Thanks to my fans for encouraging me to write more, which I definitely plan to do. And thanks to Walnut Springs for believing in me—Amy for a great book cover, and Linda for her wonderful friendship as we work together.

Prologue

A place between heaven and hell really did exist.

Morgan Thornton knew this beyond a shadow of a doubt. Hidden among the trees outside Thornton Manor—a place no longer his home but his prison—he gazed upon the smiling, carefree visage of his brother Jonathan, who was no doubt courting yet another comely lass. A stab of longing sliced through Morgan, and he stared wistfully down at his hands. Five fingers, five fingernails, all very human in appearance, but he knew better.

Was he in purgatory? Perhaps. But this purgatory was not so much a place as an altered state of being, a curse with no hope of redemption.

Morgan's thoughts often drifted to the moment he had been cast into this devil's existence—lost his humanity and become a beast to be loathed—a moment he simply called "the lighting." It was a space in time when all of life's purposes and regrets swirled into a single point of clarity, all that could have been no longer wavering in indecision, but perfectly clear, like the sky after a blistering rainstorm. To suddenly realize all he wanted from life, and know it would never again be within his grasp was a fate worse than death. In truth, death would be a blessing.

Instead, his destiny was to wander the earth not quite a man, not truly living, trapped for eternity as an entity to be feared, reviled, and hunted.

One

North Devon, England, 1880

There was no turning back now. Hannah Forester gripped the plush edge of the coach seat and stared anxiously through the window as the landscape whisked past. The village of Exmoor brought shivers to her as it was, but when she spotted Thornton Manor looming ominously ahead, chills rushed up her spine as the whispered secrets of this place whirled through her mind. Hannah's every instinct screamed to turn tail and run, yet her heart told her the answers to her father's murder lay here.

She glanced across the coach at her French maid, Francine. The younger woman sat ramrod straight with her lips pulled tight, her gaze aimed out the window. As Thornton Manor came more fully into view, the color slowly drained from the maid's face.

"We are almost there." Hannah managed a smile, twisting her hands in her lap, a nervous habit she had never managed to break.

Francine took an unsteady breath. "Are you certain this is what you want, mademoiselle? After all, Thornton Manor is haunted."

"Don't tell me you believe all those silly ghost stories."

"Oui. They are true."

Hannah suppressed her own trepidation and took hold of logic. "Do you have firsthand knowledge of this?"

"No, but—"

With a flick of the wrist, Hannah brushed away the maid's concerns. "I think the stories are told to keep people away."

Francine nodded. "It is working rather well, if you ask me. There aren't many women who volunteer to stay there."

"I have no other choice," Hannah grumbled. "According to my father's journals, Morgan Thornton, the oldest brother, was the last man to visit him. I need Mr. Thornton's help if I am to discover the murderer's identity."

"I understand, mademoiselle, but there has to be another way." Francine peeked out the window and shivered.

"When I met Mrs. Thornton in the marketplace the other day," Hannah said, "and she invited me to the manor to meet her brother-in-law, Jonathan, I knew this was the only way I could get inside to ask questions."

"Doesn't Mademoiselle Thornton think you are coming to court Monsieur Jonathan?"

"Yes, and she must continue to believe that." Hannah adjusted the cloak over her velvet traveling gown. "My father was a close friend of Jonathan's brother Morgan. I have tried to contact him, but the letters I have sent over the past year have gone unanswered. The Thorntons are purposely keeping secrets. I feel it. Getting inside the manor is the only way to find what I'm searching for."

"Then I pray you find what you need quickly. I cannot bear the thought of staying longer than a week in such a haun—" Francine glanced warily at Hannah "—*dreary* place."

The vehicle slowed as it neared the house. Hannah leaned against the seat, bunching her fingers in the folds of her dress. If only she felt as brave as the front she presented to her maid.

The vehicle jerked to stop, and her uncle's footman, Jeffries, opened the door. The older servant helped Hannah down, and as soon as her feet touched the pebbled ground, she glanced up at the towering mansion.

"I'm not afraid," she whispered, taking her first step toward the dark, foreboding structure. "And I absolutely do *not* believe in ghosts."

The shuffling of the maid's and footman's footsteps fell into rhythm with Hannah's, but the morning air settling around them was still as death. Autumn leaves of red and brown littered the walkway and crunched beneath Hannah's feet. North Devon's chilly air nipped at her cheeks, and she pulled her bonnet more tightly around her ears. The scent of burning fields hung thick as area landowners prepared for another planting season.

The place where she would find answers lay straight ahead, creeping closer with each step. As she walked from beneath the shade of the trees into the sunlight, the estate rose above her in a crescendo of magnitude. She stopped and sucked in her breath.

The redbrick manor's distinctive turrets and pinnacles rose with breathtaking splendor into the sky. The manor looked out over acres of parklands, gardens, lakes, and woods. Francine's gasp nearly drowned out Hannah's. Two large rock columns cornered the house, and at least three sections sprawled from the structure. Only a few curtains hung open at the many windows; most were hidden behind closed, dark draperies. Hannah's curiosity piqued. What secrets did the draperies conceal?

She stood still for several moments, marveling at the glory before her, yet feeling a strange eeriness about the place. Darkness lurked in the east wing of the manor as if a silent storm cloud resided there.

As she studied each window on that side of the manor, her unease grew. When the curtains of one window moved, she squinted and stepped closer but was too far away to see anything or anyone.

Slowly she continued toward the front door, gooseflesh rising on her arms with each step. The nape of her neck tingled, and she could have sworn she felt someone's eyes upon her. The bitter cold seeped through her cloak as she moved into the house's shadow, and the loss of the sun added to the eerie sensations she felt all the way to her core. Her heartbeat quickened, and her palms grew moist in the folds of her dress.

With her maid following close behind, Hannah hurried to the door and rapped on the hard oak.

Jeffries cleared his throat. "Miss Forester, permit me to do that, if you will."

She turned to him. "I have never been waited on in my life, and I'm not about to start now."

"Nevertheless, you must. Your uncle would insist, I assure you. And what of the Thorntons? They are expecting a gentle-bred lady."

She shrugged. "If they wanted a gentle-bred lady, then why did they ask *me* to come?" Everyone in town knew she was born and raised in America and was therefore practically a heathen. Only after her father earned fame from his novels had they moved to England to enjoy the isolation of the quiet countryside.

At Hannah's comment, the footman's eyes widened and his mouth gaped open, but he remained silent.

She squared her shoulders, focusing on the door as she waited for entrance. Uncle Edward was sure to hear about her less-than-genteel approach. Maybe an apology was in order. She smoothed her dress. "Forgive me, Jeffries. From now on, I shall try to act accordingly."

The door creaked open. A stooped, thin, gray-haired man dressed in butler attire stepped into the light.

Jeffries moved in front of Hannah and faced the other servant, handing them Hannah's card. "Good day, sir. May I present Miss Hannah Forester, daughter of the renowned American novelist Peter Forester. Mr. Roderick Thornton and his wife are expecting her."

The butler nodded and opened the door wider. "Please, come in."

The inside of the manor didn't reflect the dreariness of the outside façade. Instead, the marbled floors gleamed to perfection, and the dark wood furniture held a fresh-waxed glint. The Persian rugs reminded Hannah of those she had loved as a child when her mother was alive. Exquisite chandeliers, silver and gold candlesticks, and colorful tapestries brought a heavy sadness to her chest. This place almost felt like home. After her mother's passing, Hannah's father had lost the will to live and had ignored his debts. The collectors had come and, over time, confiscated everything the family had. Now Hannah lived off a small inheritance from her maternal grandmother.

The butler took Hannah's and Francine's cloaks, bidding them to wait in the hall while he shuffled into the parlor to announce Hannah's arrival.

"Mademoiselle," Francine whispered urgently, "can you feel it? There *are* ghosts here."

"Hush, Francine. You are talking nonsense." Even so, a chill ran down Hannah's arms. She glanced up the winding stairs to the second level. The sun from the window above danced off the crystals of the large chandelier, spattering rainbows across the vast walls. "My father may have written a few ghost stories in his lifetime, but I was never one to believe."

The butler opened the double doors to the drawing room and made a sweeping gesture with his arm. "You may enter, Miss Forester."

She nodded to Francine to remain in the hallway. Hannah stepped across the Persian rug to the black-and-white checkered marble floor of the parlor.

Her gaze immediately fell to the handsome man standing by the fireplace. No more than thirty, if that, he held a brandy snifter and flashed her a dazzling smile. His dark hair gleamed in the sunlight peeking through the window, and his eyes roved the length of her. Hannah gulped, suppressing the urge to squirm. To the gentleman's right sat the lovely woman Hannah had met in Exeter a few weeks ago. Bethany Thornton's red hair was wound fashionably atop her head with wispy tendrils decorating her forehead and ears—the vision of every woman's envy—and she appeared even more refined perched in her winged-back chair than she had during their meeting on the street.

Bethany settled a porcelain teacup on the small table beside her and swept her gaze over Hannah. "My dear Miss Forester, it is so lovely to see you again." She motioned to the man by the fireplace. "May I present my husband, Roderick Thornton."

Hannah gave a nervous curtsy. "A pleasure to make your acquaintance, sir."

Mrs. Thornton motioned to the chair next to her. "Please sit with me, my dear."

Hannah put on her best smile and sat in what she prayed was a delicate, ladylike fashion.

Mrs. Thornton patted Hannah's cold hand. "We shall have such a wonderful time together, you and I. Earlier I told my husband what a joy you were when we met."

Despite herself, Hannah arched her brow. "Indeed? I'm surprised you found me so interesting. We didn't converse for very long that day."

The other woman laughed, the sound forced and dry. "Nonsense. I found our brief conversation extremely delightful."

Hannah smiled uncomfortably in return. "As did I, Mrs. Thornton."

Still lingering near the fire, Mr. Thornton chuckled. "Bethany, you were correct about Miss Forester. She is charming."

For some reason, Mr. Thornton's cheerfulness seemed false, as if he was struggling to greet her in a polite manner. The awkward scene reminded Hannah of her doubts as to why Bethany Thornton would suggest matching her and Jonathan in the first place. According to society's rules Hannah was of a highly unmarriageable age. Being the daughter of an adventurous American novelist allowed her to live a life most men didn't agree with. That, and most didn't want a woman who possessed the ability to think for herself.

Hannah should not be fickle. If her upbringing didn't keep men away, her daring personality would. Her uncle couldn't wait to get her married off and out of his household, so when he had heard about her planned visit to Thornton Manor, it was the first time she could remember that he had looked pleased in her presence.

Apparently, she was not the only person in need of help finding a suitable marriage partner. Why else would the Thorntons seek out suitors for Roderick's younger brother, Jonathan? Why could not he find a bride for himself? Perhaps he was severely deformed or terribly fat. Hannah shuddered inadvertently at the thought. Or did it have something to do with the family's secrets? Gossip regarding the Thorntons' past was filled with dark shadows and unanswered questions, and Hannah's inquisitive mind could not put them to rest. Neither could she ignore the intrigue surrounding her father's death.

Where was Morgan Thornton, anyway? She could hardly blurt out the question, seeing as she had come to the manor to court his brother. Surely Morgan would make an appearance before long. According to her father, the oldest brother served as master of the house and was a very fine man indeed.

"How was your journey, my dear?" Roderick Thornton's voice brought her out of her thoughts. She startled. He had moved across the room to stand directly in front of her.

"Splendid." She shifted back in her chair. "I was surprised at how far away your estate is from Exeter. Quite a bumpy ride, I'll admit."

"Yes, that's the inconvenience of living so far from civilization," Bethany said. "Would you like to see your room now?"

Hannah smiled. "Do you not want me to meet Mr. Jonathan first?"

"In due time, my dear." Roderick helped her stand, then hooked her hand over his arm and pressed it against his side. "My brother is still out riding and probably won't return for several more hours. I will have Horace take you to Mrs. White, who will show you to your room."

"Before I go, may I ask a question?"

"But of course, my dear."

"Is there a chance I could meet Mr. Morgan?"

Her host's eyes widened, and his wife sucked in a quick breath.

Their reaction brought a flush to Hannah's cheeks. "I—I'm sorry. Is something wrong?"

"Oh, my dear Miss Forester," Roderick said. "I thought you knew, but my brother died in a house fire a little over a year ago."

Her heart sank with such force that she thought she might faint. Morgan Thornton could not be dead, for he alone held the answers she so desperately sought. Tears stung her eyes at the unwelcoming news and of the thought of the agony Mr.

Thornton must have suffered. No wonder he had never answered her letters.

She swallowed hard. "Please forgive me for speaking of such a painful matter. I'm truly sorry for your loss."

"Tell me, Miss Forester." Bethany scooted to the edge of her chair, eyes bright with curiosity. "How did you know Morgan?"

"I didn't know him, I'm afraid. My father knew him, and spoke so highly of Morgan that I had hoped to meet him." She shifted her gaze from Bethany to Roderick. "Again, I apologize for mentioning your late brother."

Roderick patted the hand still hooked over his arm. "Quite all right, my dear Miss Forester, and may I offer my condolences for your own loss."

She nodded and looked away. The anguish that must be painted on her face was real, but hardly for the reason the Thorntons would suspect. Hannah sucked in a deep breath, pondering her predicament. With or without Morgan she had a mystery to solve. She could not leave. Someone besides Morgan had to know about her father. "Did you know my father, Mr. Thornton?"

"By reputation only," he replied without looking at her. "Horace?" Roderick motioned to the butler.

"Yes, sir?"

"Kindly show Miss Forester and her maid to their quarters. See to it their needs are seen to with the utmost haste."

"As you wish." Horace looked at Hannah. "Miss, would you follow me, please?"

Francine walked beside her mistress, the maid's face a touch pinker than earlier. As the girl glanced around the hall, her eyes grew wide.

"Beautiful, isn't it?" Hannah whispered.

Francine smiled. "Extremely lovely. I have never seen anything so grand."

A woman with a curvy figure bustled in from one of the side rooms, her smile stretching from ear to ear. She wore the crisp gray dress and white apron of a housekeeper. Perhaps in her late forties, the woman still held a bit of her youth despite the silver streaks in her dark hair.

"Good morning." The woman bobbed in a curtsy. "I'm Mrs. White, the housekeeper."

Hannah nodded. "Good day."

"Miss Forester, please follow me and I will show you and your maid to your quarters."

Mrs. White led them down the long corridor and stopped in front of a closed door, where she withdrew a thick set of keys from her apron pocket and opened the door. "If you need anything or have a problem, please don't hesitate to ask me." She motioned up the hall. "I will show your maid to the attic dormitory where the other servants reside."

"Oh, no!" Hannah touched the housekeeper's arm. "I must have Francine in the room next to me, if at all possible."

The older servant's eyes clouded, her expression unreadable for several tense moments. Finally she gave a curt nod. "As you wish. The room next door is vacant."

Hannah smiled to ease the sudden tension. "Thank you."

Mrs. White rushed in and opened the green velvet curtains. Sunlight spilled into the room, and Hannah squinted against the sudden brightness.

Such beautiful chambers—much better than her room in her uncle's little cottage. The bed reminded her of the one she had as a child, nearly fit for a queen, with many pillows and with white silk hangings around the posts. An armoire and two chests of drawers stood along the walls. A small sofa and reading table sat next to the largest window, and another door opened into a private bathing chamber.

Mrs. White turned from the last window. "You may rest for a few hours, but I'm quite certain Master Roderick and his wife would enjoy your company for tea this afternoon. I will fetch you then. Mistress Bethany is hoping Mr. Jonathan will also be there."

Hannah ran her hand over the luxurious bed covering. "I look forward to meeting him."

Mrs. White released a heavy sigh and shuffled nervously, clasping and unclasping her hands.

Hannah's brow furrowed. "Is something wrong?"

Mrs. White smiled. "The whole household has been aflutter, hoping you and Mr. Jonathan will make a fine match, but . . ."

"But what?"

Mrs. White took a step closer. "There is something I must tell you," she said quietly, her dull brown eyes narrow with warning. "Neither you nor your maid are allowed in the East Wing. Under no circumstances should you wander to that side of the manor. If you are found there, Mistress Bethany will speedily dispatch you home. Do you understand, Miss Forester?"

Hannah's jaw fell. The Thorntons *were* hiding something. Determination to find out what it was surged like fire in her veins—she was her father's daughter after all. She would search the house from top to bottom after everyone retired.

Immediately, she shook such thoughts from her mind. Sneaking around after dark would only give Bethany Thornton a reason to dismiss her before she found out what happened to her father.

Hannah nodded at the housekeeper. "I understand perfectly." She tapped her chin with a finger. "But I fear curiosity is getting the better of me, and I can't help but wonder what is in the East Wing."

"What I have told you is the rule of the house, and it was set by the master himself. He is most adamant about people going there. I, for one, would like to keep my position, which is why I don't break the rules." The servant slid closer. "It is rumored there is a ghost haunting that part of the manor. A few months back a maid ventured into the East Wing and—" Mrs. White's gaze flickered between Hannah and Francine "—disappeared."

Francine gasped and covered her mouth, muttering something in French.

Hannah fought the urge to giggle. "Thank you for the warning. I will be certain not to wander that way." She folded her hands. "But why would a ghost haunt the East Wing?"

"With good reason," Mrs. White said. "The late master of Thornton Manor, the eldest brother, Morgan, perished in a fire there. Some believe his spirit still remains."

Hannah's breath caught as a tingle traveled down her neck. Mrs. White's wide eyes and the excitement in her voice led Hannah to assume the middle-aged woman was one of the believers.

Impossible. "What keeps him here?" she asked.

"His music."

Hannah arched an eyebrow. "Music?"

"Yes. Sometimes late at night you can hear him playing the organ, yet there isn't an organ in any of the rooms." Mrs. White shook her head, her salt-and-pepper bun bobbing. "The poor man died so young and before he finished any of his requiems."

"What age was he when he passed on?"

"He had not reached his thirty-second year, I'm afraid."

"Oh, that's unfortunate." Thoughts of her own mother's untimely demise floated through Hannah's head. Her mother had died giving birth to Hannah's younger brother, who had also died that day.

Mrs. White hurried to the door. "I have a few errands to run now. You are free to roam about the estate at your leisure." She paused and leaned closer. "Except for the East Wing."

"I will. Thank you again for the warning."

As the older woman swept out the door, Hannah had the impression Mrs. White was always in a rush. Hannah rubbed her forehead. *Very strange.*

Francine closed the door, leaned against it, and released a heavy sigh. "Oh, my. Do you really think—"

"No, I don't," Hannah said firmly. "Francine, you can't possibly believe in ghosts."

"Why, yes, I do.

"Well, I don't, but for some reason, the Thorntons don't want anyone going to the East Wing."

"Perhaps." Francine wrung her hands against her middle. "Do you want me to unpack for you now?"

"No. I would like to lie down before Mr. Jonathan returns from riding. I have much on my mind, and I need some peace and quiet."

"As you wish, mademoiselle." Francine spun on her heels and opened the door. "I will be in the next room if you need me."

Hannah walked to the bed and sat. She untied the ribbon below her chin, loosened her bonnet, and removed it. When her head touched the pillow, her mind swam with anticipation, just as she had expected. Resting was out of the question now.

Sighing, she pushed off the bed. Then she left the room and wandered slowly up the hallway toward the stairs. She admired the paintings lining the walls. Some were portraits, but most were scenes of nature, of animals, even biblical scenes and heaven. Hannah stopped many times to gaze upon the magnificence of the works. The paintings were unsigned, but the artist's talent was manifest in every brushstroke.

When she reached the third floor, she peeked in every room with an unlocked door. She casually glanced inside, trying not to appear obvious in her search. She found a library, a study, and another parlor. Then, finding a room with a pianoforte, she paused. Memories from years past washed over her like waves on an unsettled sea. Images of her father standing beside the pianoforte as she played a simple children's song filled her head.

She walked closer to the instrument. Brushing her fingers across the keys, she closed her eyes, wishing she remembered how to play. If only she could, her childhood memories would come to life again. Her world had been so carefree back then.

In less than an hour, Hannah finished her tour of the main and west wings of the manor. Then, trying not to act as if she had walked toward the East Wing on purpose, she studied each door, searching for the entrance to the forbidden part of the manor. Unable to locate it, she guessed she had passed it along the way.

Wondering if one might only enter the East Wing from the exterior of the mansion, Hannah wandered outside, keeping close to the edge of the house. The East Wing loomed before her, as gloomy as when she first arrived. She stopped and glanced up toward the window where she had seen a movement earlier.

The curtains moved again, and she sucked in her breath. Indeed, someone was there.

🌺

Hannah Forester must leave this place—now.

He had heard she would arrive today. Foolish woman. She had no idea what her life would be like as Mrs. Jonathan Thornton.

Morgan Thornton dropped the heavy curtain into place and stepped away from the window. He could not let her or anyone else see him. It was far safer for all if he was never seen again. Dead. A ghost.

By now, his brother's guest would know the rumors. Roderick and his wife had the servants scared out of their skin to even look toward the East Wing. It was just as well. If the rumors didn't frighten them, the truth would.

Morgan sank into a soft chair and relaxed his head against the back. He closed his eyes and drew slow breaths. Unable to stand the solitude of his banishment from the rest of the world, he had turned to music, and it was his only companion. If not for the songs he wrote, his life would have little meaning.

A vision of Hannah Forester, ethereal and lovely, floated before his mind's eye. He would love to make her acquaintance. Peter Forester had spoken so often of her that Morgan felt he knew the girl already. As usual, Hannah had been away when Morgan had visited her father for the last time, and Peter had seemed so upset at the poor timing that Morgan wondered if his friend had been trying to arrange a courtship.

With a sigh, he pushed his fingers through his wavy black hair. Once in a while he gave into temptation and dreamed of a different life. A life without worries, pain, or grueling nightmares branded in reality. A life with a woman to love . . .

Morgan turned toward the low-burning fire. Women like Hannah Forester could not be permitted to stay at the manor. She was in jeopardy because of her beauty. She was exactly the sort of woman he found himself drawn to. If a meeting had in fact occurred while her father still lived, Morgan's mentor most certainly would have seen his wish come to fruition.

But why would Miss Forester be matched with Morgan's younger brother, Jonathan? That young pup didn't have much to offer a woman like Miss Forester, other than his gentle temperament and handsome face. He was much too gullible and had not a shred of ambition, and from what Morgan knew of Miss Forester, she had inherited a fair amount of her father's drive and energetic nature.

Morgan rose from his chair and walked into the next room to his bed. Staying awake all night let him live in an existence without complications, since everyone else in the manor was asleep. The only time he rested was during the day. He needed plenty of sleep to finish composing the requiems he had been working on for a fortnight.

He shrugged out of his robe and laid the rich burgundy velvet across the end of the bed before climbing between the sheets. His eyes drifted closed, strains of music running through his mind until a lovely visage interrupted his thoughts.

Hannah Forester. The woman's beauty had captured his attention from the moment she had climbed down from her carriage. Even now he could see the chestnut curls dangling beneath her bonnet, surrounding a heart-shaped face and alert expression. Because he had loved and admired her father, Morgan knew he must protect Hannah. He must warn her away from this place. Her life depended on it.

With a grumble, he rolled over and slammed his fist into the pillow. Every aspect of the manor had changed since he had been forced to step down as master. A year ago, he was preparing to kick Roderick and Bethany out on their noses. His brother had been stealing from the coffers, and Morgan would not have any more of Roddy's deceitful ways. Morgan had also planned to dismiss some of the manor's staff at that time.

Morgan asked his secretary to write the dismissal letters. After the secretary left, *that* woman came to see Morgan. She had overheard him dictating the letters and knew he was going to dismiss her. She tried everything to get him to change his mind, even offering her affections, and when he didn't relent . . .

He took a deep breath and rubbed the ache growing in his forehead. Memories from what happened that day brought bile to his throat and made his stomach twist in horror. That was the day he learned of many more secrets that were kept inside these walls. And now he would never be completely human again.

Having Miss Forester on his mind would be disruptive, but more importantly living under his brother's roof would put her very life in peril, just as with all the women who came here to be courted by Jonathan.

To save her life, Hannah Forester must leave. There was no other way. Morgan could not have strangers coming to ask questions. He could not let them discover that something much more dangerous than a ghost haunted Thornton Manor.

Two

Hannah's thudding heart threatened to snap the ties binding her corset as she stepped into the parlor to meet Jonathan Thornton. She had to make a good impression. She dared not give him reason to turn her away from the manor before she had a chance to ask questions.

Pressing her hand to her ribs, she took a deep breath, attempting to slow her heart's wild rhythm. Jonathan stood by the hearth with one ankle crossed over the other and with his shoulder against the smooth gray stones. His waistcoat fit snug across the arms, and his white shirt and blue cravat emphasized his tan skin. His muscular frame was the opposite of what she had imagined. He lifted his gaze from the slow burning fire and looked her way.

He was handsome—devilishly so. Sandy brown hair waved back from his forehead, and when he grinned, his blue eyes sparkled. He pulled away from the hearth and straightened, his smile stretching wider the longer his gaze swept over her.

Physically, there appeared to be nothing wrong with him. A man of his quality could easily find a wife. So why was his sister-in-law matchmaking? Surely, Hannah was not the first young woman to be paraded before him. When she left, another would certainly arrive to take her place.

Bethany Thornton sat in the same chair she had occupied earlier, but Roderick was absent. "Miss Forester, may I introduce my husband's younger brother, Jonathan Thornton."

Jonathan strolled closer. "What a pleasure it is to finally meet you, Miss Forester."

Hannah smiled. "I appreciate your kind invitation to visit."

Bethany flicked a limp wrist at her brother-in-law. "Darling, when I met Miss Forester, I knew she would be perfect for you."

Hannah's throat suddenly went dry, but she managed to keep her composure. "Thank you. Please, Mrs. Thornton, just call me Hannah. And I thank you for thinking I'm perfect, but I must let you know I'm far from it."

"I happen to agree with my sister-in-law." Jonathan offered Hannah his elbow. She laid her hand on his gray coat sleeve, and he led her to the sofa and then sat beside her.

Up this close, she realized how his blue eyes danced with mischief. He was going to be a hard man to resist.

"Forgive me for being so straightforward, Miss Forester," Jonathan said, "but I have heard you are an adventurous woman. Is this so?"

She grinned and glanced at Bethany, knowing the other woman had been the one to tell him. Then again, everyone in Devonshire must have heard about Hannah's life. The way she lived was not a secret, and it didn't matter who knew. She was not ashamed of the headstrong woman she had become.

Meeting Jonathan's gaze, she nodded. "I enjoy experiencing the fullness of life."

Both Jonathan and Bethany laughed. Bethany lifted her teacup, took a sip, and then lowered the delicate china to the matching saucer. "Ah, to be young again."

Hannah stifled a laugh. Most women her age were married and had children by now. In a couple years, she would be an old maid by society's standards.

"I would not say I was young, Mrs. Thornton," she said. "However, I don't think I will ever allow life's problems to discourage me. I always search for those things uplifting to my soul. After all, that's the only way one can stay youthful in her heart."

Bethany nodded. "Well said."

Jonathan tapped Hannah's arm. "Please tell me everything about yourself. I find your spirited personality extremely refreshing."

"Not many people will confess that, Mr. Thornton. In fact, my boldness shocks most everyone I meet."

He shook his head. "I'm not like most everyone you meet, as I hope you will eventually discover."

His warm smile and charm relaxed her. She studied him closer, hoping something in his appearance would help her understand why his sister-in-law had taken charge of finding him a wife. He could be a gambler or a womanizer, but that didn't stop other wealthy men from marrying.

When he spoke, she watched his actions and facial expressions. Her father had taught her how to read people. So far, though, nothing seemed out of the ordinary. He was very well mannered, and Hannah didn't perceive him as a man with great vices.

"Miss Forester," Jonathan said suddenly. "would you enjoy an afternoon ride? I would be honored to escort you around the estate today."

"Certainly. I would enjoy an outing very much."

Bethany wagged her finger at him. "Not before we take our midday meal, I hope."

Jonathan stood, walked to his sister-in-law, and patted her shoulder. Admiration flickered in his eyes when he looked down at her. "Of course not, dear Beth. I don't want to ruin your plans."

Hannah found Bethany and Jonathan's mutual respect—their family devotion—refreshing. Hannah had missed having a mother to bring her up, and watching Bethany and Jonathan brought back that yearning, especially now that her own father was gone.

Jonathan crossed to Hannah and held out his elbow. "In the meantime, would you like to take a stroll outside? I fear I'm a restless man and cannot stay cooped up for very long sipping tea like my sister-in-law."

Hannah stood and placed her hand on his arm. "Ah, there is something we have in common. I don't like to sit idle either, and would very much enjoy a walk."

Jonathan instructed the butler to fetch Hannah's wrap, and soon she and Jonathan strolled outside. The wind had calmed since her arrival, and the sun's rays poured down on them, taking the chill from her cheeks.

A movement to her right drew her attention. Not far down the slope from the house, Roderick Thornton and a young woman stood close together behind a tree. Jonathan didn't glance their way, but from the leery grin on Roderick's face and the giggle of the servant girl, Hannah knew she was witnessing a romantic tryst. It looked as if other secrets existed in Thornton Manor.

Hannah jerked her attention to the path in front of her. Hopefully, the master of the house had not seen her watching.

"Mr. Thornton, tell me about the manor," she started the conversation, trying to get her mind off Roderick and the maid.

Jonathan slid his hand over hers and squeezed. "My great-great-grandfather was a duke and lived in Essex. He had a grand estate and stables. As lads, my father and uncle came upon this land, and my father knew this was where he wanted to live. When he had Thornton Manor built, he constructed it to resemble my grandfather's house." He pointed toward a body of water beyond the garden wall and nodded. "My father wanted it to face the small island."

"Slumbering Giant?"

"Yes."

Hannah chuckled. "Whoever created that name for the island was probably heavily into his cups."

Jonathan stopped and looked down at her, his clear blue eyes boring into her. "The name was taken from the legend."

"Well, the storyteller who created the old legend was as talented as my father."

"You don't believe the story?"

"Of course not. Do you?"

"Not about a witch turning it into a slumbering giant, but I believe there are caves of silver and gold hidden on the island."

Hannah shook her head. "For years, people have tried to find the treasure and failed. My father researched the story before he wrote a novel about it. Every bit of information he gathered about the treasure suggested it was a myth."

Jonathan shrugged. "Call me foolish, but I would like to believe it is there, hidden on the island, and that a goddess of love and beauty will remove the island's curse so that the treasure might be discovered."

Hannah was taken aback at Jonathan's naiveté, his apparent gullibility. Yet men with worse faults married and raised families. She would not judge him until she knew him better.

When they resumed their stroll, the wind teased his hair, lifting it off his collar. The smile remained on his face, as did the excitement dancing in his eyes.

"Mr. Thornton . . ." She paused. Did she dare speak what was on her mind?

"Please, call me Jonathan. When you call me Mr. Thornton, it sounds like you are talking to my brother, Roderick."

"As you wish, and you may call me Hannah."

Jonathan smiled wide. "I would love to."

"So, Jonathan, tell me about the rumors I have heard, and of the East Wing Ghost. What sort of old wives' tale is this?"

He glanced down at her with wide eyes. "You believe it to be a mere tale?"

"Certainly. I don't believe in ghosts."

He shook his head and tightened the grip on her hand. "Ah, my dear. You would do well to believe the rumors."

Laughing, she rolled her eyes. "You can't tell me there is a ghost living in your manor."

"But there is, Hannah. He does not come out every night. But when the moon is full and there is a chill in the air, he is there."

She stopped and tilted her head, gazing up at him. "Who is he—your brother? The one who died in the fire?"

"Yes. Morgan."

"And you can see him?"

"Oh, no. He does not make himself known. But you can feel him there. You can hear him. Every so often you will hear him playing the organ." Jonathan shrugged. "And we don't have an organ. It, too, burned in the fire."

"So I'm told," Hannah muttered. She pulled her hand away and folded her arms. "Jonathan, it is hard to believe a ghost plays an invisible organ at night."

"You don't understand. My brother stays in the East Wing, hoping to become mortal someday. He loves music. We must not disrupt the artist while he is composing."

Hannah wondered why anyone would believe such nonsense. Perhaps Jonathan was not single-minded but completely out of his mind.

"Come." He hooked his arm around her elbow and turned her back toward the house. "The wind is picking up, and I fear you will be chilled to the bone. I would hate to have my brother box my ears for not caring for your tender sensibilities."

Tender sensibilities, my eye, Hannah thought. He merely wanted a reason to change the subject.

※⬝⟡⟲

Night had fallen over the household, and due to the day's excitement, Hannah was exhausted. Her strength began to ebb almost as soon as she stepped into her room and closed the door. Plans had not gone according to Jonathan's schedule. The weather had turned chilly, so he had called off the ride around the estate. Roderick and Bethany occupied her time after that. Mostly Roderick.

Hannah didn't know what bothered her about that man, other than the glaring fact that he was probably being unfaithful to his wife. His gaze always followed Hannah, and it seemed he kept rather close to her whenever they were in the same room. Bethany and Jonathan must have thought Roderick's behavior normal, because they had not commented on it.

A knock on her bedroom door made Hannah jump. "Who is it?"

"Francine."

Hannah released a pent-up breath. "Come in."

Her maid bustled in. "I'm here to get you ready for bed."

Eager to crawl between the blankets, Hannah hurriedly undressed. While Francine brushed Hannah's hair, the maid babbled about the friends she had made among the Thorntons' staff.

"Although they are very kind, I fear they are keeping secrets," the maid said.

Hannah yawned. "What secrets, do you think?"

"Well, there was no mention of the East Wing Ghost, but instead they talked about the cursed white wolf that roams the land."

Hannah met her maid's gaze in the vanity mirror. "A white wolf? Are you certain they didn't mean wild dogs?"

"No dogs, Miss Hannah. They definitely said white wolf. And they said he was cursed."

"Hmm, I wonder if the wolf and the ghost share tea every evening. Do they meet on the cursed island, as well?"

"Your sarcasm surprises me, mademoiselle."

Hannah laughed. "Forgive me. I am tired."

"I believe the servants," Francine continued. "They say every full moon the white wolf comes out of hiding and feeds upon the innocent."

"Feeds upon the innocent? What does that mean? How does the wolf know if a person is innocent or not? Does he ask them before he kills and eats them?"

"It is rumored that the wolf only kills pure, chaste women."

"Once again, I wonder how the wolf knows they are chaste." Hannah rubbed her forehead. "Oh, why must you believe these stories? Have you not stopped to think the others are telling you this to frighten you?"

"Oui." Francine stopped the brush in mid-stroke and leaned closer to Hannah's ear. "Why, and for what purpose? Why would they wish to scare us away?"

"Why, indeed." Hannah tapped her finger on her chin. "I think they create these stories to cover the truth."

"Which is?"

Secrets after Dark

"I don't know, but I will find out."

"How?"

Hannah shrugged. "That's a good question, one I will ponder tomorrow." She exhaled slowly. "Because tonight I plan to rest."

Francine placed the brush on the vanity table and turned toward the door. "I shall be in my room if you need me."

"Good night, Francine. Please lock your door." Hannah tried not to grin. "With a musical ghost and a roaming wolf who seduces virgins, I'm quite certain you will need as much protection as you can get."

Francine shook her head and hurried out of the room. Hannah chuckled as she pulled back the blankets and slipped between the sheets. After switching off the lamp, she thumped her fist into the pillow and curled on her side. What she needed was a couple hours' sleep if she intended to search the house tonight. Although she did not believe the ghost stories, something was not quite right in the manor.

Just as Hannah began drifting off to sleep, the floor creaked. She snapped her eyes open to cloaking darkness and pulled the sheet up to her neck. A soft shuffling echoed in the room against the far wall. Her heart slammed against her ribs, and her breathing became ragged. Straining, she cocked her head toward the noise but heard nothing more. She squeezed her eyes shut, knowing she should pull on her wrapper and investigate.

She rolled in bed and peered toward the window. The moonlight peeked through the slit in the curtains, but it did little to brighten the room.

Her forehead pounded in a quick rhythm as she strained to listen. Then she breathed a deep sigh, tried to relax, and once more closed her eyes. Old homes settled and groaned, and certainly the manor was no different.

Just when she had convinced herself no one was there, the floor creaked again, and she heard heavy breathing. Someone was in her room! But how? Her gaze darted to the closed door. Nobody had entered or she would have heard.

As her eyes adjusted to the darkness, a tall shadow appeared at the foot of her bed. The person—a man, she assumed, from the height and the wide shoulders—wore a cape with a hood pulled low. Darkness hid the portion of his face not covered by the hood. Was this the ghost Mrs. White spoke of?

Hannah wanted to scream, but fear kept her mute, so she lay still and prayed he would disappear.

The stranger's breathing grew heavier, as did her own. Finally finding the courage to scream, she opened her mouth, but the caped figure held up his hand and pointed at her.

"You are in danger here. You must leave."

❦❧

Morgan clutched his cloak tightly around him. Although Hannah's room was dark, he always hid his face to protect his very existence.

Night and darkness were his sanctuaries. While the household slept, he wandered the halls and grounds at his own leisure. Never did he leave without his cloak in case someone spotted him. Thankfully, the fools working for his family believed in the East Wing Ghost.

Earlier, when Morgan awoke from his deep sleep, Jonathan's beautiful visitor had popped into his mind. When he had first laid eyes on her this morning, his heartbeat had knocked against his chest, and the walls built up around his heart had begun to crumble. Fear for her life hung heavy on his conscience. He needed to warn her.

"Danger awaits you here. Do not stay another night."

He stepped toward the door to leave, but the woman sprang upright in bed.

"Wait!" She reached out her hand toward him before withdrawing it. "Who—who—are you?" Her voice shook.

"Who I am is not your concern." He kept his voice low.

"It is when you have served me with a warning."

He shook his head. Brave woman. That could be a dangerous thing to have living under Roderick's roof. Mischief surrounded women like Miss Forester, and that kind also needed protection. "Just know I want to see you safe, which is why you must leave."

"Do—do I know you?"

He would not tell her he knew her father, as it would only complicate matters. "No."

"Then why—"

"Please, Miss Forester. There is no time to answer your questions. Heed my warning. You are not safe in this house." He stepped to the door and hurried out, his cloak whipping around him.

At the end of the hall, he turned the corner and plastered himself against the wall. He held his breath and listened for footsteps. She had dared speak to him without knowing his identity, so she may try to follow him. That he could not allow.

He waited a few more minutes, his chest rising and falling with each hurried breath. Thankfully, he did not hear the sound of bare feet echoing on the wood floor. He must have frightened the woman enough to keep her in bed.

He turned and made his way toward his chambers. As he neared one of the servant's rooms, a giggle stopped him in his tracks.

Curses! He needed to hide, and quickly. The linen closet was his nearest choice. He had barely shut himself inside when the door to the servant's quarters opened. Shelves dug into Morgan's back and shoulders, so he shifted his position carefully.

The woman's giggling grew louder, as did a man's deep chuckle. "Promise you will return tomorrow night," the sultry female voice said.

"I promise, my dear Sarah."

Morgan cracked the door and peeked outside. In the darkened hallway stood two figures, one of them very familiar.

Clenching his jaw, he shook his head. Roderick was at it again. When would the fool learn not to carry on with the hired help? Did the man not realize what Bethany would do if she discovered his improprieties?

Roderick yanked Sarah into his arms and kissed her soundly. She let out a heavy sigh and smiled.

Roderick withdrew. "Pleasant dreams, my sweet."

She released a throaty purr and waggled her fingers. "You have already made them come true." She stepped back inside her room and pulled the door closed.

Roderick tightened his robe around his waist before he hurried down the hallway toward his own bedchambers.

Morgan shook his head. It appears Sarah was playing her old games with Roderick. Was she trying to blackmail his brother, just as she had tried with Morgan a year ago? Foolish woman. Yet women like that were dangerous. He knew that firsthand. He also knew his brother played games with Anne, the cook's helper. Earlier today while watching Hannah and Jonathan take a stroll outside, Morgan had witnessed Roderick taking Anne out behind the stables for a moment of private intimacy.

Once silence filled the corridor, Morgan left the linen closet and rushed to his private domain. When he secured the door behind him, he breathed a relieved sigh. Everything had gone well tonight—so far.

He had done his good deed for the day. Hopefully, the pretty Miss Forester would heed his warning.

He yanked off his cloak and hung it on the hook by the door. Although Roderick had almost caught him, Morgan's visit to Miss Forester's room had been necessary. Now he could relax in the knowledge he might have saved another innocent girl from his brother's selfish clutches, and from a possible early death.

Maybe now he could concentrate on his newest piece of music. The ballad had been forming in his mind for quite a while. For some reason, writing it on paper had been harder than he had first thought.

He craned his neck as he loosened his cravat and yanked it off. He shrugged off his waistcoat and replaced it with a velvet jacket. The reason for him to dress up to impress no longer existed, but he wanted to be part of the living. Since the day of his change—the lighting—he had not felt truly alive.

That day could have been yesterday, he remembered it so well. Back then he'd had his future mapped out. Wealth had finally begun to grow in his coffers and made him a very rich man. Women admired him, but he was not ready for a permanent relationship. Now he realized his mistake for being so careless with their feelings.

That bleak day he had met with his secretary in the study to write some dismissal letters to the staff. Just as Morgan had sent him away, a creak from the floor pulled his attention to the corner by the window. There stood a woman, wearing a nearly transparent gown.

"How did you get in my study?" he had asked sharply.

She shrugged. "I have been here for a while. I wanted to give you a proper welcome home, but I realized it is not the ideal time." She glanced toward the door before meeting his stare again. "Then again, perhaps I came at the perfect time."

"You heard what I dictated to my secretary?"

"Every word. You want to get rid of me and the others."

Blowing out an irritated sigh, he moved toward his desk. "Indeed. Since you heard everything, I will not have to repeat myself, will I?"

She blocked his path and grasped his arms. "I thought you loved me."

"Good heavens, woman. You can't be serious." He shook his head and laughed. "Please leave now."

Her eyes narrowed. "I believe you are not in your right mind. I'm quite certain your rudeness comes from being overly fatigued from your trip."

Morgan arched a brow. "I have never been more clear in my thinking than I am at this moment."

Her long, thick eyelashes batted in a quick rhythm, and her lips formed a pout. "You have no heart, Morgan. You are cold and unforgiving." She blinked back tears. "Not too long ago I fancied myself in love with you. It saddens me to see you have changed into a madman."

"There again, you are wrong. *You* are the person who is mad." He walked around her and sat.

Leaning her hands on the desk, she dropped her face close to his. Her gaze stayed on his mouth as if she wanted to kiss him. He would not give her the chance. He had made the mistake once before and charmed her while intoxicated, but he had vowed he had never touch her again.

She pouted once more. "You think to play with my heart, my feelings, and then leave me to the wolves as scraps?"

"From the beginning you knew what kind of a man I was. Do not make the mistake of thinking you can change me."

Tears brimmed on her lashes and her bottom lip quivered, yet Morgan knew it was a mere performance. When he didn't respond to her antics, she was transformed into an altogether different creature. Her fingernails elongated into eagle-like talons. She laughed and her lips curled in an evil twist, almost as if she would spew venom at him at any second.

A deep, scratchy chant rose from her throat, words that held no meaning. Strong winds blew against him, yet the windows remained closed. Startled, he jumped out of his chair and swung his gaze around him.

Cool air swirled all around, and though it had been a bright, sunny day, the light shining through the white lace curtains darkened to an ominous cloud of trepidation. The only illumination came from the wicked red glow of her eyes.

Chills raced up his spine. What kind of monster was she? Or was he in a nightmare and had not yet awoken?

"Who—or what—are you?"

Ignoring his question, she pointed at him. Her long fingernail took on jagged edges. "This is the last time I let you crush my heart, Morgan Thornton." Her voice turned deep and unsettling. "You know not what I can do."

He gulped the terror lodged in his throat and scanned the room for a way out, away from this madwoman. This could not possibly be happening. Yet everything was very real.

"You know I have never held those feelings for you." He took a step back and bumped into his chair, knocking it over.

Her gaze narrowed and she shook her head. "You led me to believe you did, so if I can't have you, *nobody* will."

As she stepped closer, he pulled out one of the desk drawers. He wrapped his fingers around the pistol and pointed it at her. Laughing, she threw up her hands, and a gust of wind came from out of nowhere, knocking the weapon out of his grasp and pushing it across the floor, where it stopped against the wall. His heart pounded in a frantic rhythm. *What the devil?*

"Morgan Thornton, before I am finished with you, you will wish you were dead. I curse you from this day forward. Every time you look with passion at another woman, you shall walk the earth like a beast. When the moon is high, you shall kill for food like an animal, and only *I* can control you. Only *I* can break the spell. If I die, you die a cursed man."

"You are talking nonsense. You can't be serious."

"I am deadly serious."

The hammer of his heart increased. Panicked, he glanced around the room again, looking for a way out.

"Your destiny lies with the wolves, dear Morgan." She stretched her hands in front of her, threw back her head, and cackled.

Lightning flashed through the room. A strong wind knocked him to his knees. His limbs weakened, and then his tongue swelled, keeping him from crying out.

Heaven above, help me!

Now, as Morgan recalled the past, that day had seemed so real. The final words from the witch echoed through his memory. "You *will* be mine, Morgan Thornton. Mine. Forever!"

One year ago, he had been a man. . . .

He closed his eyes and traced his fingertips over the pitiful scars deforming the left side of his face, marks he had made that first time shifting into a wolf, the witch had told him. Apparently, he had clawed at himself. He remembered nothing of it.

He slid his hand under the collar of his jacket and over the scars on his shoulder. Yet his physical appearance was not as horrific as the beast inside.

Trying to think about something besides the curse, Morgan settled behind the organ and rested his fingers on the keys. He pictured emerald grass beneath his feet, a cloudless, aquamarine sky, and a beautiful woman gazing at him with tenderness in her eyes.

No. He could not think this way. He must not dream of what would never come to pass. But it was so very difficult. Miss Forester had brought back feelings he had buried so long ago. He missed the passionate man he once was. Now he must not even think about holding a woman or kissing her lips.

Squeezing his eyes closed, he concentrated on moving his fingers over the keys and played the song that poured from his heart. But Miss Forester's face refused to leave his mind. He had watched her this afternoon with Jonathan, enjoyed the way her wide eyes gazed up at his foolish brother in admiration. When she laid her hand tenderly on Jonathan's arm, Morgan's own arm had tingled with warmth.

Oh, to be so privileged once again! He would give anything to experience the thrill of having a woman gaze into his eyes as Hannah had Jonathan's.

Suddenly pain ripped through Morgan. Gnashing his teeth, he jerked away from the organ and stood. *Oh, no! Not again!*

Fierce heat coursed through his body. His breath became ragged. Boils rose from each pore on his skin, stretched and pulled until course hair speared its way through him. His clothes were barriers, rubbing his skin raw. He ripped at his shirt, freeing the material from his body. Where his fingers had been, white paws formed and large nails grew from each claw.

Heaviness gathered in his throat while the dizziness swimming in his head brought him to the ground. He clutched his chest, trying to slow his rapid breathing. All moisture in his mouth evaporated, leaving him parched and unable to lick his lips. Sharp canine teeth pushed past his enlarged tongue.

Heaven help him, it was happening again.

He closed his eyes and cried out, but the sound was an animal's howl rather than a human scream. Soon his heartbeat slowed, and his body began to relax into its new form.

In a few minutes, Morgan would no longer remember this nightmare or the curse that created it. But as always, when he began to shift into the wolf, his greatest fear was waking in the morning to find that another young woman was dead.

Three

Hannah's limbs shook as she stared at the open door. Was she dreaming? She pinched her arm. No, she was awake, which meant she had indeed talked to someone. *The ghost from the East Wing?* No, the intruder had clearly been alive. But who was he? And how on earth did he get into her room? He left through the door, but he definitely had not entered that way.

Perhaps he was one of the servants, playing a joke on her. Yes, that was it! She was simply the hapless victim of a prank.

Taking a deep breath, Hannah calmed her quaking body. She would find out who had sneaked into her room and scared her nearly to death. She slid her feet into her slippers and rushed out of the bedroom, pulling her wrapper on. If she remembered correctly, when her night visitor left, he had turned toward the long hallway heading to the east side of the manor.

Her feet padded on the wood floor as she hurried along. An echoed sound made her pause on the stairs leading to the third floor. As she listened closer, a man's voice and a woman's voice floated through the air.

Hannah's heart slammed against her ribs. She glanced around the darkened hall for a place to hide. The pounding of footsteps grew closer, and she skirted behind the stairs and flattened against the wall. She held her breath, praying she didn't make a sound.

A man wearing a dark dressing robe descended the marbled steps and passed close by her. *Roderick.* Marching next to him, grumbling in distaste, was his wife.

"You treat me like an unruly child," he snapped.

Bethany's arms were folded across her chest, her lips curled up in distain. "If you would stop acting like one, I would not have to scold you so often."

When they turned the corner of the hallway and walked away from Hannah, she released her breath in a loud gush. Even in the darkness, she could tell Roderick was not the man who had visited her earlier. His shoulders were not wide enough, and he was not as tall.

On shaky legs, she took two steps at a time to the top floor and the servants' rooms. It looked as if her prankster was indeed someone who worked in the manor. But who?

Inky shadows, longer than seemed natural in the dim light of the hall, stretched in forlorn warning before Hannah, but she refused to turn back. Intricately carved mahogany doors marched ahead of her as tall soldiers guiding the way toward the forbidden East Wing. She pressed an ear to each polished door, stemming the trembling in her hands as she progressed from one door to the next.

When she reached the end of the hall she frowned. A dead end. Heaving a sigh, she ran her fingers through her hair, massaging her scalp. Whoever played this trick on her would certainly try again. Perhaps she should return to her room and wait for him tomorrow night.

A draft swept across her feet, and she glanced at the corner of the hall. No windows or doors were nearby, so where had the cool air come from?

Edging her way toward the corner, Hannah tapped her toes on the floor. Within seconds, she stood in front of a potted plant. Cautiously, she touched the leaves and then reached behind it to the wall. It felt like an ordinary wall. She slid her hand along the wall and stopped. A seam sprouted from the ceiling and extended to the floor. With both hands, she pushed. The wall moved slightly.

Jumping back, she covered her mouth, stifling a scream. The East Wing. Her heartbeat thundered in her chest.

From somewhere behind the wall came the howling of a wolf. Hannah sucked in a cry of panic, then turned and ran. She didn't stop until she reached her door and rushed inside her chambers. She clicked the lock tight and climbed into her warm bed, pulling the blankets up to her chin. Staring at the shadows in the room, she listened for any signs that someone might have followed her

Nothing. But she dared not close her eyes—not yet. Would her night visitor return? If she stayed at the manor instead of heeding his warning, would he visit her again and again until she departed?

Recalling the wolf howl, Hannah exhaled. Where had the animal come from? Perhaps it was not a wolf but a wild dog, yet the Thorntons would not have allowed either inside the manor. And that chilling cry had been like nothing Hannah had heard before. The pathetic sound, as if from an animal that was injured or in pain, tugged at her heart. She shook off the thought and settled deeper into her bed, forcing herself to relax. Her eyelids grew heavy, and she curled on her side. Closing her eyes, she willed herself to fall asleep.

From outside the night's sounds crept into her room. The hoot of an owl, the branches scratching against the window with the rhythm of the wind. And the howling of a wolf.

She opened her eyes. The animal was now outside. Bits of her conversation with Francine came back to her. Did a cursed white wolf actually roam the grounds? Was he looking for another woman to kill tonight?

Shivering, Hannah pulled the covers closer around her body. Sometime after midnight, she finally fell into a restless slumber.

❦

Hannah poked her fried egg with her fork and glanced around the breakfast table. Directly in front of her sat Bethany, frowning as she stared at her plateful of food. Down at the end of the table, Roderick ate heartily as if he didn't have a care in the world. When the couple did speak to each other, their remarks were brief and derogatory. Since Hannah had heard their fight on the stairs—and witnessed Roderick kissing the maid—she knew why the married couple treated each other with such disdain.

Bethany had told Hannah previously that Jonathan was out on his usual morning ride, but since that statement, no one had spoken to her at all during breakfast. The silence from her hosts was a bit unsettling.

Hannah sipped her tea, then set down the cup. She cleared her throat and said, "I want to thank you again for allowing me to stay here at the manor. My room, and the hospitality you have shown me, is more than I could have ever expected."

Roderick nodded and sipped his coffee. "It is our pleasure, Miss Forester."

She dabbed her mouth with the linen napkin. "I was surprised to hear howling last night. I didn't know there were wolves in this area."

Both Bethany and Roderick froze, staring at each other with wide eyes.

Hannah held her breath, wondering what they would say. Her heart beat faster as the seconds crept by.

Finally, Bethany squared her shoulders and met Hannah's gaze with a smile that looked forced. "You heard a howl? How intriguing. I don't believe I have heard a wolf in quite a while."

"So there *was* a wolf?" Hannah asked.

Roderick put down his coffee cup so abruptly that Hannah thought the delicate china would break. "I cannot explain it, Miss Forester. I don't know how it came to be, and it is a little frightening, but there is a wolf that wanders the land. Usually when we hear him, someone is killed in the village."

She gasped. "Killed?"

"Yes. The legend says a great white wolf roams the land in search of his next sacrifice."

She chuckled. "Oh, yes, I believe I have heard this tale."

"Hannah, my dear," Bethany said in hushed tones, "do not take this lightly. If you fear for your safety, just as we all do, you must remain indoors at night."

"So this fierce animal only comes out at night to kill?"

"Yes," her hosts said in unison.

"Has nobody dared to capture him?"

"They cannot," Bethany said with a sigh. "It has been said that he is a cursed animal."

"Cursed, you say? How so?"

"Nobody knows," Roderick answered. "Many men have tried to hunt him, but they were all seriously wounded and vowed they would never hunt again."

"So those who live here are in fear of their lives? That doesn't make sense to me." Hannah set her utensils across her plate and leaned back in the chair.

"How long have you lived in this area, Hannah?" Bethany asked suddenly.

"My father moved us to Surrey when I was ten. A year ago when he died, I went to live with my uncle in Lynton."

Roderick shook his head. "And not one person has told you about the white wolf?"

"Not until I arrived at Thornton Manor."

Bethany chuckled. "Then I fear your father and uncle have sheltered you from the truth."

"Not to worry, Miss Forester." Roderick picked up his coffee cup again. "If you heed our advice and stay inside at night, you shall be protected."

Hannah was about to refute their assumption that she had led a sheltered life, but down the hall, the front door slammed with a resounding boom. Voices grew louder, and a women wailed. Bethany and Roderick jumped from their chairs and ran into the hall.

Bewildered, Hannah pushed away from the table and stood. As she hurried toward her hosts, the voices became clearer. Jonathan's voice overpowered them all.

"She is dead," Jonathan exclaimed as he looked at Roderick. "Killed by the wolf."

Jonathan stood with a group of servants, one with streaks of blood on his apron and hands. Clearly, he was the butcher. Next to him, Mrs. White sobbed into her hands.

"Who is dead?" Bethany asked.

"Sarah. She helps with the laundry," Mrs. White answered sadly.

Hannah swallowed hard. "Are you certain it was the wolf?"

"Mrs. White saw her." Jonathan's voice shook. "Sarah's throat had been ripped open and her face shredded by an animal's claws."

"Good heavens, man, mind your tongue. There are ladies present." Roderick mumbled a curse and raked his fingers through his hair. Bethany blinked at the tears pooling in her eyes.

Horrified, Hannah didn't utter a word.

Jonathan lifted his head and looked directly at her, his face etched with worry. Taking three strides, he stopped in front of her and took her hands in his.

"Are you all right?"

She offered a weak smile. "I should be asking you that." She glanced at the servants, then back at him. "What can I do to help?"

Jonathan shook his head. "There is nothing to be done, my sweet. The white wolf has apparently come out of hiding again. We all know he will disappear for a few months before he strikes again."

Fear lodged itself in Hannah's chest, an emotion she did not welcome. She should not be here, yet she could not leave the manor now—not until she found some answers. "Do you think I should return home?" she asked, praying he would say no.

"Is that what you wish?"

"I would very much like to stay."

"I would like that, too." Jonathan brought her hands to his mouth and kissed her knuckles.

"Is there anything I can do to assist now?"

He glanced over his shoulder at the mournful servants. "No. My brother and my sister-in-law will take care of things here." With one hand under her elbow, he led her down the hall toward the drawing room. "I would very much like to take you for a carriage ride shortly." He bowed. "If you will excuse me, I shall change before we leave."

Hannah frowned. "A ride so soon after a servant's death? Do you not fear for our safety?"

"We know the white wolf's pattern. He has gone back into hiding. We will be safe for a while, I assure you." He shrugged. "Besides, he only comes out at night."

"Very well. I shall instruct my maid to get our things ready."

"Your maid?" Jonathan's brows furrowed.

"But of course, unless you know someone else who might serve as a proper chaperone."

He smiled. "Your maid is fine."

When Jonathan left, Hannah hurried toward her own room, hoping to find Francine. After checking there, she stepped down the hall to Francine's room and knocked. Her maid opened the door almost immediately.

"Oh, good. You are here. I need your assistance, please. Jonathan is taking me for a buggy ride soon, and you will have to be my chaperone."

Francine's eyes widened. "Indeed? How exciting. Let me tell Mrs. White. I fear she has given me many duties today. But before we leave, I must tell you something I have discovered." The maid glanced up and down the hallway. "Did you know that your friend, Mademoiselle Hartley, came here to court Jonathan just a few months ago?"

Hannah grasped the maid's arm. "Amelia came here? Are you certain?"

"Mrs. White told me about the other young women who came to the manor to meet Jonathan, and she said Amelia's name."

Hannah wondered why Amelia had told her nothing of this. Then again, Hannah's uncle had not allowed her to call on her friends very frequently. "Whatever happened to her?"

"All Mrs. White said was that the ghost must have scared her away, because she disappeared after only one day."

"Scared by the rumors, or scared when he appeared in her room wearing a black robe?"

"Whatever do you mean?"

Perhaps this particular *ghost* frightened women away all the time. "My dear Francine, this is something I must think about later. Please hurry with your errand and meet me downstairs in the main hall."

Francine nodded, then left.

Now Hannah had two things to ask Jonathan about—why her friend Amelia had left the manor so suddenly, and what he knew of Morgan's friendship with her father. On more than one occasion, Hannah's father had spoken to her of the oldest Thornton brother, explaining what a wonderful, caring man Morgan was, and hinting strongly that he would make any woman a fine husband. She smiled as she thought of her father trying to play matchmaker.

Heading toward the stairs, Hannah suddenly had an idea. If she could locate Morgan's bedroom, perhaps something there would help her learn more about him—and maybe even provide a clue as to why someone would want to kill her father.

On tiptoes she retreated, creeping to the second hallway, where she knew Roderick and Bethany's chambers were located. At each door Hannah pressed her ear to the solid wood, listening for any movements inside before she opened the door and looked in.

Finally, the third door on her left led her into a man's room. She could tell immediately it was not Jonathan's, mainly because of the musty odor that hung thick in the air. The curtains had been pulled open, thankfully, so she didn't need to light a lamp.

The chamber resembled hers, except for its masculine décor in dark shades of brown and blue. She stepped softly to the three armoires that sat side by side. When she opened the first one, she gasped at the many tailored shirts and vests that lined the rack. This man obviously knew how to dress well. Gingerly, she touched a cravat, rubbing the satin between her finger and thumb.

She closed the doors and approached a dressing table. Combs, razors, and leather straps sat neatly in a row. They were well polished for a man who had been dead over a year. Strange, since she received the impression this was an unused room.

Quickly, she glanced around, looking for anything that might have been her father's. Paintings, like the ones she saw downstairs on her first day, hung on the walls. Like those downstairs, the paintings were unsigned, and they were beautifully painted with bright colors and strong brushstrokes.

The desk in the corner of the room drew Hannah's attention. Like the other furniture in the room, it was free of dust and cobwebs. As quietly as she could, she pulled out a drawer, quickly peeking inside before closing it. The bottom drawer was harder to open, so she tugged until it gave way. With a thud, she fell back on her bottom.

Holding her breath, she listened to see if anyone had heard her. After a silent minute passed, she heaved a sigh of relief. Still, she knew she should not be there, and that she had been gone too long.

Just as she placed her hands on the drawer to close it, a stack of letters tied together with a red ribbon caught her eye. In very precise writing across the top of the first were the names Roderick and Bethany.

Curious, Hannah carefully pulled out the letter from the tie, opened it, and read it.

> *This letter it to inform you that as of today, August 26, 1879, I am taking control over my household. Roderick, in my absence, you and your scheming wife have run my affairs into the ground. I was very displeased to find that you have been pilfering money from me, and you leave me no choice but to cut you from my estate and my inheritance. If you have not moved out of my house by the end*

of the week, I shall have the constable come and escort you out personally. I do bid both of you well in your new life.

Morgan Thornton

How very interesting! Thoughts swam in Hannah's head as she placed the letter in the stack, retied the ribbon, and returned the letters to the drawer. Was the fire that caused Morgan's death truly an accident?

As a noise sounded from down the hall, her heart banged against her ribs. She hurried to the door and listened closely. When the corridor became silent again, she opened the door carefully and peeked out. Praying no one would catch her, she rushed out and down the hall. Hopefully, Jonathan wasn't waiting for her.

The drawing room remained empty. Hannah breathed deeply and walked toward the fireplace, the words of the letter playing in her mind. Nothing seemed quite right here at Thornton Manor. The events of her stay had thus far felt like fiction, as if the strange happenings unfolded from a book. Nothing seemed real, especially the visitor of last night, and even the wolf attack. She felt as if she were living in one of her father's mystery novels.

Sighing, she ran her fingers over the thick stones bordering the hearth and glanced over her shoulder toward the door. Now that she had found the entrance to the forbidden East Wing, she could discover the secrets that must be hidden there. But not during daylight hours. She would go tonight once everyone had retired for bed.

Wearily, Morgan lifted his aching body off the floor. Chills ran over his bare skin, bringing him quickly to awareness. He rubbed his forehead and groaned.

He had shifted again, and for the first time he actually remembered something. Images of his hours as a wolf floated through his head. He recalled feeling a cold breeze against his body, and a woman's scream.

He looked at his hands, his chest, and the rest of his body. No cuts or marks, and thankfully, no blood. Perhaps it was his beastly presence that had caused the woman to scream. He could only hope.

On shaky legs he staggered into his room to dress. He needed to sneak downstairs through the hidden tunnels of the manor to discover what had happened last night. If there had been another killing, he would know soon enough. With a prayer in his heart, he pulled on his clothes.

After donning his long, black, hooded cape, he sneaked through the secret tunnels. He stopped at the parlor, where his brothers and sister-in-law would be at this time of the day. Since he had gone into hiding, he had regularly spied on his family. Many years ago, his father had created these magical mirrors when he had been suspicious of his servants. From inside the rooms, they appeared to be normal mirrors, but in the secret tunnels, they were used as windows into the rooms. This was Morgan's only way to stay in touch with the real world.

The cold draft coming from the dark tunnel swept across his feet. He located the spot on the wall and pulled back the covering over the mirror to look on the other side.

The only person in the room was Hannah Forester. Morgan's heart sank. She hadn't heeded his warning last night. What could he do to get her to leave? She must do so, for his well-being and especially for hers.

He knew he should not watch her, but her beauty hypnotized him. She looked prettier this morning in her bright yellow day dress. Instead of curls framing her head as they had the day before, her hair hung over her shoulders in long waves, the sides pulled back on top of her head and secured with a yellow ribbon.

Miss Forester moved through the room, running her fingers lightly along each piece of furniture as she passed it. When she reached the pianoforte, she stopped and glanced over her shoulder toward the door. She turned and sat on the stool, then placed her fingers over the keys. Closing her eyes, she smiled. Her fingers lightly grazed the keys, but she did not play. He wondered why.

Heavy footsteps pounded down the hall, tearing Miss Forester away from the pianoforte. Seconds later, Jonathan appeared. The young pup smiled, stepped to her, and took her hands in his.

"Are you ready?"

She nodded. "My maid should be here momentarily, although I still feel going out for a ride is not right while your household is in turmoil."

Morgan's heart sank. *Turmoil?*

"No need to fear, my sweet. As I told you before, Bethany and Roderick will take care of everything. Bethany will make certain Sarah's body is prepared for burial."

"I still can't believe what happened." Miss Forester sighed. "It seems unreal. Tell me, Jonathan, does this sort of thing occur often?"

"No. Three, maybe four times a year, perhaps. But do not fear. I shall protect you from the white wolf. Sarah must have gone outside after dark. That's the only way the wolf could have attacked her."

A sharp pain twisted through Morgan's chest. He squeezed his eyes closed and leaned his head against the wall. He had seen the servant girl yesterday with Roderick before they disappeared behind the stables. Morgan growled and hit his fist softly against the wall. Why her? He had never had any kind of feelings for the servant, and that was the only emotion that made him shift. Perhaps his growing attraction for Miss Forester had caused him to seek out someone to kill last night.

If only he could end this nonexistent life and become normal once more. If only he could wrap his fingers around the throat of the witch who cursed him! But if he killed her he would be trapped forever, as he needed her to retract the spell. Either way, he simply could not live the rest of his life as a wolf.

He turned away and made his way back through the tunnels toward his room. One way or another, he had to convince Miss Forester to leave. He did not want her to become his next victim.

Four

The afternoon breeze caressed Hannah's cheek as she sat bundled in a fur wrap next to Jonathan. Francine perched beside her in the landau. The ride around Thornton Manor kept Hannah enthralled, as did the beauty of the grounds. Bordering the tall iron gate were various types of plants, including a few rhododendrons still in late bloom. After the sightseers passed the garden, the carriage took them over the brown stone arches of the bridge that stretched across the lake.

Jonathan could not have been more accommodating during the ride. His sense of humor surprised Hannah, and she enjoyed his company. Still, she found it odd that not once on their ride did he mention the dead servant girl. In fact, he chatted as if nothing had happened at all.

As they rode along, he asked Hannah questions about her life. She answered in a polite manner but kept attempting to change the topic. Finally, when he asked her one more question, she shook her head. "Jonathan, I'm dreadfully tired of talking about myself. Please tell me more about you and your family."

Shifting his focus off the road for a moment, he smiled at her. "What would you like to know?"

Though she normally spoke her mind, she feared her first question might be too bold. She asked it anyway. "Why are you not married?"

When Jonathan threw back his head and laughed, she smiled in relief.

"Oh, Hannah. You are an interesting woman."

"Come now. You can't tell me no one has ever asked you that before."

"On the contrary. That question has been asked quite a bit."

"How do you reply?"

He slowed the horses and met her gaze. "I tell them I have not found the right woman."

"Then you must be a discerning man."

He transferred the reins to one hand, grasped her clasped hands, and squeezed. "Extremely."

"What makes you so discriminating?"

He shrugged as he gathered the reins in both hands and looked at the road. The laughter in his eyes disappeared. "There is much for me to think about, Hannah. I not only need to decide what is best for me, but I need to keep Roddy and Beth's wishes in mind as well."

She frowned. "Why must you think of their desires?"

"Because if my future bride can't get along with my brother and sister-in-law, then my life will be most unpleasant. Since we all will be living under the same roof, familial harmony is best for all of us."

"You intend to remain at Thornton Manor instead of finding your own home?"

He shook his head. "You don't understand. Thornton Manor is my home. And the house is big enough for several families. There is no reason for my bride and me to live elsewhere when there is plenty of room at the manor."

"Very true, Jonathan." Hannah didn't say more about the subject, although she had a strong opinion about it. Instead, she took a different direction. "So, tell me, has any woman come close to becoming your wife?"

He chuckled. "You are certainly a curious lady."

"Thank you. I consider that a compliment." When he continued to look at the road in silence, she added, "However, there is something that has been on my mind for some time."

Jonathan glanced at her. "Indeed? I almost don't dare inquire as to what it is."

"Oh, it is nothing of dire importance, I assure you," Hannah replied. "I would simply like to know about an old friend of mine."

"And you think I know this person?"

"Yes. I was told she had come to Thornton Manor to make your acquaintance, just as I have."

Grinning, Jonathan pulled on the reins and brought the horse to a complete stop, then turned to look at her.

"You want to know about another woman I courted? Why, Hannah, you surprise me at every turn."

"Thank you."

He shook his head. "What a brave woman you are."

"I certainly try."

"So who is the person you would like to ask me about?"

"Miss Amelia Hartley."

Hannah studied his eyes, waiting for an expression of remembrance.

Jonathan seemed to think for a moment, then said, "I have never courted anyone named Amelia. Are you certain that was her name?"

Beside Hannah, her maid gasped. Hannah's heart lurched.

"Yes. Amelia Hartley," she confirmed. "Mrs. White said Amelia came to the manor only a couple of months ago."

Francine leaned forward. "That she did, monsieur. Mrs. White told me personally."

Lines appeared on Jonathan's forehead and he frowned. "Mrs. White said that? How strange. As far as I can recall, I have not met anyone named Amelia Hartley."

Tears sprang to Hannah's eyes, and she tried to blink them away.

"Hannah, my dear." He grasped her hands. "Why are you crying?"

"I'm—I'm not."

"But you are about to." He placed a finger under her chin and tilted her face until she met his gaze. "Why are you upset?"

She wiped her eyes. "Amelia was a good friend of mine. If she never arrived, that means . . . that means . . ." She shook her head and took a deep breath. "What if something terrible happened to her?"

"Shh. No need to fret, my dear. I shall contact the constable and have him look into the matter. We will find your friend, I assure you."

Hannah tried to be brave, but fresh tears threatened to stream down her cheeks. She bit her lip and breathed deeply. She had lost her father in a tragic way, and she didn't know what she would do if she learned Amelia had the same dreadful end. Where could her friend be?

Hannah must believe Jonathan would help her. That was the only hope she could hold on to at the moment.

❦

The hour was late, well past midnight. Morgan walked softly down the corridor toward Miss Forester's room, listening carefully for any sounds.

Thankfully, tonight his amorous brother had decided to stay in his own bedroom instead of visiting one of the maids. Morgan shook his head. One day Roderick would pay for his infidelity. Hadn't his brother learned from their father's mistakes?

It had been no secret that Jonathan was the product of their father's dalliance with a servant. Morgan didn't know who she was, but he had been told the woman killed herself shortly after she bore the child because Henry, Morgan's father, would not marry her.

Due to the dubious status of his birth, Jonathan had never been treated properly as a child by the other children his age. It wasn't fair, but children like Jonathan were always disadvantaged.

Morgan stopped in front of Miss Forester's door. Glancing up and down the hall, he made certain the corridor was clear. He took the key from the pocket of his hooded cape, gently slid it into the keyhole, and turned.

Taking a deep breath, he edged open the door and slipped inside. Just as the night before, the room was dark. A small sliver of light passed between the heavy drapes, barely outlining the form beneath the bed covers.

He crept to the foot of the bed, giving his eyes time to adjust to the darkness. Miss Forester didn't move, so she must be asleep.

He had thought about her all day, wanting to talk to her as a man, not a beast. Yet he *was* a beast! Not wanting to tell her the truth, he must convince her to leave in other ways. He could not allow anything tragic to happen to her.

Her beauty tempted him more than he had anticipated. Feeling passion for her would wreak havoc with his isolated world. He didn't want to shift into the white wolf and kill another woman.

From behind, the floor creaked, and suddenly something hard pushed into his back. Morgan sucked in a quick breath.

"Do not move or I shall shoot!"

The female voice shook, as did the gun barrel pressing into him. *Shoot me?* he thought. *If only the bullet would pierce my heart and end my tortured life.* Unfortunately, nothing could kill him, not while the curse still held him captive.

Miss Forester's bravery made him smile. Not many women would act with such boldness.

Morgan held out his arms. "I'm not going to move."

"Why are you here?"

"I came to warn you again."

"As I surmised. Turn around and let me see your face."

"That is an impossible request."

"Who are you?"

He chuckled. "Have you not heard of the East Wing Ghost?"

"Sir, I don't believe in ghosts." She jabbed the barrel into his back a little harder. "Besides, if you were a ghost, I would not be able to accomplish this."

She was a very intelligent woman—a trait she must have inherited from her father.

Morgan remained still for several seconds. Her ragged breathing did not slow, but she pulled the gun back slightly.

In a quick motion, Morgan spun around and grabbed the weapon from her hands. A squeak came from her throat as she backed against the wall. She clutched her nightgown near her neck and gasped.

"Please don't hurt me."

He looked at the weapon in his hand and almost laughed. "Miss Forester, I'm not going to hurt you, especially with a broomstick. I'm only here to protect you."

She shook her head. "I don't even know you."

"And I would like to keep things that way."

"I—I don't understand."

"Just understand this. You are in danger. You *must* leave. I don't know how else to make you believe the risk you undertake by staying here. Please heed my word. Take your maid and leave first thing in the morning."

Morgan swung around and left her, clutching the broom handle in his hand. With each footstep closer to his domain, he prayed she would follow his counsel. He could not live with himself if he so much as harmed a hair on her head.

The witch had told him it was passion that changed him into the beast. But he certainly had not felt anything for the laundry girl, Sarah, and she had ended up dead.

If only he could think of a way to break the curse. The witch came to him every so often and demanded that he love her. This he could not do. Ever. Recently, though, the witch had demanded something else. She now wanted Morgan to turn over the treasure map. Apparently she thought Peter Forester had given him a map that led to the treasure on the nearby island, Slumbering Giant. Morgan didn't know where the map or the treasure was; if he had he would have gladly traded it for his freedom from this terrible curse.

After reaching the East Wing, he made certain the door closed behind him securely, and then he hurried down the long, dark, cold hallway to his chambers. He stopped at the fireplace and threw in a couple of logs to last through the night. Then he straightened and stared into the growing fire.

Perhaps the key to breaking the curse lay with Miss Forester. Had her father known about a treasure on the island? If so, had he told his daughter? Morgan shook his head and moved away from the fire. It didn't matter if she knew or not. If the witch suspected she did, Miss Forester's life would indeed be in peril.

Fear clenched Morgan's gut. Although the witch might break his curse if he could find the map, Hannah's life was more important. One way or another he needed to get her out of Thornton Manor—and fast.

❦❦❦❦

Hannah could not stop her body from trembling. That blasted man had won again! She should not have let him walk out of her room the second time without asking him about her father. She swallowed hard and wobbled to her bed to sit. After taking a few reassuring deep breaths, she felt her confidence return. It was time to get some answers.

On slippered feet, she quickly retraced her route to the wall she had found the night before. Where one hall met another, she peeked around the corner, making certain no one lingered there. She reached the familiar plotted plant and pressed her hands against the wall until she located the seam.

Did she really want to enter his lair? This was the East Wing, the very area she was forbidden to enter, lest she and her maid be sent away from the manor. Ignoring her trepidation, Hannah pushed the wall as hard as she could. This time it opened.

Holding her breath, she peeked inside. A dim light shone through the long, shadowed corridor, and a cold draft swept over her legs. She pulled the wrapper tighter around her and stepped into the shadows with only scant light to show her the way. As her feet touched cold stone, a shiver passed through her. Swallowing hard, she forced herself to continue. She simply could not stay at the manor and wonder every night if the prankster would come back.

The further into the wing she walked, the warmer the air became, until even the cold floor no longer chilled her. Soon, bright light at the end of the tunnel revealed a large room, and Hannah crept inside. Against the far wall stood a fireplace, where flames licked the stones in a gentle welcome. Scattered candles lent more light to the room. This was someone's sanctuary, a place kept hidden from the rest of the world.

A spicy scent wafted through the air, bringing memories of her father. He used to splash his face with this same cologne, and when he would sit next to her while she played the pianoforte, his smell had surrounded her.

The sound of a beautiful organ chord made her jump. She gasped and slapped her hand over her mouth. In the far corner, a man with a deep purple evening jacket sat on the bench, his head tilted back, the ends of his black hair brushing the collar. She recognized his wide shoulders and his tall frame. He was indeed her nighttime visitor.

Hannah's mouth turned dry, and she twisted her hands against her stomach. She hadn't realized she had been holding her breath until it came out in a rush.

Behind the organ, the man stiffened. "Is someone there?" he asked without turning.

The deep timbre of his voice added to her terror and caused her to tremble. She cleared her throat. "You came to my room. I thought I should come to yours, as we never finished our conversation."

He cursed and reached for a black scarf at the corner of the organ. "Miss Forester, you should not be here." He fastened the silk over his head to partially cover his face, but he didn't look at her.

"Why not?"

"Do not play coy with me. I know you have heard of the East Wing Ghost."

"And I remember telling you I don't believe in ghosts."

"You should. Being here is not good for you."

She folded her arms and rubbed the length of them to stop the chills. "So we are back to discussing the danger I am in, are we?"

He turned on the bench. His left eye, part of his nose, and his mouth were all Hannah could see of his face, but she almost gasped at how attractive he was.

"Miss Forester, leave this very moment, and never think of this place again."

"This place? Meaning your chambers?"

"Yes."

"And what about your earlier warning about leaving the manor altogether?"

He stood, his hands fisted at his sides. "You are a most impetuous woman, and I'm growing weary of your questions. Leave now or suffer the consequences."

Hannah's knees knocked together, and she feared she would swoon. No, she must be strong! She must learn why he resided here, hiding from everyone.

Slowly, he made his way toward her, and she forced herself not to back away.

"I will leave your chambers, but know this." She took a deep breath. "You can't scare me away, so don't sneak into my room and threaten me again. I don't understand why you gave me such an outlandish warning, but I'm not frightened of you, or any other servant in this house."

He stopped in front of her and tilted his head to the side, his anger seeming to fade. "I'm not a servant. And you are a stubborn child."

"I am no child, sir."

He folded his arms and tapped his finger on his chin. His gaze slid over her in a slow caress. Tingles rushed through her body, feelings she didn't quite understand.

"Obviously."

She licked her parched lips. "I—I came to tell you that you can't frighten me. I will not leave the manor until the Thorntons ask me to." Her voice cracked, and she cleared her throat. "So please cease these warnings. They fall on deaf ears."

Straightening, Hannah turned to make her way back down the long, cold tunnel. Rapid footsteps reverberated behind her. When strong fingers gripped her arm, she let out a sob.

The so-called ghost yanked her around to face him. He hovered over her, his face only a few inches away. She had to tilt her head back sharply just to look at him. Although the scarf concealed half of his face, his one eye held her prisoner.

"Miss Forester, you must heed my word. You should not stay here. I don't want to see you put in danger."

"D–danger of wh–what?" Her teeth chattered, and a shiver of fear ran through her.

"Do you really want to stay and find out?" he ground out. "Why can you not simply listen and believe what I say?"

"Because I don't know you."

A heavy sigh fell from his lips, and he released her. He folded his arms, keeping his stare on her. "How will knowing me make a difference?"

"I only trust those I know." Hannah shook her head. "You, sir, are a stranger, a man who has played with my emotions by coming into my room trying to frighten me."

According to what she had heard, Roderick's and Jonathan's older brother had died in a house fire, and he remained as a ghost in the East Wing. If there was supposed to have been a fire in this section of the house, it certainly did not appear that way now.

Was this man Morgan, the older brother? Did he cover half of his face to hide his hideous burns? If this was indeed him, it would definitely explain why the clothes in his room were not dusty or covered with cobwebs. Obviously, he still dressed every day. So why would he hide and pretend to be a ghost?

"I only want to help you. Can't you see?"

"No." She inched her hand forward to touch his arm, but withdrew before making contact. "I need you to tell me why you think I'm in danger."

He backed away, his gaze narrowing with each step he took toward the fireplace. "I can't tell you any more. Please leave." His voice softened. "If you are caught in this room, you will certainly be in grave danger. The Thorntons don't want people knowing of my existence."

"Is that why you think I'm in peril? Are you Morgan Thornton, the oldest brother who they say died in the fire?"

He closed his eyes. "Please leave and do not come back again." He turned and without a word strode into another room, then slammed the door behind him.

Hannah stared at the closed door. He had not answered her question about his identity, but she felt strongly this was Morgan. Yet this man was nothing like the loving, kind, gentle person her father had admired. Something had definitely happened in Morgan's life to make him so sinister. And she wanted to find out what it was. She would learn every detail of his life and find the man her father had talked so much about. She wouldn't leave this place until she talked to Morgan about her father and uncovered the secrets only the eldest Thornton brother must hold.

On steadier legs she retraced her path back to the secret opening in the wall, then quickly passed through it. Once she stepped onto the hardwood floor of the mansion's main corridor, the door clicked shut behind her before she had a chance to pull it closed. She jumped and placed her hand on her chest.

Had he followed her out?

Five

The sky darkened with gray clouds. It was fitting for a funeral. The breeze turned cold, and Hannah tightened her fur-lined cloak around her throat to ward off the chill.

The staff of Thornton Manor wore black for Sarah's burial, but Bethany Thornton adorned herself in a shimmering silver gown, the only sign of mourning a black veil covering her eyes. Hannah sighed, studying the woman. Why would Bethany flaunt her wealth on a day such as this?

Roderick was distant and didn't say anything unless it was to mutter a word to the servants. As Hannah stood by Jonathan near the grave, she once again felt out of place, and she wondered at this curious family. Bethany and Mrs. White had forbidden her to enter the east wing of the manor, yet they clearly had no idea she had already ventured there twice. Hopefully, she could keep it that way, since she hadn't yet found what she had come to Thornton to find.

Horace, the butler, sang a mournful song while everyone else stood in silence. Hannah tried to concentrate on the song, but her mind replayed her encounter with the so-called ghost the previous night. Now that she had a chance to compare him to

Roderick and Jonathan, she concluded the ghost was indeed the older brother. She also realized that while Morgan had a scarred face, he had displayed more masculinity in his mannerisms and speech than either of his younger brothers. She had been captivated by Morgan's presence. Her body had quaked at his nearness, and more from exhilaration than fear.

Familiar prickles of awareness danced over her skin. Someone was watching her again. She glanced around the small group at the gravesite, but everyone was focused on the simple wooden coffin on which sat a single white rose. She glanced over her shoulder toward the East Wing. In an upper window, the curtains moved.

Turning back to the grave, Hannah fought to keep herself from smiling. Morgan was watching her. Warmth spread through her. The memory of his dark eye, his full lips, and his robust frame brought feelings to her heart that she had never before experienced. What was it about him that made her limbs quiver so? Why hadn't any other man raised a similar reaction in her?

After the service, Jonathan escorted her back to the house, while Francine, acting as chaperone, followed behind. Once inside, Jonathan took Hannah's cloak and handed it to Francine. Then Jonathan stroked Hannah's arm and smiled.

"Would you care for a game of cards?" he asked.

She took hold of his hand to halt his caresses. "Thank you, Jonathan, but if you don't mind, I would like to spend some time in my room this afternoon. I fear I didn't sleep well last night, so I was hoping I could rest now."

"As you wish, my sweet. Please don't hesitate to ask Mrs. White to get you anything you need."

Hannah shook her head. "I would not dream of bothering her now. I'm certain this is a bad day for many of your servants."

"You are very thoughtful." He cupped her chin. "We are very fortunate to have you with us."

She pulled away and started up the stairs, but Jonathan followed, his hand resting low on her back. Right away she noticed his touch didn't stir feelings inside of her like Morgan's brief touch had. She shook away such thoughts. How could she possibly have these feelings for a man who tried to frighten her? But Morgan was the last person to speak with her father, and somehow she needed to convince him to confide in her.

Outside her room, Jonathan took her hand and placed a kiss on her knuckles. She smiled, then pulled away as politely as she could.

"I hope you get some rest, Hannah."

"I hope so as well, or I will be out of sorts for the duration of the day."

She closed the door and leaned against it, exhaling a heavy sigh of relief. Although she did need to get some rest, sleep was not on her mind at this very moment. What she truly wanted was to return to the East Wing and talk with Morgan. Maybe if she explained her true reason for visiting the manor, he would soften toward her and confess the truth. No, that would never happen, she decided, especially when he did not want her here in the first place. But she would not leave, not yet.

She lay on the bed and stared at the ceiling. Hours slipped by. How many, she didn't know. The sky grew dark, casting shadows on the walls. Hannah turned her eyes to the window, where rain sprinkled against the glass in a constant rhythm. No matter how long she stared at the rain, her eyes would not close. Trying to rest was useless.

Sliding off the bed, she decided to find Francine, to ask if she had heard any more tales from the servants. Between what her maid had heard and what Hannah knew, maybe she could figure out the some of the secrets of this place.

She exited the room and knocked on Francine's door, but there was no answer. She opened the door and peeked inside. It was empty. Hannah crept farther into the room. The space was so immaculate that it seemed as if nobody occupied it.

She walked to the long, lightly frosted window and peered outside. A movement from the courtyard caught her attention. The cloaked figure of what appeared to be a woman hurried toward the wooded area beyond the lawn. Suddenly, she stopped and looked back toward the house.

Hannah's heart jumped. Was that her maid? What was Francine doing outside, alone in this weather, especially when the poor girl was afraid of her own shadow? Knocking on the window, Hannah shouted at Francine. But the maid turned back toward the thicket of trees and rushed out of sight.

Grumbling, Hannah hurried to her room and grabbed her own cloak. She dashed down the stairs and outside. Shielding her face from the drizzling rain with one hand, she ran toward the wooded area.

"Francine?" She hurried faster through the trees. "Blast it, Francine, answer me!"

Hannah paused, taking deep breaths as she looked through the trees. The rain had stopped and a thick sea mist settled around her, making it impossible to see which direction her maid had gone.

As Hannah studied her surroundings, a noise in the distance grew louder. *The white wolf!* She strained to listen closer. No, according to everyone, he only came out at night. Yet the sound had definitely come from a dog.

Fear chilled her bones and left her breathless as she realized it was not just one dog, but several. The fierce barking grew closer. With a sharp cry, Hannah turned and ran back into the mist in what she hoped was the direction of the house.

Branches caught on her cloak as she hurtled through a cluster of trees. Low branches caught at her hood and pulled it off, and sharp twigs tangled in her hair. She yelped and jumped away.

The barking dogs grew closer. Her feet slipped in the mud and she fell to her knees. Frantic, she scrambled to stand. Now the animals' growls rose right behind her. She tried to rise from the mud puddle and found her cloak caught in a bush. With a sob, she yanked at her garment and turned, tears stinging her eyes.

Three large, snarling dogs crouched in front of her. Foam drooled from the jaws of the hairy hounds, and their eyes seemed covered with a milky blue film. Her heart wrenched. They were rabid.

Slowly, the animals circled her. She dared not scream for fear they would attack. On the ground, she searched for something—a broken limb or a rock—to use as a weapon. Her hands found nothing.

One dog crept closer. "Get away!" she screamed. Another snapped at her, catching the end of her cloak. "No!" She jerked on the garment, but the dog pulled back until Hannah shrugged out of the covering and threw it to the animal. The other two jumped at it, and all three began tearing it into shreds.

Hannah held her shaking hands close to her chest. On unsteady legs, she stepped back. She had to get away or the dogs would tear her to pieces as they were doing to her cloak.

With the dogs momentarily distracted, she took another step back, then another, until her feet quickened and she put some distance between them. The dogs snapped their heads in her direction before leaping toward her.

Disoriented, Hannah had no idea which way the manor was, so she simply screamed and ran. All that loomed before her were a jumble of black tree trunks and a white, swirling mist. Branches whipped at her face and caught her hair, but she didn't dare stop. The animals were close on her heels.

Suddenly, she slipped on a moss-covered log and fell to the ground. Sobbing, she covered her face, knowing she would soon feel the canines' sharp teeth piercing her skin.

Another sound ripped through the air. Some other animal had joined the threesome. One dog yelped, then the other two joined in. The cries of the fourth animal seemed to become a man's voice, booming into a growl-like hiss.

Hannah peeked through her quivering fingers. Yellow, glowing eyes caught her attention. She blinked, not believing what she saw. Wearing a hooded black cloak, a tall man with wide shoulders stood between her and the dogs. She recognized him immediately. Lowering her hands, she watched. The glowing color of his eyes disappeared. Had she imagined it? After all, he wanted her to believe he was the East Wing Ghost.

Morgan turned his attention toward the beasts and growled like a wolf. Cocking their heads from side to side, the dogs whined.

Hannah gasped. Could this man actually talk to them? *Impossible!* Yet the dogs acted as if they understood him, or at the very least, feared him.

He growled again, and the three beasts yelped and ran into the forest with their tails between their legs. Morgan turned and knelt beside Hannah. Her entire body trembled uncontrollably.

"Miss Forester, are you all right?"

She nodded, her chest tight. Tears welled in her eyes, and instinctively she reached for him. He scooped her up in his arms. She buried her face in his neck and breathed in his spicy scent while tears flowed down her cheeks.

The rain started again and beat against them as he carried her back toward the house. He did not enter through the front doors or the servants' quarters; instead, he used a door Hannah had not seen before. Inside, darkness surrounded them, and Morgan set her down on the floor to light a candle. A long tunnel loomed straight ahead. He swept her up into his arms again and carried her as if she weighed no more than a feather.

He climbed stairs that circled upward into a tunnel that looked well used. No cobwebs filled the corners, and remarkably, no mice scurried across the floor. Soon, they arrived at a room lit with many candles and with a fire roaring in a deep hearth. Immediately, Hannah recognized his sanctuary.

He carried her to the fireplace and set her on the rug before it. He doffed his cloak and knelt beside her, then took her hands in his and rubbed warmth back into them. His eyes remained downcast, so she studied him more closely. A scarf still covered the left side of his face, yet he looked remarkably handsome.

She swallowed the lump of emotion lodged in her throat. "Thank you for saving me."

His dark gray eyes met her stare. "What were you doing wandering in the rain by yourself?"

"Chasing after my maid."

"What was she doing outside in this weather?"

"I don't know. That's why I ran after her."

Silence stretched as her encounter with the dogs replayed in her mind. She shivered, then finally spoke. "Tell me, how is it that you can talk to those dogs in their language."

He shook his head. "I didn't."

"I heard you."

"It must have been your imagination, then. Nobody can talk to animals in their own language." His brow creased and he lifted his hand to her face, running the pads of his fingers over the scratches there. "Do they hurt?"

Apparently, he was not going to tell her what she wanted to know. "A little."

"I have some ointment that might help."

He rose and strode across the room. After digging through a black medical bag, he returned to her side with a small jar. He gave her a kind smile and removed the lid.

"It will not hurt." He touched his finger to the ointment and dabbed it on the scratches on her face.

She jerked at first, but then warmth blended with the sting. "Who are you? Are you Morgan?"

Sighing heavily, he lowered his hand. "Will knowing my name really make a difference?"

"It will to me."

"I'm surprised you are not screaming and fleeing as fast as your legs will carry you. Those who have seen me think I'm a beast."

"No." She softly touched his arm. "Anyone who would save a woman from rabid dogs is no beast."

He didn't speak. His gaze swept over her hair and her face, then rested on her lips. Her heart hammered. Once again, she became breathless, and fear of a different kind invaded her senses, warming her even more than his fingers had.

"I am Morgan Thornton. I died a year ago."

Hannah shook her head. "Are you trying to tell me I'm not only talking to a ghost, but touching him as well? Impossible." She ran her hand over his arm, and his muscles tightened beneath her fingers.

"Believe it or not, I died. I am not human."

Hannah touched the side of his cheek not covered by the scarf. He inhaled sharply but remained still. Her hand drifted to his black, wavy hair and brushed a lock away from his brow. "You feel human to me."

Eyes of dark gray bore into hers. She shivered, but it had nothing to do with the damp gown sticking to her body.

"You are cold." His voice was husky. "We must return you to your room before my imbecile brother discovers you missing."

He moved again, but she clasped his hand. "No, Morgan. I don't want to leave. Not yet."

Morgan's gaze dropped to her mouth, making her stomach flutter. Her heartbeat quickened and she licked her dry lips.

"You must, Hannah."

"Please, just a few moments more. Jonathan thinks I'm sleeping. I'm certain he will not come to get me for a little while. Can I not just stay and talk to you?"

Morgan turned his hand and entwined his fingers with hers. Her heart skipped a beat.

"What is it about me that intrigues you so?" he asked quietly.

She smiled. "I'm a quizzical woman by nature. Because my father was a novelist, he thrived on the mysteries in people's lives. Perhaps I'm much like he in that regard."

"I knew your father. I have read all of his books." He chuckled and shook his head. "He would have quite a story to write with my life, I'm afraid."

She frowned. "Are you aware my father is dead?"

"Yes, I heard. My condolences to you. He was a good man—a trusted friend."

Tears pricked Hannah's eyes, and she blinked them away. "I live with my uncle now."

"I sense you are unhappy with your living arrangements."

"Just as I can sense your sorrow." She squeezed his hand. "Please, Morgan. Let me help you." She desperately wanted him to talk to her, to tell her the secrets of Thornton Manor, and why he was hiding.

"Helping me will only cause us both pain. No, Hannah, it is dangerous enough that you are talking to me, touching me. I must take you back."

Her heart sank as he went to a closet, retrieved a thick cloak, and brought it back to her. "Put this on. It will warm you until you can change your clothes."

She nodded. Her legs shook as she tried to stand. She wobbled and lost her balance, but Morgan caught her with strong arms. She clung to him, staring into his eyes and then at his parted lips. The urge to press her mouth to his was overpowering. Yet such a thing would be improper. Even a lady with a spirited personality did not act so boldly.

Suddenly, his arms tightened around her, drawing her closer. Her chest constricted with anticipation.

"Morgan." The word left her lips in a whisper as her fingertips slid down the side of his face. "Why do I feel as if I know you? I should be frightened, yet I am not."

He closed his eyes and brought his forehead against hers. His breathing quickened. "Hannah, this is why you need to leave. Being here with me now puts you in tremendous danger, and I have no power to stop it."

"I'm not frightened. Being with you calms my soul."

With a moan, he swept his lips across hers. She wrapped her arms around his neck, meeting his mouth with tiny kisses. His heartbeat pounded against her chest. His hands moved tenderly over her back, drying her dress quicker than the fire. Warmth infused her, and she pulled him even closer.

Just as Hannah crushed her mouth to his, he pushed her away. She almost stumbled backward. Morgan stared at her, his eyes blazing with passion. Agony clutched her heart. More than anything, she wanted to be back in his arms with his lips on hers.

He shook his head. "You don't understand, Hannah. I can't do that. I can't think of you this way. It is dangerous for both of us." He picked up the cloak and handed it to her. "Please don't ask questions. Just trust me."

She pulled the heavy cloth to her chest. Trust him? How could she trust him when he could not tell her everything? Yet how could she not when he had saved her life?

Wrapping the cloak around her, she nodded. He lifted her in his arms again without a word and carried her from his room and back through the tunnel. She cradled her head in the crook of his neck, relishing the time in his arms. It was a privilege she might never have again.

Six

Hannah had a difficult time trying to explain to Jonathan and the Thorntons how she obtained the scratches on her face. She didn't exactly lie. She told them she had seen her maid outside, so she had wandered into the thick trees to find her. However, she told them nothing about her adventure with the dogs—and the handsome man who had saved her.

What began as a nightmare had turned into a wonderful dream. She had always imagined a knight in shining armor coming to rescue her. Morgan did not wear armor, but he had most certainly rescued her and carried her away.

No matter how he tried to convince her he had not spoken to the vicious dogs in their own language, she knew differently. And they had responded! It was very strange indeed, no matter how hard she tried to explain away the events in the forest.

Whatever Morgan was hiding, Hannah wanted to help him, regardless of the danger he thought she would be in. Clearly, he was suffering somehow, and she knew her father would want her to help him.

That evening at dinner, Jonathan was very attentive. As much as Hannah wanted to pull away when he took her hand, to have him not look at her with such longing, she had to go along with it to keep up pretenses. If she did otherwise, he would send her away. She could not return home now.

He took her into the parlor after dinner and closed the door. Immediately, the expression in his eyes became serious. Her heart sank.

"I'm certain you are having second thoughts about your stay at Thornton Manor," he began.

"Nonsense, Jonathan. I'm having a splendid time."

Chuckling, he moved closer. When he stood in front of her he swept the back of his fingers across the scratches on her face so very gently. "You don't lie very well, my sweet Hannah. I can't fathom how you would want to stay a minute longer, especially after the afternoon you have had thus far. Anyone else would have turned and fled hours ago."

She smiled and stepped away. "I will admit it has been one adventure after another. But you seem to forget with whom you are speaking. Because of the way my father raised me, I'm used to such escapades."

Hannah turned and walked to the sofa, then sat and smoothed her gown. "I have not been disappointed in the least. Your family has been most accommodating."

Jonathan followed and sat beside her. He took her hand and brought it to his mouth, his lips brushing her knuckles. If it had been two months ago and under different circumstances, she might have encouraged his attentions. But now she had learned that though he was kind, he was not the sort of man she wanted to marry.

"I admire your courage." Jonathan caressed her hand with his lips once again. "Any other woman would have left the first day."

She suppressed the urge to pull her hand from his grasp. "Why do you say that?

"Most young women I meet are frail and timid. By now, my brother and sister-in-law would have scared them away."

It was strange that Jonathan would say such a thing when it was Bethany who was trying to find him a wife. Why would she scare the young women away once they arrived at the manor?

The harder he clasped Hannah's hand, the more she wanted to pull away. He didn't act like this with Roderick and Bethany around. And where was Francine, Hannah's chaperone? When she had spoken with her earlier, the maid claimed she had not gone outside all day. Hopefully she was busy helping Mrs. White.

"Jonathan, what makes you think your brother and sister-in-law would frighten me away?" Hannah asked him. "They have been exemplary hosts."

"You don't know them as I do. They can be very forceful at times."

Withdrawing her hand, she stood and moved to window. "Then I must be blind to that side of them, because I have not noticed that trait at all."

Once again, the determined young man followed. He stood directly behind her and placed a hand on her shoulder. Just then, the door to the parlor opened, and Bethany and Roderick strolled in. Jonathan jumped away from Hannah, folding his hands in front of him. She breathed a sigh of relief.

Bethany's gaze narrowed on Jonathan, and she tilted her head curiously. With wilted shoulders, he moved further away from Hannah.

"Hannah, my dear," Bethany began as she settled into a chair. "I hope you don't mind discussing your father for a bit."

Hannah smiled and sat on the sofa, her heart suddenly beating in a different rhythm. Did they know anything about her father's death? Could they help her solve the mystery surrounding the day he died? "Not at all. I love talking about my father. What do you wish to know?"

"I read a book he wrote about the Slumbering Giant."

Hannah nodded. "He researched the island and wrote a novel about it. That was his last publication."

"What kind of research did he do, may I ask?" Bethany kept her gaze directly on Hannah.

She folded her hands in her lap and straightened her shoulders. "He went to the island and walked around to get a feel for the layout. He even looked inside the caves. He had heard the legend about the old curse, but he didn't believe it."

"He actually stepped foot on the island and nothing horrid happened to him?" Bethany arched a brow.

"There have been a lot of tales circling about. I think my father proved them false, because he searched the island and returned a whole man."

Roderick laughed as he poured himself a brandy. "If he survived all that, he would be considered a god among the people here."

"Hannah, why do you suppose there have been so many tales about the island if they are not true?" Bethany asked.

Hannah shrugged. "Perhaps someone started the tale a long time ago to keep everyone away."

"That could very well be the reason." Bethany nodded. "However, I have known many men who went there and never returned. If, by chance, they were fortunate enough to come back, they were not whole."

Hannah lifted her hands in surrender. "I can't tell you what I don't know. But my father survived, which was how he was able to write the book."

Roderick cleared his throat. "But your father is dead now. Do you suppose it had something to do with the curse of the island?"

Her heart ached as doubts filled her mind. "My father died a year after writing the book, Mr. Thornton. In fact, the book had already been published by that time. I don't think his death and the curse were related."

"There is another tale," Jonathan said as he sat by Hannah and took her hand. "Only a pure woman with a kind and loving heart, more beautiful than anyone can imagine, will be able to lift the curse on the island." He rubbed her hand. "Do you believe that?"

"There are a lot of stories I don't believe," Hannah replied.

"But that does not mean they are not real."

"Possibly."

"Perhaps one day, Miss Forester," Roderick said, lifting his glass, "I shall take you there to see firsthand."

Hannah blinked at him, surprised he would suggest such a thing. "Pardon me?"

He took a sip from his glass, his gaze wandering over Hannah's figure. His grin made her stomach churn.

"What if *you* are the woman who is pure in heart?" His eyebrows waggled. "And you are very comely, you know."

Without really meaning to, she snorted and rolled her eyes. "I fear, Mr. Thornton, if you believe that rubbish, you need spectacles. Or perhaps you have consumed more spirits than usual tonight."

The others laughed, which relaxed Hannah just a bit.

Jonathan stood and held out his hand to her. "Hannah, my sweet, would you care to accompany me into the music room?"

She didn't want to be alone with him, mainly because the sparkle in his eyes warned her he wanted to continue their earlier conversation. Yet she had no choice; she could not discourage him by breaking off their courtship just yet—not until she found more answers.

Forcing a smile, she slipped her hand into his. "I would love to." She turned back to Bethany and Roderick. "Would you excuse us?"

"Most certainly." Roderick grinned.

As she walked out of the parlor with Jonathan, she could feel Roderick's stare on her. Chills of disgust spread over her and made her shiver. There was no way she could have mistaken the heated look he gave her earlier. She would have to watch him closely.

❦

Bethany waited until her brother-in-law and Hannah were far enough down the hall before she stood and hurried to close the room's double doors. Once they clicked securely, she swung around and faced her husband with a glare.

"You imbecile! What was that all about?"

Roderick arched his brow and took another sip of his brandy. "Pray, woman, what are you harping about now?"

"I saw the way you ogled Miss Forester. Can you not have a decent conversation with a woman without flirting?"

He lifted a shoulder and watched his drink as he swirled it in the snifter. "She is quite lovely. It is hard for any man to miss that."

"She is here for your brother, you jackanapes! Can you not keep your disgusting hands off women long enough for them to get to know him? Or do you think it is your job to seduce all of them first?"

He narrowed his gaze on her. "If my wife kept herself for her husband and her husband only, I would not have to go elsewhere."

She flipped her hands in the air. "You are impossible."

"Besides, how else are we supposed to find the pure and beautiful woman who can lift the curse on the island?"

"Not by you seducing them all, that's for certain. We need to find the woman who holds the power to lift the curse."

He shook his head. "I look at it this way—if the woman is willing to let me charm her, then she is not the pure-hearted woman we are looking for."

Bethany marched up and stopped in front of her husband, folding her arms over her chest. "Am I to assume Hannah will not allow your attentions?"

"I have not tried. I thought to give the girl a few more days to get to know me better."

"Why give her that long? I'm certain she already knows what a leech you are."

Roderick set down his glass and stood. He brought his face close to his wife's until their noses nearly touched. His alcohol-laced breath made Bethany want to retch.

"My dear wife. I think you have a soft spot in your heart for my brother."

She widened her eyes and gulped.

"Jonathan is a simple-minded boy." He cupped her chin. "He will never be able to make you happy, I am afraid."

She slapped his hand away. "You don't know how wrong you are."

He shrugged. "And I happen to think differently. We each have our faults, but we learn to live with them, do we not?"

Bethany pushed past him and stalked to the door. Before she opened it, she looked at him over her shoulder. "For once will you keep your hands off this woman? She just may be the key to getting us onto that island. After all, her father was able to go there."

"I doubt we will be able to persuade Hannah to help us in our quest anyway." Roderick shook his head. "Have you seen the way her maid keeps an eye on her? Not only that, I have caught the servant eavesdropping several times. I fear that girl will be our stumbling block."

"Then I suppose we shall have to dispose of the maid."

"And how do you think we should accomplish that, my dear, scheming wife?"

She chuckled. "Try to charm her. That will make her run far away."

He cocked his head and glared at Bethany. "My, are you humorous today."

"No need to fear, Roddy. I shall think of something."

"The sooner the better, I trust."

Smiling with anticipation, she walked out of the parlor, plotting a way to make Hannah's maid flee from the manor as fast as her little feet would carry her. The maid would only complicate matters if she stayed. It was essential to Bethany's plan to gain Hannah's confidence, just in case she knew where her father had hidden the treasure map. Bethany would make the young lady talk.

Greed burned in Bethany's chest. For her entire adult life, it had been her ambition to become an extremely wealthy woman. Marrying one of North Devon's wealthiest men had helped considerably. Too bad Roderick wasn't as handsome and charming as Morgan. She had actually been in love with the older brother, but when he never paid any attention to her, she had set her sights on Roderick. Her decision had been a bad one, since he could not stay faithful. But it didn't matter now, since getting the gold and silver from that cursed island was all Bethany really cared about. The treasure was there—somewhere—and she would not give up until it was hers.

Jonathan escorted Hannah into the music room and closed the door behind them. He walked past her and sat at the pianoforte, then rested his fingers on the keys. "Hannah, do you play?"

Without waiting for an answer, he played a simple tune, one she remembered from her childhood. She smiled and crossed the floor to stand behind him.

"I used to play when I was small," she said. "I don't remember much now."

He motioned to the space next to him on the bench. "Come. Let us play a tune together. I shall teach you one that is very easy."

She sat. "How long have you been playing?"

"Several years. Morgan taught me."

Hannah's heart softened for the man hidden away in the East Wing. "Oh, how lovely. I heard Morgan wrote music."

Jonathan nodded. "Many ballads."

She touched his hand, and he stopped playing and looked at her. "Can you tell me how he died?" she asked.

He scratched his head. "I don't recall much about the fire. I was on extended holiday in Italy with friends during that time. Roderick and Bethany told me there was a fire in the East Wing and that Morgan burned to death trying to stop it from spreading."

"Were you very close to Morgan?"

Jonathan nodded. "Most definitely. He looked out for me when Roderick would not."

She squeezed his hand. "I'm sorry. I hope I didn't bring up bad memories for you."

He looked at her and smiled. "No. I do miss Morgan, though. We used to have long talks, and he helped me through my problems."

"I can imagine. My father was the same way with me."

Jonathan slipped his arm around her waist and pulled her closer. When his gaze dipped to her mouth, her chest tightened. Automatically, she stiffened, but Jonathan must not have noticed because he still looked at her with desire in his eyes.

"We are a lot alike, don't you agree?" he asked huskily.

"I suppose."

His arm tightened, bringing her nearer. Quickly, she placed a hand on his chest to keep from pressing into him.

He cupped her chin and grinned. "Hannah, I'm certain you are aware of my feelings for you."

She gulped. "I think so."

"You are unlike any woman I have ever met."

"Thank you."

His thumb swept over her bottom lip. *He is going to kiss me!* Her heart hammered, but the feeling was totally different from when Morgan had been about kiss her. Thoughts of fleeing as fast as she could sprang to mind, but she told herself she must allow Jonathan to court her, even to kiss her. After all, she simply could not leave the manor yet.

Leaning forward, he closed his eyes. Hannah squeezed her eyes shut and waited for it to happen. His lips brushed hers back and forth before he pressed his mouth to hers. She fisted her hands, trying to keep herself from pushing him away. Although her lips were stiff, she let the kiss linger.

Finally, he pulled away, and Hannah opened her eyes. He smiled at her, his eyes sparkling with passion. "There, now. That was not too hard, was it?" He stroked her cheek.

She cleared her throat. "Of course not."

"Maybe we can try it once more when you aren't so nervous."

A laugh sprang from her before she had time to stop it. She quickly scooted away and stood. "Yes, that's a splendid idea. Perhaps tomorrow."

His smile dropped into a frown. "I suppose tomorrow is fine, but I was in hopes of giving it another try now."

"Jonathan, you are so bold. Can you not give me time to catch my breath and get to know you a little better first?"

He stood and took hold of her trembling hands. "I shall give you all the time you need. I'm not in any hurry."

Hannah breathed a sigh. "Thank you for your patience with me."

He kissed her knuckles, then placed her hand in the crook of his arm. "Come. I will take you back to your room now."

"I would like that."

As she walked by his side up the stairs, she glanced out of the long, colored windowpanes. The fog outside had thickened. The cold, misty weather made the atmosphere in the manor that much more foreboding.

From outside, the howl of a wolf echoed in the night. Jonathan froze on the steps, then turned and looked at her with wide eyes.

"What's wrong?" she asked softly.

"He's out again tonight." He shook his head. "It's not midnight yet."

"Who?"

"The white wolf." His voice shook.

"Has he not done this before?"

"No. Usually after he kills, he goes back into hiding for a few months."

Hannah frowned. "Very strange indeed."

Jonathan smiled and patted her hands, his fearful expression disappearing. "Not to worry. I shall stay by your side and protect you."

"Oh, Jonathan, you are so heroic. But I shall be safe in my room, I assure you."

Once they reached her chambers, he stopped and put his arms around her. She was relieved when he only kissed her forehead.

"Please don't go chasing after your maid tonight. It is dangerous outside."

"So I have been told."

He kissed her mouth this time, but briefly. "Tomorrow I shall take you into Exeter. Would you like that?"

"Yes, very much." She touched his arm. "And perhaps we can ask questions around town about my friend."

Jonathan looked puzzled. "What friend?"

"The friend I asked you about yesterday afternoon—Miss Amelia Hartley."

He shook his head. "I don't recall you asking about your friend. What is wrong with her?"

Hannah gasped. "You know . . . my friend who came here a few months ago so you might court her."

"Hannah, my sweet." He stroked her cheek. "I don't know what you mean. You haven't mentioned anyone named Amelia."

Her heartbeat quickened. "Yes, I did, when we went for a ride yesterday afternoon."

He chuckled and squeezed her shoulders. "My dear, I believe you have been daydreaming again. I don't recall you saying anything about your friend."

Panic threatened to close off Hannah's throat. *What is wrong with him? Why doesn't he remember?* "Perhaps I have been in another world," she muttered. "With everything that has happened of late, it is no wonder."

"Very true." He pressed a kiss to her forehead one last time and pulled away. "Please get some rest tonight. I fear you are not sleeping well, and that is the reason you are not yourself."

"I believe you are correct. Thank you for understanding, Jonathan."

She hurried into her room and closed the door. Tears welled in her eyes, and she fought the lump forming in her throat. She *had* told him about Amelia—she knew she had!

Taking deep breaths, she roamed aimlessly around her room, trying to sort her thoughts. This house was full of secrets, and it was enough to drive *anyone* mad. Then she thought of the irresistible man who had tried to convince her he wasn't real.

A knock sounded on the door. Francine peeked her head inside. "Will you need my assistance? Mr. Jonathan mentioned you were out of sorts this evening."

"Yes . . . no . . . I don't know." Hannah motioned with her hand. "Please come in and close the door." Once Francine was inside, Hannah asked, "Where were you earlier this evening?"

"I've been helping Mrs. White since the graveside service."

Hannah rubbed her forehead. "Something very strange is happening around here."

Francine rushed to her and took hold of her cold hands. "I know. I think we should leave posthaste."

"We can't, for I haven't yet found any answers about my father's death. And today I'm more confused than ever about my friend Amelia."

"Why? Will Monsieur Jonathan not help you locate her?"

"That's the strange thing, Francine. Jonathan does not even remember me asking him about her yesterday."

The maid's eyes widened.

"That man confuses me." Hannah shook her head. "Sometimes he acts like he is oblivious to everything. It is as if he is not well most of the time."

"Very strange indeed, which is why we must leave here, mademoiselle."

Hannah pulled her hand away. "Not until I have discovered what happened to Amelia. She was heading to this manor before she disappeared. If anyone knows what happened to her, I'm quite certain it will be someone here." For that she needed Morgan's help.

"What are you going to do?"

"I don't know." Hannah threw her hands in the air and paced the floor, her head pounding with each step. "They are keeping secrets, and I must find out what they are."

"Will you ask Monsieur Roderick?"

"Oh, heavens no." Hannah faced her maid, planting her hands on her hips. "I don't trust anyone here. Especially him."

"Why?"

Hannah shrugged. "I don't know what it is, but he has a deceitful way about him. Worst of all, his wicked gaze follows me around the room. When I catch him looking at me, I feel undressed."

Francine scrunched her face and stuck out her tongue.

"See? You know exactly what I mean," Hannah replied. "I don't trust Bethany, either. She is too sweet, and she is often overly dramatic."

Francine giggled. "Yes, mademoiselle, that is so."

Hannah rubbed her forehead and resumed her pacing. What could she do?

Morgan. Her heart soared with excitement at the thought of him. He knew his family better than anyone. He could tell her what was going on at Thornton Manor—*if* she could get him to open up to her.

"Is there anything you would like me to do?" Francine asked.

"Tomorrow, ask the other servants. They know things that happen in this house. See if anyone knows what happened to Amelia. I know my friend was here." Hannah placed her hand over her heart. "I can feel it."

"I shall help. I promise."

Relief poured through Hannah while the maid helped her undress and brushed her hair. Hannah would find her friend, even if she had to stumble over the Thorntons' secrets to do so.

Seven

The kiss had done it! Morgan groaned and lifted himself off the floor after another night of shifting. Weariness filled his body as he staggered toward his bed to grab his robe. Passion brought out the beast in him, literally. He could not let it happen again.

Yet as he had watched Hannah and Jonathan in the music room through the secret mirror in the wall, Morgan's chest had ached with longing. And jealousy. He wanted to be the one sitting next to her at the pianoforte, teaching her how to play. He wanted to be the one to hold her and kiss her sweet mouth.

There was more to her than mere beauty. When he had rescued her from the dogs, she had looked upon him as if he were the most perfect man she had ever seen. His heart softened, and forbidden feelings crept inside of him. Hannah should have run away from this place. She should have seen him as a beast as everyone else did.

In his attempt to save her, however, something quite remarkable had happened. Up until now he had never remembered much about shifting or his night hours as the wolf. But the previous day, he had spoken to the wild dogs in a language only they knew. He had warned them to leave, promising to kill them if they did not. The dogs had understood him, and Hannah had noticed and questioned him about it.

Morgan shook his head and slipped the robe around him, then tied the sash tightly around his waist. She would definitely want to know more. That he couldn't tell her. He would certainly become a beast in her eyes if he confessed the truth.

Groaning, he sat on the edge of the bed and buried his head in his hands. Sunlight spilled through the heavy velvet curtains, threatening to make his headache worse. Perhaps he should tell Hannah about his secret—the truth about the East Wing Ghost. Maybe then she would leave this place and never return.

He rubbed his hands over his legs, trying to ease the pain that always tortured his body after he shifted. When would his curse be lifted? He scowled. Never. The witch wanted one thing—the one thing he didn't know.

Unless . . . what if Hannah knew? If her father knew about a map to the island's treasure, had he passed it on to his daughter? If they could find this map, perhaps the witch would lift Morgan's curse. He could only pray it would be the case. But asking for Hannah's help would put her in danger, unless he protected her from the witch.

Suddenly, the floor creaked and heavy perfume permeated the air. Morgan jerked upright as the woman of his nightmares swept into his room. It had been several months since she had paid him a visit, but she had not changed. Her outward beauty had been destroyed by the evil lurking inside her.

Wearing a long, transparent gown, with her hair in disarray, she looked as if she had just gotten out of bed. Morgan knew she did this to try to entice him. It would not work. Not ever.

"Tsk, tsk, tsk." She shook her head and sashayed closer. "Shifting twice in one week, Morgan. That has to be a record for you."

He glared, wishing he could literally shoot daggers from his eyes and destroy her. "How did you know?"

"I know everything, my darling man."

"Go away," he grumbled. "You are not welcome here."

She stopped in front of him and caressed his face. "I'm starting to wonder if you actually have some feeling for your brother's newest conquest."

He pushed her hand away. "You are mistaken."

Throwing back her head, the witch cackled. "Oh, my dear Morgan. You can't lie to me. I'm the one who cursed you. I know when you are smitten."

He stood and walked past her, stopping at the bookshelf. "As you mentioned before, she is my brother's conquest. Why should I care one thing about her?"

"Because I know you well. Although you are a cursed beast, you are still a man. Miss Forester is a lovely woman, after all."

Soft footsteps on the floor behind him crept near, warning him of her intent. But he could not do anything about it. He would never be able to hide from her.

She stopped behind him and ran her hands up his back to his shoulders and then down each arm. "I have always thought your body was muscular, you know. I think shifting has made you even stronger." She squeezed his forearms. "I long for the day you will be mine."

"Give up that dream. I will never happen.

"Tell me what I want to hear, and I'll free you from the curse."

Angrily, he spun around and grasped her arms in a tight hold. How he wished he could grow the beast's canine teeth now. He would love to sink them into her neck and rip out her throat. But killing her would make his curse a life sentence.

"I don't know where the map is, or the blasted treasure. Why can you not understand that?"

"Oh, I think you do know," the witch said. "You were with Mr. Forester before he died, and he had the map. I believe he gave it to you."

Morgan groaned. "He did not, I tell you!"

"When you finally tire of turning into a wolf, you will come to me, begging me to remove your curse. I'm quite certain you will do anything to make me happy then."

"Think again." He shoved her away and stormed past her into the next room. He knelt by the hearth and threw more logs onto the dying cinders. He was not alone for long.

"If you want Miss Forester to live, you will remove her from your thoughts." The witch's voice came at him like shards of glass, the message just as painful.

"Do you remember what happened to the other women?" she continued.

He squeezed his eyes closed and gnashed his teeth. "No. I remember nothing. You know that."

She bent over him, running her hands down his chest through the opening of his robe. Her hands stopped over his heart. "Deep inside you know what happened. I need not tell you."

Morgan's chest ached from her words. "Please leave."

She nuzzled her face against him and kissed his earlobe. Bile rose in his throat, nearly choking him.

"I shall go but will return soon," she whispered. "You love me. You are just too stubborn to admit it."

He didn't turn to watch. He didn't have to know when she left, because her disgusting scent disappeared with her.

Sighing, he pushed his palms against his closed eyes, hoping to relieve the throb that grew deeper by the second. There was only one way to keep the witch from coming to see him. He had to convince Hannah to leave. If the witch knew how deep his attraction for Hannah went, he would be cursed for sure.

The witch would not leave his side, not if she knew there was competition. And if the beast didn't kill Hannah, the witch might do it instead. He could not live with himself either way.

Wearily, he stumbled to his bed. Shifting always drained him. He removed his robe before climbing between the sheets. Exhaustion filled his head, but with it came the beautiful vision of the woman he had kissed the day before.

When he watched her kissing Jonathan, Morgan could tell she didn't enjoy it. Her body was too stiff, her lips too tight. But she had enjoyed the kiss *they* shared, he thought with a smile.

As his eyelids grew heavy and his breathing slowed, his body felt so weightless it was as if he floated on air. He closed his eyes. In his mind, he left his chambers and made his way through the secret tunnels to Hannah's room, where he took her in his arms and kissed her endlessly.

Hannah held her parasol to block the sun as she rode beside Jonathan in the open two-seat buggy. Francine sat in the back reading a novel and keeping to herself. They drove past the small village on the other side of the Thornton estate, and people waved and called out greetings. Though she didn't know the villagers, Hannah nodded at them in return.

"Most of these people work the Thornton lands," Jonathan explained. "Several of them have been in our employ since before I was born."

"How amazing." Hannah smiled.

"In fact, did you know Bethany's mother used to work for us?"

Hannah blinked at him with wide eyes. "Indeed? I would have never thought that."

"I know. It's hard to believe her family labored for a living. She plays the mistress of the house so well that most people think it has been in her blood for generations."

"My thoughts exactly."

Jonathan shook his head. "Her father used to work the land, but he died when Bethany was ten. That's when her mother started working in our house as a maid."

"Very interesting. Had Bethany ever been a servant in your house?"

"No. Because her mother worked for us, my father helped support Bethany in school. Not many of the servants were educated, and my father wanted them to have the knowledge." He glanced at her. "Not very often do men in my father's position do this for their servants."

"No, they don't," Hannah replied. "I'm very impressed with how well your father cared for them."

Beaming, Jonathan puffed out his chest. "My father was a great man."

Hannah touched his arm. "And I can tell you are following in his footsteps."

Jonathan's face reddened. "What a sweet thing to say."

She smiled, then continued, "Tell me about your childhood. Were you a close family?"

"Oh, yes." He nodded. "My brothers and I are only a few years apart, so as children we played together and teased each other as all siblings do. Being the youngest, I was spoiled a little more than the others, but since Morgan was oldest, he had gotten his fair share of attention. Father trained him from the moment Morgan could walk—he wanted him to excel at everything. That's one of the reasons Morgan was forced to take music lessons. He didn't like them at first but later learned he had a talent for playing and writing music." Jonathan sighed. "Father wanted to make certain Morgan would be able to take his place as master of Thornton Manor one day."

"What about Roderick?" Hannah wondered. "What was he like?"

Jonathan shrugged. "I remember he got in trouble a lot. Morgan told me Roddy craved that kind of attention. Another thing I remember is that Roddy always competed with Morgan, and when Roddy could not measure up, it upset him. Sometimes he would take it out on Morgan."

"What did Morgan do?"

Jonathan chuckled. "Most of the time he ignored Roddy, which upset him even more."

Hannah laughed. "I can see how that would be maddening, especially when someone is vying for more attention."

"You know" —Jonathan glanced at Hannah again— "another thing I remember is Roddy being sneaky. As we were growing into men, he became a secretive person. Both Morgan and I knew he was up to no good, but Roddy would not confess what he had been doing." He chuckled. "Of course Morgan figured Roddy was sneaking out after dark to meet girls."

Hannah glanced in the back seat at Francine, who looked her way and nodded.

"I don't doubt that one bit," Hannah told Jonathan.

"If you ask me," Jonathan continued, "he has not changed that much."

"No?"

Jonathan shook his head. "Roddy still sneaks out after dark and meets women."

So, Jonathan was not ignorant to his brother's faults. "How very sad for Bethany."

"Indeed, it is. If not for me, I'm certain that woman would have gone insane by now. I cheer her up the best I can."

Hannah patted his arm. "What a wonderful brother-in-law you are."

He turned to gaze at her and winked before focusing on the road again.

Soon, they arrived at their destination. Hannah didn't usually come this far into town, only because her uncle forbade it. The older man ruled over her as if she were a disobedient child. If only she could have been sent to another family member after her father died, but alas, Uncle George was the closest relative—and unfortunately, the only one who could afford to take her in.

Jonathan stopped the buggy in front of the mercantile. He helped Hannah down, then turned and helped Francine. He smiled at Hannah and offered his arm, so she wrapped her hand around it and he escorted her down the street.

As they walked past the shops, Jonathan told her stories about the businesses. Hannah could not believe how well he remembered things like this, yet could not recall discussing her friend Amelia the other day.

At Hannah's reminder, he took her to the constable's office, where she explained about her friend Amelia. At first the older man looked confused.

"Would her family not report her missing?" he asked.

Hannah shrugged. "I sincerely hope so, but since she lives with her aged grandfather, I wonder if the old man even realizes she should have returned from her visit with the Thorntons."

"Miss Hartley has no other family?"

"None."

"Then I will do some investigating into this matter."

Hannah sighed with relief. "Thank you. I pray you will find answers to her disappearance soon."

"As do I."

When Hannah turned, Jonathan was not inside. She hurried out the door and glanced up and down the street. He stood across the way talking to a few younger women. She rolled her eyes. Jonathan was a charmer like his brother, yet in a different way.

She strolled across the street and stopped by his side. He smiled at her. "Forgive me for leaving you, Hannah. I saw some acquaintances and thought to visit a little."

"There is no need to apologize." She nodded to the other women. "Pleasant day for an outing, is it not?"

"Very pleasant, indeed," one of the ladies replied.

Jonathan tipped his hat. "If you will excuse us, Miss Forester and I will continue our walk."

Hannah slipped her hand in the crook of his elbow and allowed him to lead the way. She found it strange that he had not asked her about her talk with the constable.

They came upon a bakery, and Jonathan led her inside. As he talked with the man at the counter, another customer walked in. Hannah didn't know Mary Beth Williams very well, but the middle-aged woman lived down the lane from Hannah's uncle. Hannah smiled and approached the other woman.

"Good day, Mrs. Williams."

The older woman's smile deepened the wrinkles around her mouth and eyes. "Hello, Miss Forester. What a pleasure to see you in town." The lady's gaze darted to Jonathan. "Are you here with Mr. Thornton?"

"Yes. We are taking a stroll and visiting the shops." Hannah glanced again at Jonathan, who still talked with the baker.

Concern etched Mrs. Williams's brow and she leaned closer. "My dear Miss Forester, are you perhaps . . . um . . . courting Mr. Thornton?" she asked with a lowered voice.

"Yes. I was invited to the manor to stay as their guest so that Jonathan and I might become acquainted."

Mrs. Williams frowned, pulling on Hannah's arm to move her further away from Jonathan. "Have you not heard what goes on in that place?"

"Well, I have heard a few things. Why? What have you heard?"

"That family has not been in their right mind since the oldest brother died in the house fire."

"Indeed?" Hannah glanced again at Jonathan, who had not looked her way. "Jonathan seems fine to me."

"He is not. He is actually worse than the others." Mrs. William gripped Hannah's arm. "Please assure me you will not stay with them for long. That place is not safe for good women like yourself."

Hannah shook her head. "Why do you think such a thing? Haven't you heard that Jonathan's sister-in-law has brought many women to the manor in hopes of finding him a wife?"

Mrs. Williams crinkled her brow. "Many, you say?"

"Yes. In fact, my friend Amelia Hartley was one of them."

"Emmet Hartley's granddaughter?"

"Yes."

"How did she find the Thornton family?"

"I wish I knew." Hannah sighed heavily. "She has disappeared. She went to meet Jonathan but apparently left after staying at the manor only a few hours. That was several weeks ago."

Mrs. Williams sucked in a quick breath, placing her hand on her bosom. "Amelia has not returned?"

"No. And nobody knows where she is."

"That is dreadful." The older woman pursed her lips. "I suspect the Thornton family knows more than they are telling."

"What makes you think that—"

"Miss Forester," Jonathan called as he hurried to her, handing her a sweet roll. "I hope you don't mind that I bought you one."

Pulling away from Mrs. Williams, Hannah smiled at him. "Not at all." She glanced back at the other woman, who nodded to her and gave a small curtsy to Jonathan before mumbling an excuse and leaving.

Slowly, Hannah stepped out of the bakery beside Jonathan. While people treated him politely, Hannah wondered if most of them thought him insane.

"Jonathan?"

"Yes," he responded before taking another bite of his roll.

"Did you talk to the baker about my friend?"

Jonathan narrowed his gaze on her. "What friend?"

"Amelia Hartley. Remember, you brought me to town to ask people questions about my friend."

"Hannah, my dear, I have no idea what you mean. I promised you no such thing."

Her chest clenched. *Why does he not remember?* Poor Jonathan really was losing his mind, it seemed. She turned and bit into her roll as tears stung her eyes. As much as she didn't want to live with her uncle, she could hardly wait to return to his little cottage. *Soon,* she told herself. Soon she would discover the answers she needed and leave Thornton Manor as quickly as she had come.

They didn't stay in town much longer before Jonathan brought her home. Hannah rushed to her room, then shut and locked the door. With a sinking heart, she threw herself on the bed and pressed her face into her pillow. She could not ask Jonathan for assistance when the poor man needed help himself. And what bothered her more, Bethany and Roderick knew this and still continued to try to find him a wife.

A tear slipped down Hannah's face, and she wiped it away. Perhaps she should admit defeat. No, she told herself. While her father was alive, he would not hear of his daughter cowering, so for his sake, she must not do it now.

Not bothering to extinguish the lamp in the corner, she stripped to her shift and crawled into bed, pulling the blankets to her chin. Tears filled her eyes again, but she blinked them back. Trying to think of something pleasant, she pictured Morgan. Even though he crept around in the night and refused to tell her his story, he had been kind to her, and he had saved her life. She felt drawn to him, and it was his secrets she wanted to discover more than anything.

She smiled sleepily as she thought of the kiss they had shared. What she wouldn't give to kiss him again and be in his strong arms once more. She could practically feel his embrace now, his fingers stroking her face and sliding down to touch her neck. She would caress his face, and he would let her remove the scarf to see the scars she knew must be beneath it. In her mind, he was the most handsome man she'd ever met.

"Hannah," a deep voice said, pulling her from her thoughts.

Morgan? She glanced at the door, but it remained closed and locked. She shook her head. She must be dreaming again.

"Hannah." The voice grew louder. The floor in the corner of her room creaked, and the heavy drapes moved mere seconds before a tall figure emerged.

She blinked. "Morgan?" She sat up and clasped the sheet to her chest.

He removed his hooded cloak and set it on the chair near the window. As before, half of his face was hidden by a black scarf. His clothing was as dignified as Roderick's and Jonathan's, but Morgan's frame was more muscular.

"How did you . . . where did you . . ." She shook her head. "I am going mad."

He rushed to her side, knelt by the bed, and grasped her arms. "No, you are not. Remember when I took you through the tunnel yesterday?"

"Yes."

"There are secret passageways all over the manor. Behind your curtains is a door in the corner of the room."

She gasped, her hand going to her throat. "Do you spy on me often?"

"No, of course not, but I needed to see you today."

She smiled and put her hand on his chest. "I wanted to see you, too."

"Why were you crying a few minutes ago?"

It relieved her that he didn't know what had been playing in her thoughts right after that moment of weakness. "Staying with your family is most confusing."

His chest shook with silent laughter. "Alas, someone else understands my pain." Using his knuckle, he wiped at the tears on her cheek. "But what is it about my family that disturbs you so?"

"Their secrets, of course."

Morgan's smile disappeared. Dropping his hands, he stepped away. "Which is why you must leave."

"I can't do that."

"Why are you so stubborn?"

"What about you?" She cocked her head and folded her arms. "You keep secrets from me, just as I do from you."

"My secrets will cause you harm if I disclose them."

"So you have been telling me. You asked me to trust you yesterday, yet you will not trust me." She threw off the sheet, grabbed her wrapper, and shrugged into it. She walked to the window and pushed aside a curtain just enough to peek out. The weather had changed drastically since afternoon. Dark clouds covered the sun, and as usual, fog threatened in the distance.

What could she do to change Morgan's mind? She needed his help, just as he needed hers. Yet the emotions running through her from her dream were so real, she would be satisfied to throw herself in his arms and kiss him to distraction.

Morgan's heart twisted as he watched Hannah. So beautiful. So kind. What could he tell her to make her leave? The truth? As much as he wanted to, he knew she would not believe him. And even if she did, he didn't want her to know he was not a man but a beast.

He crossed the floor and stopped behind her. Her chestnut curls hung down her back. How he wanted to stroke the satin locks and feel them glide through his fingers, but he knew what would happen if he did that—the same thing that always happened since he had been cursed. But looking at her now, he didn't care. He needed to feel her touch, to just *feel.*

If he convinced her to leave his family and this cursed manor, he would never be able to touch her again. It was now or never.

Hesitantly, he slid his hand down the soft waves of her hair. He closed his eyes and inhaled her sweet scent of lilacs. This was wrong. He should have the decency to beg her forgiveness and excuse himself. But he could not.

She turned and faced him, and his hand fell to her shoulder. He opened his eyes. Her wide brown eyes met his gray ones.

He cleared his suddenly dry throat. "As you have surmised, this house is full of secrets. Dangerous secrets that might take your life."

"What do you mean? Your family doesn't seem dangerous."

His heart clenched. "I can't explain, sweet Hannah. I would fear for your safety if you were to know the truth."

"But Morgan, I know you will protect me."

"I can't always protect you. Have you forgotten I'm in hiding?"

She placed her hands on his chest. His breathing grew ragged, and he didn't know how much more of her closeness he could take. Yet he didn't push her away. Indeed, he was a fool for taking this kind of punishment, as sweet at it was.

"If you are in hiding, how do you know where I am at all times?" Without taking her eyes off him, she motioned her head toward the secret door. "Through the tunnels?"

"Yes."

"Then you know when I'm in danger."

He shook his head. "You don't understand."

She stepped closer, sliding her hands up his arms. He held in a groan.

"Then help me understand," she said.

He cupped her face. Closing her eyes, she tilted her head back, letting his hands glide down her neck. Tonight he would pay dearly for feeling these emotions.

"Morgan," she whispered. "I have never felt these feelings for a man. What is this power you hold over me?"

He held her face again and ran his thumb along her bottom lip. Her beautiful eyes opened, and her gaze held his.

"I wish I could tell you all would be made right, Hannah, but I can't. I don't dare give you false hope."

She took his hand and nuzzled her lips against his palm. "Please let me stay with you."

With a sigh of surrender, he pulled her face to his and captured her lips. She clung to his shirt, pressing herself against him as her mouth answered his. He pulled her closer still. She gasped and wrapped her arms around his neck. Moaning, he deepened the kiss, tilting his head with hers in wild abandonment.

Kissing her made him feel human—like a man again—and he didn't want to stop. The more he kissed her, the more passion he felt. Yet, his feelings went deeper than just passion. He wanted to make Hannah his and only his, body and soul. But he knew he could not love her, as it would only hurt them both in the end.

Finally, he jerked away from her and stepped back. She swayed, then lowered to the bed and sat on the edge. Wide, questioning eyes stared up at him.

He breathed deeply and stroked her chin. "Hannah, my darling, we don't know each other, but it feels as if I have known you all my life."

"I know," she said with a smile.

"I'm still amazed that you would want to kiss a beast such as me in the first place, but—"

She jumped to her feet and scowled. "You are not a beast. Why would you say such a thing?"

"Yes, I am a beast. And I wanted to come and see you this afternoon to warn you. You are not safe here."

"Will you ever stop telling me to leave?"

"Not until you are safely back home with your uncle."

Hannah shook her head and turned toward the window again. "What makes you think I'm any safer with my uncle?"

Morgan's chest tightened. Were there other secrets she hid from him? If only he could trust her with his, maybe she would divulge hers. Yet the truth was, his secret could kill her.

He swallowed hard. "Hannah, please try to understand. My family is insane—every last one of them. They can't be trusted, and you must leave as soon as possible before something terrible happens." Morgan took slow steps until he reached her. She hadn't turned to look at him, so he softly touched her hair. "I don't know what I would do if something tragic happened to you."

Hannah straightened her shoulders and lifted her chin in defiance. "I'm sorry, but I can't leave, not yet."

He shook his head. "Although I don't understand, I shall try. At least I have warned you of the dangers that might befall you and your maid."

She placed her hand on his arm, and his temper calmed. "When will I see you again?" she asked.

"I don't know."

"Tomorrow night? I shall come to your room."

A sigh escaped him, and his heart melted. He took her back in his arms and kissed her forehead. "You are tempting fate by coming to my room, Hannah. Don't you know how hard it is to resist you?"

She looked up at him with a smile. "That's what I had hoped you would say."

He turned and walked toward the hidden doorway that led to the tunnels. "And whatever you do, keep away from Roderick," he said over his shoulder.

She drew her brows together. "Why?"

"Trust me." Morgan turned and hurried through the passageway before he told her everything. As hard as it was not to bear his soul to her, he must not. She would be safer if he simply said nothing.

Eight

A satisfied smile sneaked across Hannah's face as she stared at her plate of food. She pushed the piece of fish with her fork and thought about Morgan. Seated across from her at the table, Jonathan and Roderick talked about one of the tenant farmers, and she didn't bother to listen closely. However, she did notice the disapproving glares Bethany threw her way.

Hannah sipped her red wine. Perhaps Bethany sensed her reluctance to become seriously attached to Jonathan. But Hannah could not help the way she felt about Morgan. He occupied her thoughts more than his youngest brother did, and though Hannah was not sure how it had happened, Morgan had crept into her heart, as well. She had kissed other men, but it had never felt like it did with Morgan.

Setting her glass down, she glanced around the table. She truly didn't know anyone very well—not even Morgan. But she trusted him. Her heart told her to. Her father had wanted her to.

Bethany placed her fork beside her dish and cleared her throat. "Hannah dear, Roderick and I have decided to have a masked ball to celebrate Jonathan's birthday. I do hope you will help me plan it."

Hannah blinked as a bit of food stuck in her throat. She coughed and managed a smile. "I would be delighted to help make the arrangements. When will it be, and how many guests will be attending?"

"We will have it Friday after next."

Just as Hannah lifted the glass to her mouth, she stalled. "Friday after next? That's All Hallows' Eve."

"Yes, it is. Jonathan was born on that day." Bethany smiled broadly. "As for the guest list, I hope you will help me with that. I fear I don't know as many people in town as you."

Hannah wiped her mouth with her linen napkin. "I shall certainly help in any way I can." She looked at Jonathan, whose wide eyes revealed that the party was a surprise to him, too. "Jonathan? I didn't know it was your birthday. How old will you be?"

"Twenty-six."

"A perfect age." She glanced back at Bethany, who was glaring at her for some reason. "May I ask why you wish to have a masked ball?"

Bethany let out a low chuckle. "Since Jonathan was a young lad, he has always had a masked ball to celebrate his birthday."

As Hannah took a bite of her food, she realized why this family disturbed her so. They were dark and mysterious, just like All Hallows' Eve. The masked ball theme only added to her suspicions.

Perhaps Morgan was right and these people were dangerous. If it was true, then *he* could not stay here, either.

There was no other way—she must convince Morgan to leave with her.

"Let's start making plans immediately," Bethany continued. "Tomorrow I shall have Horace send out the invitations."

"Splendid idea." Hannah gave the lady of the house her best smile.

Bethany pushed away from the table and stood. "Gentlemen, if you will excuse us, Hannah and I will be in the parlor."

As Hannah followed her hostess, she felt a sudden eeriness overtaking her. Something was wrong, dreadfully wrong. But the only way she would know for certain was to go along with Bethany to see what lay ahead.

They sat in the parlor, writing down names and addresses, and planning the menu for the party. Mrs. White hung back in the corner of the room, seemingly preoccupied in dusting some bookshelves and then fiddling with a silver tea set that was arranged on a large platter. Hannah didn't pay much attention to her at first, but after half an hour, she realized the housekeeper was eavesdropping. Surprisingly, Bethany said nothing to the servant. As time passed, Hannah decided Mrs. White was simply curious about the plans for Jonathan's party.

After a few hours of pouring over names and jotting notes, Hannah wearily climbed the stairs to her room. Not too far behind her lurked Mrs. White. When Hannah reached her room and opened her door, she stood and waited for the servant to approach. The older woman drew near, her eyes wide.

"Mrs. White, may I speak with you in private?"

The woman glanced up and down the hall as if making sure no one else was around. She nodded and followed Hannah inside the room.

Once the door was closed, Hannah took a deep breath. "You may think I'm bold for saying this, but that is just my nature. Was there a reason you were in the parlor listening to Mrs. Thornton and me?"

The other woman lowered her gaze as she wrung her hands against her waist. "I beg your forgiveness, Miss Forester, but I was waiting for a chance to talk to you."

"Indeed?"

"I have been with the Thorntons for several years. I feel as if I'm a part of their family."

Hannah nodded. "That's understandable."

"Out of all the young women Mrs. Thornton has asked to come to the manor to make Jonathan's acquaintance, I like you the best. You are not afraid to speak, and you seem very intelligent."

"Thank you, Mrs. White. You are very kind."

The older woman stepped closer and touched Hannah's clasped hands. "But I fear you are withdrawing from Jonathan, just as the other women have done. Please be patient with him. His mind is not what it used to be, but he is a very kind, loving man. He would make a wonderful and attentive husband."

Guilt washed over Hannah, making her smile waver. She did not want Jonathan for a husband, but she could not allow anyone to know her thoughts. "I shall keep that in mind. I do enjoy Jonathan's company, and I'm very much looking forward to his birthday ball."

Mrs. White straightened. "I'm very happy to hear that, Miss Forester. Once again, forgive me for being so audacious, but I had to tell you."

"Not to worry. I understand you now." Hannah smiled. "But before you leave, may I ask you a question?"

"Certainly."

"The other day you told my maid that Miss Amelia Hartley had come to the manor to court Jonathan, but that she left quickly. Is this correct?"

"Yes, it is. She didn't even stay the night."

Hannah's heart hammered quicker and she stepped closer. "Please, Mrs. White, I must know what happened. She is a friend, and I have not seen her for quite a while."

The housekeeper shrugged. "There is nothing to tell, really. She came, took the midday meal with Master Roderick and

Mistress Bethany, and left. I didn't talk to her at all, but I had heard the reason she didn't stay was because she thought the manor was . . . haunted."

"I wish I knew what happened to her when she left here. She didn't return home."

Mrs. White's eyes went wide, and she lifted her hand to her mouth. "Oh, heavens. You don't suppose—"

"What?"

"Forgive me, but with the white wolf nearby, it is hard not to come to the conclusion that the wolf killed your friend." She ended in a whisper.

Tears stung Hannah's eyes as she shook her head. "I refuse to believe that. If the wolf killed Amelia, wouldn't someone have found her body by now?"

"Perhaps."

Breathing deeply, Hannah tried to calm her herself. "My friend's disappearance is most worrisome."

"I understand." Mrs. White curtsied. "Good night, Miss Forester."

Afraid she would start crying again, Hannah didn't speak another word as the woman hurried out of the room. Too many questions needed answers, and she was not a patient person.

On weary legs, she stumbled toward her vanity. She hadn't seen or heard from Francine tonight, but she didn't want to wait for the maid to help her undress. As soon as she removed her outer clothing, she would climb into bed and fall asleep instantly.

She glanced at the open curtains. Hadn't she closed them before leaving her room? Perhaps Mrs. White or one of the maids had opened them while straightening the room earlier.

Hannah hurried to the window and grasped the gold cord so she could close the curtains, but then paused to take in the view. Outside, the fog was heavy in patches, and the moon loomed large in the sky. Suddenly, shadows moved near the wooded area, drawing her attention. She narrowed her eyes, trying to see more clearly, but to no avail. With a sigh, she shut the curtains.

Just then, from outside, a voice rang through the night, screaming Hannah's name. She yanked the curtains open and peered into the night. Gradually, shadows took the shape of people. One wore a black, hooded cloak, but the figure was too short and slender to be Morgan. The cloaked person pulled a struggling woman along behind.

Hannah rubbed her eyes and looked again. As before, her name was called in a panicked voice. Fear gripped her like icy fingers. *Francine!* This time there was no mistaking the scene below. Her maid struggled with the person grasping her wrist, who now forcefully yanked her toward the forest. Francine glanced back at the manor and screamed her mistress's name again.

Renewed strength filled Hannah as she grabbed her cloak and rushed out of the room. Her heartbeat hammered as she ran down the stairs, up the hall to the front door, and out of the house into the cold night.

"Francine! Where are you?"

When there was no answer, Hannah's heart jumped to her throat. Her chest tightened and she ran faster. The fog grew dense in spots, making it almost impossible to see more than a few feet in front of her, but she surged forward, calling for her maid.

Deep into the woods she ran, with no idea where she was going. With every step she prayed she would come upon her maid, or hear her voice. Tree branches tore at Hannah's cloak and her hair, scratching her face and arms, but she didn't care.

After what seemed like hours, she stopped. She heaved quick breaths that parched her aching throat. She had not dreamed it this time. She had seen Francine, and someone was taking her away!

Hannah glanced around and listened. It was surreally quiet, especially for the woods.

"Francine?" she called out again, her voice raspy.

When no answer came, she sobbed and sank to her knees on the cold ground. Tears streamed down her cheeks and fell into the clasped hands she held against her mouth.

In the distance came the cry of a wolf. *The white wolf?*

Hannah shook her head. No matter how everyone around here tried to convince her, she didn't believe in such legends.

When she stood, her limbs quaked from both fear and fatigue. Step by step, she tried to retrace her path back to the manor. If only she could remember which way she had come.

The wolf howled again, closer this time. Hannah clasped her cloak, pulling the garment tighter around her body to ward off the coldness. With every step, she searched through the fog and strained to hear something—anything.

All of a sudden, bushes rustled and twigs snapped nearby. Someone was coming! Hannah glanced at the trees, wondering if she should climb one to try to hide. Another twig snapped, and the growl of an animal rumbled through the air. Hannah froze in fear, afraid to even breathe.

Through the fog, yellow eyes moved toward her, and within seconds the outline of a wolf appeared. A white wolf. He bared his teeth, stalking closer.

Hannah whimpered. "Please don't." Against her ribs her heartbeat thundered. Would he kill her immediately?

The wolf stared at her. Even through her fear, she realized she had never seen a more beautiful animal. Pure white fur covered the wolf, and perfect ears stood straight on top his head. The long, bushy tail didn't move as the animal stared her way.

Several long moments passed. Hannah dared not move for fear of provoking the animal further. If the rapid speed of her heart didn't kill her, the wolf certainly would. Silently, she prayed Morgan would save her as he did the last time, but as each second passed, her hopes sank lower.

Finally, the white wolf moved, taking a step closer. Clutching her shaking hands against her chest, Hannah squeezed her eyes closed and whimpered. The heat of his breath fanned her face. She waited for his sharp teeth to sink into her skin, but instead she felt soft fur rubbing gently against her hand.

She peeked at the wolf, keeping as still as she could. He looked up at her, his large, yellow eyes staring wondrously into her eyes for a brief moment. Then he whined and nudged her with his nose before rubbing his head on her hand again.

The beast seemed friendly, but how could that be? Hadn't he already killed several women, including Sarah, the Thorntons' servant?

Now, the wolf sat in front of her and lifted his paw. Letting out a whine, he rested the paw on Hannah's leg. Her heart leaped in terror. She had heard once that some animals play with their victims before they kill them, and perhaps this was the case now.

Keeping his eyes on her, the wolf touched her again. He let out a soft whine and tilted his head at her.

Hannah licked her lips. "Wh–what do you want?" she whispered.

The wolf rose to all fours and stepped in front of her as if he was leaving. He took a couple of steps then turned and looked back at her. He whined once more before turning and taking a few more steps, then stopping again to peer back at her, his eyes glowing.

Perhaps all the rumors of the white wolf had been false. Obviously, the animal was not trying to hurt her, but help her. Hannah clasped her cold, shaky hands and walked toward him on quaky limbs. She kept a few steps behind him as he led her through the trees. Every so often, he turned and looked at her as if to make certain she followed.

Soon, the lights from the manor shone through the night like a beacon in the fog. Tears gathered in her eyes, and a shudder of relief ran through her body.

The wolf stopped at the edge of the cluster of trees and looked toward the house as if motioning to Hannah. Her lips quivered as she smiled at the animal, and with a shaky hand, she softly patted his head. "Thank you."

She hurried to the house. When she reached the door, she turned and glanced back at the wolf. He looked at her once more, then retreated into the ominous night. She could scarcely wait to tell the Thorntons how wrong they were about the animal.

As Hannah staggered into the house, her legs went weak, and soon she crumbled to the floor. She could not stop the sobs wrenching from her throat. Heavy footsteps pounded in the hallway, and soon Roderick appeared.

He sucked in a breath and ran to her side. "Hannah! Good heavens, what happened to you?"

She could not speak; all she could do was cry and shake her head. Roderick lifted her in his arms and brought her to the drawing room, depositing her on the couch next to the fireplace.

He knelt beside her and rubbed her cold hands. "My dear, what happened? Were you attacked?"

"No," she managed to squeak.

"Why is your face so pale?" His hands moved to cup her face. "You are as cold as ice."

She shook her head. "The white . . ." She cleared her throat. "White wolf."

His eyes widened. "Did you see him?"

She nodded. "He . . . saved me. I was I–lost in the thick–thicket, and he found me."

Roderick's brows creased. "How did you escape?"

"The wolf didn't t–try to k–kill me. He showed me the way back to the m–manor."

He gasped. "Impossible."

"It is true, I tell you." Hannah wrapped her arms around herself, trying to stop the trembling.

"My poor, dear girl. Your ordeal has made you forgetful, or insane." He hurried to the liquor tray, poured her a drink, and brought it back. "Here. Drink this wine. It will calm your nerves, I assure you."

With his help, she lifted the glass to her lips and sipped. Fiery liquid scorched her throat, making her cough. Roderick encouraged her to take another sip, and another. In the back of her mind, she reasoned that what she was drinking tasted too strong to be wine, yet in her confused state, she followed Roderick's instructions.

"What were you doing out at this time at night when we instructed you not to go out after dark?" He stroked her arm.

For a moment Hannah's brain seemed to shut down. Why had she been out? Then in a flash, she remembered her maid, Francine, and the haunting memory of her voice calling Hannah's name.

She sat up and grasped Roderick's hand. "My maid, Francine. Someone has taken her. We need to find her!"

"What?" Roderick brows creased. "Are you addled? Why would anyone kidnap your maid?"

She tried to stand, but he held her on the couch. "You don't understand! I saw her outside. Someone dragged her toward the trees. I heard her calling me for help."

"Calm now, my pet," Roderick cooed as he ran his fingers down the side of her face. "You have been through quite an ordeal. I am certain your mind is playing tricks on you. Francine is probably helping Mrs. White as we speak."

"No!" Hannah tried to push past him again, but he held her to the couch with his upper body, pressing her against the cushions.

"Take another drink. I am certain you will feel better soon."

Tears gathered in her eyes as utter helplessness spread through her. "But I *did* see her! She needs my help."

"Shh." He stroked her hair. "Calm yourself now. I will have Horace locate your maid posthaste, but you need to relax, my dear. It is not good to be in such a dither."

Hannah nodded and took another sip of the strong wine. Slowly, warmth spread through her body, forcing her to relax. This time, the liquid didn't burn as much as it coursed down her throat.

"Now there." Roderick smiled. "Feeling better?"

"A little."

As she sank into the cushions, she became heavy with exhaustion. The weight of Roderick's torso continued to press against her, and she hoped she would be able to remove him. Their position was quite improper, even if she had been through a mind-scrambling ordeal.

His gaze dropped to her lips, and fear sliced through her again. Pushing the heels of her hands against his chest, she again tried to move him, but he did not budge.

"Please, Mr. Thornton. I—I don't think I need your assistance any longer. I'm well, I assure you."

His fingertips slid down her cheek to her bottom lip. "I am pleased to hear this, but nonetheless, I feel as if you are too weak to fend for yourself."

"Please, Mr. Thornton—" She turned her head, trying to avoid his hand.

"I insist that you call me Roderick."

She gulped. "Please. I—I can't breathe with you on me like this."

He adjusted his body to lift off her chest only briefly. His gaze darkened, and Hannah wanted nothing better than to slap his face. But the liquor had weakened her limbs, and she found she was losing the ability to control her movements. Would he take advantage of her in her condition?

Morgan, where are you?

"As it is, Mr.—um—Roderick, I would very much like to retire for the evening."

He nodded and lifted himself off her. A loud *whoosh* came from her throat as she could finally breathe properly.

Roderick held out his hand, and hesitantly she took it.

"Hannah, let me help you to your room."

"That's unnecessary, Roderick. I will be fine." To prove it to him, she took a couple of steps toward the door, but her legs shook and she swayed.

He grabbed her arm with one hand, while his other arm slipped around her waist and pulled her against him. Biting her bottom lip, she allowed him to walk her out of the room.

Roderick said nothing as he helped her up the stairs. Tears glistened in her eyes as she silently prayed nothing unforeseen had happened to Francine. Perhaps all of this was in Hannah's imagination, but she didn't think so. It all seemed so very real.

When they reached her room, she tried to remove herself from Roderick's arm as he opened the door. "Thank you. I will be fine now."

"I think I should help you inside. You might need assistance getting undressed."

She managed to place her hand on his chest in an attempt to hold him away. "Don't be ridiculous. I assure you, I am fine."

Ignoring her protests, he walked her to the bed, then gently pushed her onto it. She struggled to an upright position, but Roderick promptly sat beside her, his hands caressing up and down her arms.

Terror filled her heart, and she shook her head. "I don't think you should be helping me. If you get a maid—"

"Nonsense, my dear. I am capable of readying a woman for bed."

Her limbs suddenly weighed more than she could bear, and she was helpless to fight him. She squeezed her eyes shut to avoid his desire-laced gaze.

His hands brushed over her shoulders and down her back. One by one, he unfastened the buttons at the back of her gown. When her dress fell forward, she whimpered.

"Here now, Hannah." His voice came out deep. "I beg you to allow me to finish undressing you."

Collecting her courage, she opened her eyes. His face blurred, and she blinked to clear her vision as she tried to fight the effects of the strong drink. "Roderick, I insist you leave. This is improper, and you know it. What would Jonathan think if he knew you were in here?" She lifted her chin in defiance. "Please leave now!"

Roderick pulled back. "As you wish, my dear." He leaned forward and placed a kiss on her forehead. "Rest tonight, and on the morrow you will feel better."

"Thank you." She held her breath until he left her side, walked out of the room, and closed the door.

Crumbling onto the mattress, Hannah sobbed into her hands. Why did she feel so out of sorts? What had Roderick put in the liquor? Why didn't he believe her about the white wolf? What was going on at the manor?

She must convince Morgan to help her. The sooner she could locate the information she sought, the sooner she and Francine could get out of this place.

Oh, yes—Francine! What had happened to her? And where was Morgan tonight? He had not come to Hannah's rescue as she had thought he would.

As she tried to focus her thoughts, her eyelids closed and her muscles relaxed. Somewhere in the recesses of her mind, she knew the strong drink was putting her to sleep, but she simply could not find the strength to care. Without climbing under the covers, she drifted quickly into a deep slumber.

Nine

Bethany shoved the maid into the boat before climbing in herself. Morris, her henchman, helped Bethany sit before he rowed them toward the island. She gathered the hood of her cloak around her face, warding off the breeze while she kept an eye on the maid.

Francine shivered, her wide eyes searching the surroundings— probably looking for a way out, Bethany guessed. She smiled grimly. The girl would never find a way to escape. Her prison for the next little while, or until she died, would be the island.

Francine wrapped her arms around her middle and looked at Bethany. "W–where are you t–taking me?" she asked through chattering teeth.

"To a place I need you more than at the manor."

"Wh–what of Mademoiselle Forester?"

"Do not fret. Hannah will be well taken care of. She will play a part in my plans, too."

"But she does not know where I am. She will be distraught over my absence."

"Nonsense. Jonathan will entertain her, I assure you." Bethany lifted her chin and straightened. "Besides, once she reads your note, she will believe you have returned home."

The maid gasped, and tears welled in her eyes. "She will not believe it."

Throwing her head back, Bethany laughed. "Oh, I'm not worried about that. I have ways of convincing her."

The small rowboat rocked with the waves that splashed against the sides. Bethany tightened the cloak around her.

Morris pushed and pulled the oars, his muscles straining against the sleeves of his overcoat. A black patch covered one eye, but it did not hide the pockmarks scattered across his face. Although hideous to look upon, he served Bethany well.

Ahead of them, the island grew closer. Tall trees lined the shore and hid the secret path to the caves. The ghost stories about the island kept people away, except for the stubborn, curious ones—people like Peter Forester, Hannah's father.

Bethany had wanted him to search the island and its caves. While Mr. Forester studied every crevasse, every stone, and the ancient drawings on the walls, she had watched from afar with interest. She had waited for the curse of the island to kill him. It had not, and this led her to wonder if the curse was false. But she had not dared test it until a year ago.

She had bided her time and waited until Forester wrote his novel. Bethany's ancestors had spoken of a great treasure on the island, and of a map that revealed its location. She knew Forester had the treasure map, and she wondered if he would mention it in the book. And while she was disappointed when he didn't, what he *did* say hinted that the cache of gold and silver indeed existed.

Determination surged through Bethany, making her more headstrong than ever to find it. She had confronted Forester the day he died, but the insipid man had refused to divulge any information. She had threatened to kill him, and when he would not budge, she was forced to follow through with her promise, using the poker from the fireplace to crack his skull. Of course, that was after he had mentioned Morgan's name.

Unfortunately, Bethany still didn't have the treasure map, and she didn't feel any closer to obtaining it than she had a year ago. Lately, she had felt Hannah Forester was a key to the mystery, whether the young beauty knew it or not. Miss Forester's father made it to the island without the curse taking him, and his daughter might possess the same ability.

With Francine out of the way, Bethany could get closer to Miss Forester. Perhaps she was the woman who could break the curse after all. Bethany had brought many young women to the island, but none of them had found the treasure. None of them died, either, which proved a portion of the island's curse untrue. However, Bethany still believed that only a woman with a pure heart could find the treasure. And Bethany *would* have the treasure to herself, no matter what.

Morris climbed out of the boat and grasped the lantern. Holding it high above his head, he reached for Bethany and helped her out. Francine probably would have resisted had he not yanked her from the boat. The girl cried out and struggled but could not break free of the large man's hold.

In the cave, the maid grew quiet and still. Darkness enveloped them, except for the lantern Morris held aloft to lead the way down a narrow, rocky pathway. Musty smells tickled Bethany's nose, and she very nearly sneezed. Above their heads, a large group of bats hung upside down, and when Francine saw them, she sobbed and moved closer to Morris. The winged animals didn't frighten Bethany any longer.

A light at the end of the tunnel grew larger. As they reached the heart of the cave, Francine halted and gasped, her hand flying to her throat. Bethany grinned as she glanced at all of the girls she had gathered in the past year. Each one had originally come to Thornton Manor to meet Jonathan, but then left quite suddenly, never to be seen again by the outside world. Bethany needed them here, digging, just as she needed Hannah's maid.

The girls looked up from their shovels. The pathetic creatures no longer resembled gentle-bred ladies. Their dresses were dusty rags now, and dirt and mud caked their hands and faces. Grimy, disheveled hair replaced the refined styles they had worn when they arrived at the manor.

Bethany stepped over the rocks to move past Morris and their newest slave. "Welcome to your new home, Francine."

Shovels and buckets were propped against the wall. Bethany took one of each and handed them to the maid. "From now on, the only thing you are required to do is dig. When my guards feel it is time to feed you, they will do so, but not a moment sooner." She swept her hand toward the seven burly men. "And when they feel it is time for you to sleep, they will lay out blankets." Smiling even wider, she faced Francine. "Do you have any questions?"

Tears streamed down the girl's cheeks, and she shook her head. "I d–do not understand. Why . . . why am I here?"

Bethany stood before the cowering girl and lifted the maid's chin until their eyes locked. "You are my prisoner. You will dig for gold. You will dig for silver. And you will not stop until it is found."

Turning, Bethany brushed her hands against her cloak. "I must return to the manor. I'm quite certain my foolish husband has gotten into some sort of mischief in my absence."

Morris pushed Francine toward the closest guard, and the maid stumbled to her knees. She sobbed loudly and covered her face with her hands. One of the women ran to Francine and helped her stand.

Bethany shook her head and tsked. "Amelia Hartley. Always the brave one, always the kind-hearted helper." Bethany sighed. "Still trying to soften the hearts of my guards, are you?"

Amelia glared at Bethany. The younger woman's face was smudged heavily with dirt, but her fiery gaze bore deeply into her master's. "I'm waiting for the day when you will get your comeuppance, and I will be privileged to see it happen. It will be soon, Mrs. Thornton. Mark my words."

"Bah!" Bethany threw her hands in the air and turned to depart. "Come, Morris. I grow weary of these imbeciles. How dare they doubt who is in control here."

"Yes, mistress."

Morris led the way down the tunnel with the lantern held high. Bethany followed, but her mind was not on the prisoners. Instead, she plotted how she could continue befriending Hannah Forester. The young woman knew something important about her father's work on the island; Bethany merely had to dig deep enough in Miss Forester's mind to recover it.

Soon, Bethany would have the treasure, and the world would be at her disposal. Being raised poor had made her covet that which she didn't have. But even though she would soon be extremely wealthy, she could not forget the one thing she would never have—the man she had loved as a child. As a young girl in pigtails, she would sit atop the hillside to watch Morgan exercise his horses, secretly dreaming of a happier life with him as her husband.

Her smile dropped into a frown. Why hadn't she been able to make him love her? Perhaps she *was* a worthless creature, just as her mother had drilled into her head since infancy. Mother had said Bethany would never acquire a wealthy husband. The family came from a long line of poverty, and poor women didn't have a chance to fulfill their dreams.

Balling her hands into fists, Bethany clenched her jaw. This time was different. She was not a worthless creature, but a goddess. Never again would she live in squalor. She would prove her mother wrong. If the older woman was alive, she would beg on her knees for Bethany to forgive her.

❦

Morgan blinked his eyes open and felt his cheek resting on the cold floor. Straight ahead, his bed beckoned.

Wearily, he stood and took a step forward. He stumbled but righted himself. When he made it to the bed, he slumped down on the edge. Running his fingers through his hair, he closed his eyes.

Images and sounds floated through his head. A dark night. Fog. A wolf's howl. Tree limbs whipping across his body. Ahead of him, a woman ran, screaming. Her long, chestnut hair flew in her face as she looked behind. She stumbled and fell. Fear must have paralyzed her, for she didn't move. Her wide eyes stayed on him as he crept closer.

The memory faded, and Morgan covered his face. *No! Not Hannah!* Agony wrenched his heart as he realized the beast had killed her. Never before had Morgan remembered any of his time as a wolf, and now he wished he had not. His sweet Hannah was dead because of his feelings for her.

He squeezed his eyes shut as tears burned behind his eyelids. Why hadn't he stayed away from her? Why had he made excuses to be near her, to touch her, to taste her sweet lips? Poor Hannah! Why hadn't she heeded his warning and left the manor? If she had, she would still be alive.

His chest ached so deeply that he cried out to release the pain. He jumped to his feet, anger flowing through him like molten lava. The witch did this to him, to Hannah. That evil woman had to be stopped! If killing the witch killed him too, then so be it. He could not stand to hear of yet another helpless victim being slaughtered by the white wolf.

Morgan grabbed his black velvet robe and draped it around him, tying the sash around his waist. He would like to strangle the witch with his bare hands, but she would certainly cast another spell on him. So how could he catch her unawares and put an end to her wickedness?

The creak of the floor in the adjacent room caught his attention. *Someone is here.* The witch had probably come to torture him further. Hatred burned inside him.

The footsteps came louder, closer, and he detected a faint scent. But it was not the perfume the witch always wore to try to hide her stench. Instead, the smell of lilacs hung in the air. His heart beat faster. Only one woman smelled that intoxicating. *Hannah.*

He hurried to the bedroom door and stepped out. Hannah jumped, her hand flying to her mouth. Her gaze swept over him from the top of his head to his toes, and a blush reddened her cheeks.

Praise the Almighty! She was alive. Unable to stop himself, he scooped her up in his arms and crushed her body against his, burying his face in her neck. Emotion choked his throat.

"Oh, my dear, sweet, Hannah," he muttered against her skin before leaving light kisses along her neck. Her body had been stiff for a moment, but as he kissed her, she relaxed.

His mouth moved over her chin and met her lips. Delicate fingers threaded through his hair as she held his head to her, kissing him back. He thought he had lost her! Now he must show her how much she meant to him. True, he would shift, but not until tonight.

"Morgan, please."

"Hannah," he muttered, still kissing her face. "Oh, my dear Hannah. I'm so thankful you are alive."

Her body stilled, and she braced her palms against his shoulders to move him away. She stared at him in confusion, her lips already swelling from his ardent kisses. He swept his fingers over her cheek, her chin, her throat, then kissed her again.

"No, Morgan." Her gaze moved over his face and rested on the half he had always kept hidden from her. Suddenly he realized why she stared. In his excitement to see her, he had not put on the scarf.

Morgan let her go as if she were a hot coal. His heart twisted as he watched her, waiting for her to turn and run away, screaming in horror.

She did not. Instead, she looked at him in interest. Her hand moved as if to touch him, but he jerked back.

"Please don't," he whispered.

Nodding, she withdrew her hand and sat on the edge of his bed. "I'm sorry to have disturbed your sleep, but . . ." She licked her lips. "I had to find you, to talk to you. I must know why . . . why . . ." Hannah drew in a deep breath and met his gaze fully again. "Where were you last night? Why didn't you come to my rescue when I needed you?"

Fear crawled up his spine. "What do you mean? What happened?"

Tears brimmed in her eyes and clung to her long eyelashes. "Francine—my maid—she is gone. From out my bedroom window, I saw someone take her. When I ran into the thicket of trees to search for her, I became lost." Hannah wiped a hand across her cheeks, but more tears replaced the ones she had brushed away. "I could not find her." Her voice choked. "Then the white wolf came."

Morgan sucked in a heavy breath and held it, his heart hammering against his ribs.

"I can't explain it, but the wolf didn't try to attack me. Well, he did at first, but when I spoke, he—he—"

Morgan knelt on the floor before her and grasped her clutched hands. "He what?"

"He became calm. And then he showed me the way back to the manor."

Morgan's eyes widened. "He helped you?"

"Yes. He even allowed me to pet him." Hannah wiped her eyes again. "Oh, Morgan, I was so scared, but then I realized he was not dangerous like everyone said." She sniffled. "When I stumbled into the house, Roderick took me to the parlor and gave me a very strong drink, unlike anything I have tasted before."

Her bottom lip quivered, and more tears flowed from her eyes. Morgan gritted his teeth. *If my brother touched her at all . . .*

"A different fear crept over me then. The look in Roderick's eyes told me what he wanted, what he planned to do." She shivered. "I prayed you would come to help me, but you—you didn't."

Hannah buried her face in her hands and sobbed. Morgan's heart ached, his guilt tearing him apart with her every cry. He took her in his arms, but she thumped his chest with her fists.

"You didn't even come." She cried harder before pressing her face against his shoulder.

Sliding his hands up her arms, he drew her closer and kissed the top of her head. "Oh, my darling Hannah. I tried to tell you the other day. I tried to warn you I might not always be there." He kissed the side of her face, and her tears dampened his lips. "Please forgive me. I would move heaven and earth to try and protect you if I could."

He held her tight until her crying ceased. Finally, she lifted her head and looked at him with red-rimmed eyes. "What a fool I am. How do you tolerate me?"

"What on earth do you mean, my dear?"

"I'm blaming you when I should not be. I was just so frightened last night, and I wanted so desperately for you to come to my rescue." She sniffed and shook her head. "You must hate me."

"Oh, Hannah, I could never hate you."

"I should not have blamed you, not when you tried to warn me." Her body stiffened, and she drew back to stare at him quizzically. "How did you know to warn me about Roderick?"

Once more, anger surged through Morgan. "Roddy is a conceited, ignorant, man. He thinks only of his own pleasure, and he does not give a whit about anyone else. He is dangerous, especially for innocent young ladies." Morgan ran his thumbs gently underneath Hannah's eyes, drying her tears. "Did he touch you?"

Slowly, she nodded. "He had me drink something vile that burned my throat. When I felt as if I was losing control of my limbs, he helped me to my room. I wanted him to leave. I asked him to, but he ignored me. He took me to my bed . . ."

Morgan gritted his teeth. He would kill his brother for touching her! "Oh, Hannah." His voice broke as he held her close. "Please forgive me for not being there."

She sniffed. "Roderick tried to remove my dress, and again I asked him to leave. Finally, he did."

Morgan looked down into her eyes. "He didn't . . . force you in any way?"

"No, but I had never been so frightened in my life."

Cradling her in his arms, Morgan stroked her back. "I swear, I shall do everything I can to keep him away from you. Even if it means . . ."

He sucked in a deep breath. What was he thinking? He could not come out of hiding.

Hannah lifted her head and met his stare. "If it means what?" She touched the burned side of his face, tenderly running her fingers over his scars. "What are you keeping from me, Morgan?"

"You would not understand."

"Why do you hide from everyone? You are not a ghost like your family has declared. So why hide? You are the master of the manor. Can you not reclaim your title?"

Shutting his eyes, he rested his head against her forehead. "If only it were that easy. You don't know how I long to take back the life I used to have." He opened his eyes and peered into hers. "You don't know how badly I want to be a man, to be free to touch and kiss you." He ran a finger across her bottom lip. "You are the first woman I have touched in a year, Hannah. Being with you has brought back feelings I can no longer deny."

She caressed the side of his face. "What happened to you a year ago, Morgan? Why can you not be the man you once were?"

"It is too complex a story to tell now." Groaning, he closed his eyes and tilted his head back. "And I fear telling you the truth will put you in more danger."

She rose up and kissed his lips lightly. "Then take me away from here. Today. You and me, together."

He took her head and pulled her down for another kiss. She responded the way he had hoped she would—the way he had dreamed about for so long now. How he wanted to forget his beastly existence and run away with her.

He withdrew and stood. "Hannah, my love, I will take you away from here, only because it is dangerous for you. But I must return."

She frowned. "That's ridiculous. Why would you want to come back to this?" Her expression softened. "Do you not want to be with me?"

Anguish filled his soul once again. "More than anything, but not now. It is impossible."

She rose to her feet, then folded her arms across her chest and began pacing the floor. "Then if you will not leave, neither will I."

"Hannah, be reasonable."

"No, I mean it, Morgan." She faced him and planted her hands on her hips. "My feelings for you run very deep, and I think you have the same kind of feelings for me."

He nodded.

"Then if you want me to leave, you must be honest with me. You must tell me the truth."

Morgan cupped her face as dread seized his stomach. Could he? Would she understand? Would she still look at him as a man and not a monster?

He swallowed hard. "If I'm forthright with you, will you answer what I ask of you?"

"Yes, certainly." She clutched his shoulders. "There is nothing I want more than to tell you my true reason for coming to Thornton Manor, if that's what you mean to ask me."

His brow furrowed. "Why are you really here, Hannah?"

"I came to find you."

"You are here for me? I thought you came here to meet Jonathan and to allow him to court you."

"That was just an excuse to come to the manor to talk to you. You were the last person I know of who spoke to my father before he died. I need your help to find out who killed him."

At the mention of her father, Morgan smiled. "I will tell you anything you want to know, but I don't know who killed him."

Tears moistened Hannah's lashes as she clasped his hands. "Thank you. My father talked highly of you, and I know he loved you."

"When I last visited with him, he talked of you, his beloved daughter. He wanted us to meet, you know."

Her cheeks darkened, and she lowered her gaze. "Yes, he mentioned it a few times. He said you were the kind of man he wanted me to . . . marry."

"Yes. I received the same impression when I visited your father." Morgan winked. "Before I left, he gave me some paintings."

Her eyes widened. "Paintings?"

"Yes. I assumed he painted them, yet he never told me he had such a talent."

Hannah shook her head. "He didn't paint, at least not that I know of. Do you still have these paintings?"

"Actually, some of them are still hanging on the walls in the manor. You may recognize them because they don't have the artist's signature."

She gasped. "I remember seeing them."

"I kept some in my room." Morgan glanced around the semi-dark chamber. "Not this one, but my other room."

"Father would have been pleased you thought so much of them. It would also have made him happy to know you are going to help me."

Morgan lifted her hands to his mouth and kissed her knuckles. "Being with you lightens my heart. I would do anything for you, Hannah."

"Anything?"

"Yes."

"Then tell me why you are hiding."

Ten

Hannah held her breath, praying he would trust her with his secret. Despite her initial misgivings, and despite hardly knowing him, she had fallen completely and irretrievably in love with him. If he did not trust her enough to tell her, it would break her heart because she would know he did not return her affection.

Morgan pulled away and paced the floor of his bedroom, his jaw tense and his lips tight as he ran his fingers through his hair. Could his past be that horrible?

Finally, he stopped in front of her and heaved a deep breath. She waited for him to speak. He squared his shoulders and met her gaze.

"Hannah, as hard as this is for me to say, I'm quite certain it will be harder to believe. I'm—I'm not human."

He paused as if waiting for her to say something, but she didn't. She had already told him she didn't believe in ghosts.

"I have been cursed." He swallowed. "My family is embarrassed by me and bade me to hide away in the East Wing. They spread rumors that I am a ghost so nobody would be tempted to come into my sanctuary. But as you can see, I'm not a ghost. Unfortunately, though, the truth is harder to believe."

She shook her head. "You are not making sense."

He fisted his hands by his sides. "A year ago, a witch cursed me."

Hannah gasped.

"I was about to dismiss some of my staff and throw my brother and sister-in-law out of the house. To put a stop to my plans, the witch put a curse on me, a curse so bad I'm afraid to show myself. That's why I'm in hiding."

Fear clutched Hannah's chest. "Why, Morgan? And how did she curse you?"

Growling, he ran his fingers through his hair once more, still meeting her stare. "She wanted me to love her, but I would not, so she cursed me so I would not feel passion for other women." He took a deep breath. "Every time I do, I turn into a beast."

Hannah brought her hand to her mouth. "A beast?"

"To be more precise, I shift into" —he paused— "the white wolf."

Shock vibrated through her body, and she stepped back until she bumped into the bed. She sat on the edge of the mattress, her limbs trembling. This could not be. A throb pounded in her forehead and she rubbed the spot, hoping to make it disappear. "You—you killed Sarah?"

Morgan groaned. "I suppose. I don't remember. I have never remembered what happens when I shift."

"Then how do you know?"

"The witch tells me." He moved beside Hannah and knelt in front of her. "I swear I don't remember. I don't understand why I kill. Not once have I desired Sarah or the other girls who were killed."

"Could the witch be lying to you?"

"I don't know. All I know is that whenever a woman is killed, I have shifted."

Questions swam in Hannah's head, but she asked the most obvious one. "Do you know who the witch is? I mean, is she someone you know?"

"Yes."

"Why can't you kill her?"

Releasing a sigh, Morgan reclined and rested his head on Hannah's lap. "I cannot kill her," he said without looking up. "If she dies, my curse remains intact. Only she can break the curse, which means she has to live. You don't know how many times I have wanted to kill her, but I don't wish to be a beast for the rest of my life."

"Is there anything you can do to make her break the curse?"

He lifted his head and met Hannah's eyes. "No. In the beginning, she wanted my affection, which I could never give. Lately, she has wanted something I do not have. I try to tell her, but she does not believe me."

"What does she demand of you?"

"She wants the treasure map to the island."

"Slumbering Giant?" Hannah's jaw dropped. "Did you tell her there is no such thing?"

"Yes. She refuses to listen."

"Then we have to *make* her listen."

Morgan shook his head and frowned. "She is stubborn. I have tried for a year now."

"Then I shall talk to her. My father—"

"Absolutely not." He jumped to his feet. "You must not even think about that, Hannah. You do not know how dangerous she will become if she thinks you have the answers."

"But I don't. My father's last book was about the island. I will tell her to read it—"

"Hannah." He grasped her hands and pulled her to her feet before sliding his arms around her and bringing her close to him. "Promise me you will stop thinking like that. I cannot put you in harm's way. I will deal with the witch on my own. Nobody else can be involved."

Her heart ached for this man, and although she wanted to help, she knew he was right. There was nothing she could do without opening herself up to danger. Her heart cried out in angry protest. Finally, she had found a man who fulfilled her, made her complete. Now she learned their future was not meant to be. Merely standing this close to him was tempting fate. He shifted into the white wolf if he felt passion, and as much as she wanted to hold him by her side forever, she could not put him through the pain of knowing he had hurt someone he loved.

Tears filled her eyes as she lowered her head. She pushed away from him until they were not touching. "I need some time to think." Her voice trembled.

"As you wish," he replied softly.

On shaking legs, she made her way through the tunnel to her bedchamber. With each step away from him, her heart seemed to break, especially when he didn't try to stop her.

When she reached her room, she flung herself on the bed and sobbed, praying for relief. After she finally stopped crying, she lay on her back and thought about the way Morgan had kissed her earlier, as if he could not get enough. No wonder he had acted in such a manner—he thought he had killed her.

She sighed and clutched the pillow to her chest. How could she help him? He had mentioned that the witch wanted the treasure map. But there was no treasure, at least according to her father's book. Had her father known something she did not? Could he have known his life was in danger? Her father had given Morgan some paintings, yet her father did not paint.

She jerked upright, dropping the pillow. Perhaps the paintings held a secret, and that was that why her father sent them to Morgan!

With a lighter heart, she climbed off the bed and splashed water on her face. She peered into the mirror on the dresser and sighed. Her eyes still looked puffy and red. But if anyone were to ask, she would say she was worried about her maid, which was certainly true.

She walked into Francine's room. It was just as it had been before, clean and untouched, only now Francine's clothes were missing from the armoires. Hannah grumbled under her breath. Indeed, something was going on here, something unnatural. The Thorntons were hiding her maid—Hannah just knew it. She had to figure out the family's secrets, and how Morgan's curse was related to the other strange things going on at the manor.

She hurried out of the room to the paintings she remembered seeing the first day she arrived at the manor. Trying to act as if she admired them, she trained her attention on the small details. But after studying each painting, she came to the decision there was no treasure map—no clues—hidden within the strokes of a paintbrush. Then again, perhaps the clues were not in these paintings at all, but in those located in Morgan's room.

Wandering through the house, found it odd that she didn't see Bethany, Roderick, or even Jonathan. Hannah did pass a few servants on her way to Morgan's old room, so she waited until the hall was empty to approach the room. After listening at the door for a few minutes, she concluded the room was empty, so she hurried inside and closed the door behind her.

Everything was exactly the way she remembered, even the smell. Closing her eyes, she took in a deep breath, memorizing Morgan's scent all over again. Then she frowned as she reminded herself he could never be hers—not as long as he turned into the white wolf and might kill her.

Her mind caught hold of that thought. If he was able to kill her, why hadn't he done so the night before? As the white wolf, he could have easily done so. But when he had heard her voice, he had stopped growling and helped her find her way back to the manor. Because of Morgan's feelings for her, perhaps the white wolf would never hurt her.

Hannah moved away from the door and looked at the walls of Morgan's bedroom. Four beautiful paintings hung close together. She pushed aside a curtain to get a better look at the paintings, but saw nothing unusual.

She walked to the desk and stared at the bottom drawer where she had found the bundle of letters, including the one Morgan had written to Roderick and Bethany. This time, the drawer didn't stick as Hannah pulled it out. The letters were still there, and she flipped over Roderick's letter and pulled out the next one. On the top was written "Gretchen White." Hannah scratched her head. *White? As in Mrs. White, the housekeeper?* She read the letter.

> *You have been with the Thornton family for ten years now, and it is most difficult to inform you that we no longer require your services. I shall give you a letter of reference for your future employment, but for personal reasons I will not explain, you cannot stay. You will receive two months' pay, which is more than enough to establish you elsewhere. Please accept my gratitude for all you have done for my family.*

Clearly, neither Roderick and Bethany nor Mrs. White had received their letters.

Hannah put the missive back and pulled out the next one. "Anne Shultz" was written across the top. Anne was the servant from whom Roderick had sneaked a kiss on Hannah's first day at the manor.

Due to my dissatisfaction with your services to the Thornton family of late, you are hereby released to seek alternative employment. No letter of reference will be forthcoming, but you will, however, receive a month's wages.

All of this was very intriguing, and Hannah could hardly wait to ask Morgan why the letters were not sent. He mentioned he had been writing them when the witch came. Perhaps that was the reason they were not delivered—because he had been cursed and gone into hiding.

Hannah placed the bundle of letters back in the drawer and pushed it closed. She stood and glanced around the room, wondering where to look next. Heavy footsteps vibrated outside the bedroom door. Her heart raced. She was going to get caught!

✦❀✦

Bethany sashayed into the parlor. Jonathan sat at the table, staring at the untouched chess set as he leaned forward on his elbows. His hands bracketed his face, his fingers rubbing circles against his temple. It appeared as if the weight of the world rested on his shoulders.

She pitied him, as she had done since they were children. He was a little younger than she, not only in body but also in mind. Now, it was as if Jonathan was her younger brother—the brother she never had. It pleased her to look after him and take care of his needs, especially now as his mind grew weak. Since Roderick had not given her any children, caring for Jonathan made her feel like a mother.

Bethany closed the door behind her and moved quietly to Jonathan. When she reached him, she stroked his wavy hair.

"What is on your mind this afternoon?"

He jumped slightly but didn't turn his head. "The same thing that has always been on my mind."

"Finding a wife?"

"Do you think I will find one before . . ." He sighed heavily. "Before I meet my Maker?"

Bethany moved to his side and sat on the empty chair. She slipped her hands over his and removed them from his head.

"I'll not hear you talk like that." She met his gaze directly. "You are not going to die before you are married."

A weak grin tugged at the corners of Jonathan's mouth. "My mind is getting worse, you know. I wake in the morning and can't remember much about the day before." He stared at their clasped hands, his smile disappearing. "I can see it on Hannah's face. She thinks I'm insane."

"Nonsense. She's still getting to know you. Give her time."

He shook his head. "I feel as if this is my last chance. How many women have we invited to the manor in the past year? A dozen? More? And they have all disappeared within a few days."

Bethany squeezed his hand. "Yes, they have. But Hannah has been here the longest. I think she is the one."

He stared blankly into the distance as his mouth slowly widened into a smile. "You are right." He looked at her. "She is still here."

"Jonathan, you need to be more charming. Women like that in a man."

"They do?"

"Oh, yes, and our Miss Forester is no different. There is passion in that woman, but you need to bring it out. Let her get a taste of the real Jonathan—the loving, kind, gentleman inside this shell." She tapped his chest.

Sighing, he closed his eyes and let his head fall back. "If it were only that simple."

"Why don't you believe me?"

"Because I know she thinks of me as a simple-minded boy." He paused and shook his head. "And perhaps I am. All I want is to marry and have children. Isn't that what all men want?"

"I suppose, Jonathan, though I know many men who put wealth and power above everything else."

"Bah! Those things are insignificant unless a gentleman has a wife and family to support."

"Don't give up. A family will be yours soon. And the wealth . . ." Bethany shrugged. "You know how that can happen."

"Slumbering Giant?"

"Yes."

"You really believe the treasure is hidden on the island?"

"I do, just as my ancestors did. We are very close to finding it."

Jonathan scooted closer to her. "Indeed?"

"I believe Hannah is the key. She has a pure heart. She is the one."

Still smiling, he nodded. "She is a very kind woman. I do like her very much."

"Then you must convince her to marry you. We must make her your bride as soon as we can."

His grin widened. "That would be fitting for my birthday present, wouldn't it?"

Bethany chuckled. "Indeed, it would be most fitting." She clasped his hands. "Between you and me, we shall convince her of her love for you. Mark my words, Jonathan. Hannah will be ours!"

Hannah glanced around Morgan's bedroom, her heart fluttering in panic. Where could she hide? She ran to the corner of the room and slipped behind the heavy drape. A cool breeze blew across her feet, and suddenly the wall moved. She gasped as the secret door opened to reveal Morgan, looking breathtakingly handsome. He held out his hand.

"Hannah, in here. Quickly."

She did not ask questions, but slipped her hand into his large one and allowed him to pull her through. Just as he closed the heavy barrier, voices floated into the bedroom. She sighed with relief and leaned against him.

"How did you know?" she asked, looking up at him.

"I didn't. I was coming to look at the paintings."

She chuckled. "We think alike."

He placed his finger over her mouth. "Shh. Although we are separated by a wall, they can still hear us if we are too loud."

"Who is in your room?"

Morgan pulled her toward a window on the wall, flipped back the black covering, and peered through what looked like a mirror from the other side. "Roderick and one of the maids." His jaw hardened.

"Anne."

She sucked in a quick breath. "Oh, my! You don't think Roderick and Anne—"

Morgan glanced at her, his eyebrows raised. "Indeed, I do."

"Did you know," she began, putting her hand on his arm, "that Roderick and Sarah were . . . you know . . ."

"Lovers?" Morgan nodded and covered the window so they could no longer see the trespassers inside. "I saw them together the night before she was killed—before the wolf killed her."

Hannah's heart clenched and she squeezed Morgan's arm. "Please don't say that. What if you didn't kill her?"

"Oh, my dearest." He wrapped her in his embrace and rested his chin on her head. "You don't know how much I want to believe that."

"Do you think those wild dogs could have killed her?"

He pulled back slightly to look into her eyes.

"Remember? The dogs that almost attacked me?"

"Yes, I remember," he replied. "Do you truly think it was them?"

"I would rather believe they killed her than the white wolf. You told me the curse only makes you shift if you feel passion for a woman, correct?"

"Yes."

"And you said you didn't have those feelings for her."

"I have never had those kind of feelings for any of the women that have died this past year."

"Then perhaps it was the rabid dogs doing the killing."

Holding her closer, Morgan buried his face in her neck. "I would like nothing better than to believe that."

"Then let's do so," Hannah replied. "Let's put aside the idea that you kill."

He kissed her neck. "How did I ever live without you?"

From the other side of the wall, the voices grew louder. Morgan pulled away from Hannah and moved the window covering so they could peek through.

"You are nothing but a scheming wench," Roderick yelled.

Hannah gasped and met Morgan's surprised eyes.

"Scheming? How did you come to that conclusion?" Anne sobbed in between words.

"I know you had your eye on my brother a year ago, and now you want to weasel your way into my life. Well, I am telling you right now, it is not going to happen."

"I don't know what you're talking about. I love you."

Silence lasted a few minutes as Roderick paced the floor, raking his fingers through his hair. Anne remained sitting on the bed.

"What do you expect me to do? I am married," Roderick growled as he faced her.

"But I'm carrying your child."

Morgan's groan overrode Hannah's gasp. He closed his eyes and rested his forehead against the wall. "My brother is a fool."

Roderick threw his hands in the air. "Do you really expect me to believe that when I have seen you with the stable hands?"

Anne wailed loudly, and Hannah cringed.

"I cannot think with your crying," Roderick exclaimed. "I will be in my study, so please do not disrupt me."

The slamming of the door confirmed his departure.

Morgan took a deep breath and held Hannah's hands. "I'm sorry you had to hear that."

"I don't mind. What do you think he will do about Anne?"

"I'm more worried about what Anne will do if Roderick chooses to ignore him."

"Why do you say that?"

Morgan shook his head, turned, and led her down another passageway. "Let us not worry about my brother, but rather concentrate on finding that map."

"Do you think my father left it in the paintings?"

"Either that or his journal."

She gasped. "His journal? You have that as well? I found one after he was killed. I had assumed it was his only one."

"Right after he died, the journal arrived by messenger. I think your father might have sent it before he was killed. I was too distraught to think about it, so I hid it in my room. Earlier today, after you left, I started thinking about it. Now I believe he might have known he was in trouble. Why else would he send it to me?"

"It is still in your room?" Hannah asked.

"Yes, but I will look for it later—tonight after everyone has gone to sleep. Obviously, my room is still being used during the day." He shook his head. "Is nothing sacred anymore?"

"Morgan, what do you want me to do?"

He stopped, pulled her into his arms, and kissed her forehead. "Whatever you do, do *not* let anyone in my household know that you are studying the paintings. I don't want anyone to become suspicious of your actions."

"All right. I think I can do that."

"And . . ." He pulled her closer and placed a gentle kiss on her lips. "Don't kiss Jonathan the way you kiss me."

Her face burned with embarrassment. "You saw him kiss me the other day?"

"Yes, and I didn't like it. I was insanely jealous."

She stroked the scarred side of Morgan's face and smiled. "If you saw him kiss me, then you know I didn't want it. While his lips were on mine, I wished you were in his place."

"Oh, my darling." Morgan buried his face in her neck, his lips sweeping across the skin by her ear.

"I wish I didn't have to be in Jonathan's company, other than as a good friend, but I must make your family believe I wish him to court me. That's the only way they will allow me to remain at the manor."

Morgan pulled away and nodded. "You are wise. But please try not to entice my feeble-minded younger brother. He is a helpless creature, and I fear for his state of mind."

"Has he always been this way?"

"Not always, just for the last five years or so."

"Why do you think his mind is going?"

"I wish I knew so I could help him." Morgan took her hand and kissed her fingertips. "But I would rather not discuss him.

As much as I would like to carry you to my chambers and kiss you senseless, I think we should concentrate on finding that treasure map."

"I agree. Things will be better once the witch lifts your spell."

"Exactly. And afterwards, I must kill her."

Eleven

Hannah floated down the stairs, hoping to appear peaceful when she felt far from it. As she stepped into the dining room to join her hosts for the midday meal, she noticed Bethany's lips drooped and her eyes held an evil glint.

"Oh, my dear girl!" She stood and took Hannah's hands. "I heard about your ordeal last night. How completely dreadful!"

Hannah glanced at the woman's wayward husband, whose gaze pierced right through her. It was a look meant to intimidate, she was certain, especially when his eyes swept over every inch of her with undisguised lust.

Her stomach churned, and she fought the urge to slap Roderick's face. Instead, she looked at Bethany and nodded. "It was certainly an ordeal, but the worst is not over."

"Whatever do you mean, Miss Forester?"

"My maid is still missing. As I told Mr. Thornton last night, someone has kidnapped her."

Bethany's eyes twinkled with humor. "Your maid, Francine?"

"Of course. Do I have another?" Hannah walked to her chair and sat.

Bethany moved back to her seat, lifting two fingers to her mouth as the corners pulled wide in a grin. "But why would someone want to kidnap your maid? Any maid, for that matter."

"I wish I knew the answer, Mrs. Thornton. I heard Francine screaming for me last night, which is why I ventured outside. I saw someone pulling her into the forest."

"If you think someone has kidnapped her, we will certainly find out, though it is a difficult thing to comprehend. What possible reason would anyone have to kidnap a mere maid?"

Hannah forced herself to be civil. "I would love nothing better than to find those answers."

Bethany turned to her husband. "Roderick, dear, would you ride into town and summon the constable? Our Hannah will not rest until she knows what happened."

"As you wish, my sweet." His words dripped with honey.

He motioned to the kitchen maid and pointed toward Hannah. "Please bring our guest some food. She is probably famished."

While the maid served her, Hannah studied the master and mistress of the manor. She knew they had no intention of asking the constable to help find Francine. In fact, Hannah had no doubt Bethany and Roderick were responsible for her maid's disappearance. But why on earth would they want to take Francine away?

After the kitchen maid left, Hannah picked at her berries, trying not to look at Bethany or her husband.

From the doorway, someone cleared her throat. Hannah looked at Mrs. White, who stood just inside the double doors, holding a folded piece of paper.

"What is it?" Bethany asked.

Mrs. White's blue eyes met Hannah's for a brief moment before she frowned. "I found this in Francine's room, mistress."

She moved to bring it to Hannah, but Bethany held out her hand. "Let me see it."

Hannah dropped her fork, pushed away from the table, and rushed to Bethany's side as the mistress opened the letter.

Dear Hannah,

Please forgive me for leaving in the middle of the night, but I simply could not stay any longer. I believe there is a ghost in the East Wing, and I am so terrified that I cannot sleep at night. Since you wanted to stay, I decided to leave without you. Please forgive me.

Francine

Bethany slowly raised her gaze to meet her guest's. Hannah's stomach clenched. Indeed, Francine didn't like Thornton Manor, but she would have never left without her mistress, especially in the middle of the night.

Inspecting the letter more closely, Hannah realized it was not composed in Francine's handwriting. The maid's schooling had not been very advanced, yet the penmanship was smooth and precise, with not a word misspelled. Not only that, but Francine would have called her "mademoiselle" instead of Hannah. What was Bethany up to?

Hannah glanced around the room. All eyes were on her. She couldn't possibly tell the Thorntons she knew someone else wrote the letter. So, with shoulders lifted and chin raised, she took a deep breath for courage. "Apparently, I was wrong. Indeed, Francine was afraid of her own shadow, but I never thought she would leave by herself."

Seeming relieved, Bethany patted Hannah's hands. "I'm dreadfully sorry, my dear. Rest assured we will take care of you.

In fact, I shall assign Mrs. White to be your maid during the remainder of your stay."

Hesitantly, Hannah looked at Mrs. White, who gazed at her with sympathetic, motherly eyes. "Thank you, Mrs. Thornton," Hannah said quietly. "I appreciate the generous offer, but I really don't need a maid. I can dress and undress myself without any help."

From across the table, Roderick chuckled beneath his hand, and Hannah fought the urge to glare at him.

Bethany shook her head. "Regardless, Hannah, you are my guest, so you will receive the best treatment. Mrs. White will be your maid."

Hannah moved back to her chair, silently gnashing her teeth. During the rest of the meal, she managed to endure Bethany's constant, mindless chatter and Roderick's leering grins and ogling eyes. Hannah prayed Jonathan would come into the room, but she knew he was probably out riding his horse as usual.

When she finished the last bite, she quickly excused herself. She hurried down the corridor to the drawing room, where she had admired several of the paintings she now knew had been gifts to Morgan from her father. A few of them were missing. Biting back a grin, she figured Morgan had taken them and hidden them. Clever man. Hopefully, the other members of the household would not notice.

She glanced back at the door and listened. From what she could tell, she had not been followed. As she cautiously walked to the corner of the room near the long, heavy drapes, she held her breath. There should be a secret door around here somewhere. And where was Morgan's magic looking glass?

"Can you see me or hear me?" she whispered with a smile. "I miss you." Although she guessed he was not there to hear her, warmth crept up her cheeks at her admission.

Slowly, she walked to the wall, studying each painting, each crevasse to see if she could locate the entrance to Morgan's secret passageway. "I want to be near you again. You are all I can think about," she continued in a low voice.

"Whom are you talking to, Hannah?"

She jumped and twirled around, placing her hand over her wildly beating heart. "Oh, Jonathan. It is just you. You gave me a fright."

Still in his riding clothes, he stepped into the drawing room and grinned. Quite handsome in his deep brown coat, trousers, and black knee boots, he would make any woman's heart flutter. It was a pity the poor creature was insane like the rest of his family—except Morgan, of course.

"Forgive me for startling you," Jonathan said. "I didn't mean to make you jump."

She smiled. "I was not expecting to see you until later today."

"To whom were you talking?" He glanced around the room. "Or were you talking to anyone?"

"I—I—" She took a deep breath, trying to decide what to say. She hated lying, but she couldn't tell him about Morgan. "I was actually thinking out loud." A light laugh escaped her throat. "I do that on occasion."

He moved closer and stroked her cheek. "I heard you say you could not stop thinking about someone." His grin stretched wider. "Who could that be?"

It was unfair to lead him along, yet she must. Hopefully, he would forgive her someday.

"I—" She swallowed hard. "Actually, Jonathan, if you must know, I was thinking about you."

He grasped her hands. "And what were you thinking about?"

"Well . . ." She licked her dry lips. "I was wondering . . . thinking about your birthday party. Yes, I was pondering as to what I should get you for a birthday present."

He threw back his head and laughed before taking her in his arms and pressing her against his firm chest. "Oh, my lovely Hannah. You are such a dear."

"Thank you." She rested her palms on his waistcoat, ready to push him away if necessary.

"Don't you know the only gift I need from you is your affection?" He bent his head and swept his lips across her forehead. "I think of you constantly, and the one thing you could give me that would be the best present in the world right now is a kiss." His voice lowered, and he looked at her lips. "The kind lovers share."

Her heart sank. She wanted to save those kisses for Morgan. "So soon? It is not your birthday."

Jonathan's hands wandered down her back and came to rest just above her bustle. "No, it is not my birthday, but we could call it an early present. Do you not agree?"

When his mouth covered hers, Hannah willed her lips to relax. He kissed her tenderly, his lips caressing her mouth, and tears sprang to her eyes as Morgan's request echoed in her head. She must lead Jonathan to believe she had feelings for him, and she prayed Morgan would understand.

Hesitantly, she moved her lips to encourage Jonathan's ardor. He sighed heavily and tightened his hold on her, kissing her with greater passion. She squeezed her eyes shut so as to not let the tears slip through.

Finally, Jonathan pulled back, a satisfied smile on his lips. He stroked her cheek. "That was a wonderful birthday present."

"I'm pleased you think so," she said softly, trying not to let him hear the emotion in her throat and mistake it for something she did not feel for him.

He linked his fingers with hers and led her out of the drawing room. "You can have no idea how happy you have made me since your arrival. You are a fine woman, Hannah."

She smiled. "Thank you for such a sweet compliment. You are a charming man yourself."

"I hope you don't mind if we take a stroll outside."

"Not at all. With the sun out, it shouldn't be too chilly."

If she could keep him from kissing her again, everything would be splendid, Hannah thought, grimacing to herself.

"I heard Mrs. White was appointed as your new maid," he said after they left the house.

How does he know that? Hannah wondered. She had not been in the drawing room long enough for Bethany and Roderick to tell Jonathan of their decision. Now she wondered if the youngest Thornton brother could be trusted.

"Yes. Francine left quite suddenly," Hannah said, "so I'm relieved Bethany and Roderick found me someone to replace her."

Jonathan stroked his thumb across her hand. "I'm sorry to hear she was afraid of staying here."

"I know she was, but I still can't believe she left without me. She is such a timid girl."

"Mrs. White will be a very good maid for you. She has been with us for many, many years."

"She has? I had no idea. How long?"

He shrugged. "Since I was a boy, I believe. She has a loving heart."

"She sounds like a special woman."

Jonathan nodded, keeping his gaze on the path ahead of them. "She is. Out of all the women Roderick had tried to seduce, she is the only one who has not fallen for his charms."

His comment took Hannah unawares, considering Mrs. White's age, but she laughed and said, "Then I like her even more."

Jonathan looked down at her. "And because of your reply, I like *you* that much more."

Hannah smiled. "Thank you."

"Just know that whatever you need, Mrs. White will take care of you. She has been supervising our staff for quite a while. We are like family to her."

"That's good to know," Hannah said. And it was, for now she worried what would happen if the housekeeper discovered she was in love with Morgan. She now had no doubt Mrs. White knew he was still alive.

✱❊C❧

Morgan's chest was heavy as he trudged back to his hidden sanctuary. It was his own fault for spying. Until he met Hannah, he had never experienced the pangs of jealousy. Then again, he had never truly been in love before. Although he tried to convince himself she kissed Jonathan the way she did because she had to, it still made him angry to see them together.

His brother had looked so happy with Hannah in his arms. She was perfect for Jonathan, and he was an infinitely better match for her than Morgan was. First of all, he was human, not a cursed beast that roamed the land at night seeking innocent women to kill. Even though Jonathan was simple minded, he could carry on a normal life, which was more than Morgan could do.

Morgan removed his waistcoat and cravat and unbuttoned the first two buttons on his shirt before relaxing in the cushioned chair by the fireplace. It was late in the afternoon, but not late enough for him to shift. That would happen once the sun disappeared and darkness covered the land. He had a few hours. Undoubtedly, he would shift tonight just as he had the night before, and the night before that.

Sighing, he picked up the book lying on the table next to him. He had returned to his old bedroom to find Peter Forester's journal. Now he opened it and started to read, but weariness soon came over him, and he closed his eyes. It was so warm next to the fire.

As he started to doze, thoughts of Hannah drifted through his mind. The taste of her sweet lips still lingered on his own. Her fragrance of lilacs filled his head, and even now the scent was so strong . . .

"Morgan?"

A soft hand touched his shoulder, and he jumped, suddenly fully awake.

Hannah gasped. "Oh, forgive me, Morgan. I thought—"

Quickly, he stood and pulled her into his arms, burying his face in her neck. "Hannah, my love. You are here."

Her body melted against his as she clung to him, filling his soul with happiness. He withdrew and looked into her eyes. Sliding his fingers over her face, he kissed her mouth, then grinned. "I'm so happy you are here. You must have heard my silent plea for your company."

Her lips stretched into a smile as she pressed her face into his hand. "My heart must have, because I knew I needed to be here with you."

He tugged on her arms and pulled her down to the couch with him, then picked up her father's journal. "I have something for you. I thought we could read it together."

When he brought forth the book, Hannah gasped, then grabbed it and pulled it to her chest. "You found it."

He slid his arm around her shoulders. "Yes."

"Oh, Morgan. You are so wonderful." She turned and kissed his cheek.

Holding his breath, he waited for her to cringe or appear disgusted, since she had just touched the scarred side of his face, but she did not. In fact, she acted as if she did not realize what she had done. His heart soared with the realization that she was not bothered by his deformities.

Hannah snuggled against him as they read aloud her father's journal. Peter Forester wrote about the research he had done while visiting Slumbering Giant. He mentioned the tales circulating about the island, explaining that none of them were true. As far as Peter knew, there was no treasure hidden there—no gold, no silver. And there was certainly no curse.

Several times as they read, Morgan caught Hannah wiping a tear from her cheek. His heart mourned with her. Peter had been a good friend and mentor, and Morgan knew the older man would be pleased to know he had fallen in love with Hannah.

Further into the journal, Peter wrote about his love for his daughter and how dear she was to him. Hannah wept silently again but continued to read. Toward the end of the book, Peter wrote of a visitor he had, a very old man who had read Peter's novel set on the island. The stranger had told Peter there was gold on the island, but that only someone with a pure heart would find it.

Hannah chuckled and looked up at Morgan. "Your family believes this, too. The first day I was here, this is what Jonathan told me. Even Roderick commented that I might be that woman."

Morgan stroked her cheek. "For once, I agree with my brother. You are certainly a treasure."

Blushing deeply, she quickly looked at the book again. As she read on, Morgan sat back and enjoyed the sound of her voice.

In the journal, Peter mentioned the stranger giving him a large number of paintings, suggesting they were special works of art that had something to do with the island. Peter wrote how overcome he was at the stranger's kindness, but he didn't know what he would do with all the paintings.

Hannah looked up at Morgan again. "Do you think those are the paintings Father sent to you?"

"They would have to be. But why would he send them to me?"

"Let's read more. Maybe he will say."

As they read on, Peter didn't say more about the paintings, but there was an entry that made Morgan extremely curious. Peter mentioned a woman coming to see him—another stranger. She was very beautiful, and she asked about the secrets of the island and what Peter had discovered while doing his research.

The next entry talked about Morgan's visit, and how much Peter had enjoyed it. Morgan smiled when Hannah read aloud how Peter wanted his daughter and Morgan to meet. Peter thought of Morgan as a son, and from what he had written in the journal, he very much wanted Hannah and Morgan to marry.

In the last entry, Peter wrote about how the strange woman came back, more aggressive this time, and even angrier when he didn't answer her questions to her satisfaction. He said he would not allow her into his house if she ever came calling again.

Sighing heavily, Hannah closed the book and relaxed against Morgan. He pulled her closer and stroked her arm.

"It makes me wonder," she began, "if this woman was the one who killed him."

"It is a possibility. But why?"

Hannah looked up at Morgan. "The paintings."

"How did she know about them?"

"I don't know, unless she had been watching my father all that time."

"That's something to consider." Morgan kissed the top of her head as she pressed her cheek against his chest. "I wish I knew what to tell you. I want to help you discover who killed your father, because this person needs to be hanged for such a crime."

"I agree."

"Tomorrow we will take a closer look at those paintings—see if they might give us a clue to why that man gave them to your father."

"I like that idea." Hannah looked up at Morgan again. "Can we meet here, in your chambers?"

"Yes."

She smiled. "Splendid, because I enjoy being alone with you."

He groaned and placed tender kisses on her eyelids, cheeks, nose, and then her mouth. She lifted her fingers to his hair and pushed them through his waves to hold his head close to hers. As much as he wanted to hold her all night, he knew he could not. Soon it would be dark, and then the beast would make an appearance. He could not have her witness that, for he could not bear to see the disgust in her eyes, her horror at what he really was.

Twelve

Morgan pulled back and rested his forehead against hers. "Hannah, my love, I could kiss you all night."

She withdrew slightly and smiled. "There is nothing wrong with that."

"Oh, but there is." He cradled her face in his hands, his thumbs tracing her bottom lip, still swollen from his kiss. "Being with you like this puts you in danger."

"I beg to differ. Have you forgotten? When the white wolf came to me the other night, he was very gentle. He didn't harm me at all."

"I'm not thinking about the white wolf. I'm thinking about the witch."

She frowned. "Oh, her."

"Yes. If she knew you were with me now, I fear what she might do."

"I understand."

Hannah's disappointment tugged at his heart. "The problem is, although I know I'm putting you in danger, I can't seem to let you go. I want to be with you every moment, Hannah. I want for us never to be apart."

"Oh, Morgan. I want that as well."

He gathered her back into his arms and covered her mouth with his. She clung to him and answered with an urgent kiss. Pushing his fingers through her hair, he released the pins holding the coil together until thick locks cascaded over her back. She was so beautiful, so tempting.

"Morgan," she sighed as she kissed his forehead.

From down the hall, he heard creaking on the floor. His heart slammed against his chest.

The witch!

Cursing, he pulled Hannah off the couch and pushed her into the adjoining room. Her mouth opened to speak, but he put his finger to her lips.

"Don't make a sound. The witch is here."

He quickly hurried out of the room, closing the door behind him. He ran back to the couch and sat before the witch entered.

She sashayed through the doorway and leaned against the wall. As always, her overpowering perfume made him gag.

"Do you ever knock?" he snapped.

Her throaty laugh hung in the air. "Oh, Morgan. Why would I knock? I'm the only one who comes here."

"And I would be most grateful if you never came back."

Smiling, she moved away from the door and slunk toward him.

He held his breath, waiting for her to say something about his visitor, but as he studied her face, he realized she didn't know Hannah was there. He said a silent prayer of thanks.

The witch sat on the armrest and ran her hand over his chest. "Have you grown weary of shifting, my dear? You know what to do if you want me to change you back to a normal man."

Morgan pushed her aside, stood, and moved away. He linked his hands behind his back and paced the floor between her and Hannah, who remained behind the closed door.

"Since you know I will never love you, I assume you have come to harp about that treasure map." He shook his head. "I grow weary, not simply of shifting into a wolf, but of your inability to accept what I tell you." He stopped in front of her and glared. "I do not, nor will I ever, have that cursed treasure map. There is no such thing. If there was, do you not think someone would have found it by now?"

"Oh, there is a treasure there, I assure you. It has been spoken of for centuries. Peter Forester gave you the map—I know he did."

Anger poured through Morgan, and his animal instincts took over. He stepped to her and wrapped his hands around her throat. Her eyes widened and she gasped, but she said nothing.

"Do you know how I loathe you?" Morgan asked, seething. "Every day I want to kill you with my bare hands. I want to choke the life right out of you just to be free."

He caught a glimpse of terror on her face, but then she grinned. "You will not kill me, because if you do you will never turn back."

It would be easy to strangle her or snap her neck, but she was correct. The curse would die with her.

Releasing a frustrated growl, he yanked his hands away and stepped back. He drove his fingers through his hair as he paced the floor again, breathing deep and slow, trying to control his hatred. He accidentally kicked the paintings he had taken off the walls in the manor, and two of them toppled over, the wooden frames breaking as they hit the floor.

He glanced back at the witch. "Would you please leave?"

She tsked. "Morgan, you are out of sorts today. " She walked toward him, a smirk on her face. "Does this have anything to do with Miss Forester?"

He stared hard into her eyes. "If you touch one hair on her head, I swear—"

The witch's cackle floated through the air as she stroked his cheek. "I can't believe these threats you are throwing at me, my dear man."

He pushed her hand away. "You forget that you don't frighten me any longer."

She shrugged and turned away, moving toward the door. "I hope you have not fallen completely in love with Miss Forester," she said over her shoulder. When she reached the door, she stopped and met his gaze. "Jonathan is madly in love with her. Did you know that? I believe he will ask her to be his wife soon."

Morgan's gut clenched, and he gritted his teeth. He should not be surprised. He had suspected as much when he saw Jonathan kissing Hannah.

"Then I wish them a happy life together."

The witch arched an eyebrow. "Oh, you can't fool me, Morgan. You have become infatuated with her, too. Why else would you shift so often?"

"Good night. I'm weary of your chatter, and I need my sleep."

She flipped her hand through the air. "As you wish. I shall see you again very soon."

When she walked out of the room he listened for her footsteps and the creaking of the door as she closed it. Sighing with relief, he sank to the couch and covered his face with his hands. That had been the closest he had ever come to killing her—or anyone, for that matter, since he did not recall his nights as the wolf.

He glanced at the door Hannah hid behind and groaned. They had almost gotten caught. He shuddered to think what the witch would have done if she had seen Hannah in his arms.

He stood and released a deep breath before walking to the door and opening it. Hannah's wide eyes, moist with tears, stared up at him. His heart crumbled, and he gathered her in his arms. Her body trembled against him, and he tightened his hold.

"Oh, Morgan," she sobbed. "We were almost discovered."

He kissed the top of her head. "I know."

"It is my fault. If I had not come here—"

"Shh." He lifted her chin until she met his eyes. "It is not your fault. It is mine. I could have told you to leave several times, but the truth is, I wanted you here. You make me whole. When you are with me, I'm a man instead of a beast."

He bent and captured her mouth, but only kissed her for a few moments before pulling away. "But I think it is best if you return to your room."

She nodded.

Taking her hand in his, he led her through the tunnels. Because knowing him put her in danger, he wished he had never met her and fallen in love with her. But she had brought happiness and hope back to his life, and now he could never let her go. That thought frightened him more than anything.

❦

Morgan had shifted again—because of her. The wolf's howls during the night brought tears to Hannah's eyes. She had tried to block out the mournful cries with her pillow over her ears, but to no avail.

The next morning her eyes were heavy with fatigue, and all she wanted to do was sleep. Yet much needed to be done. With Morgan shifting every night, and with the witch suspicious that he loved Hannah, they must find a way out of this curse, and quickly.

At breakfast, Bethany chattered about their last-minute plans for Jonathan's birthday ball. Hannah's emotions were such that it physically hurt her to smile, but she had to keep up appearances. She must not let Bethany and Roderick suspect she was unhappy, for they would only ask questions—questions she could not answer.

Suddenly, from down the hall, a door slammed and voices rose. Hannah's heart sank. The last time this happened, the white wolf had killed a young woman. Hannah prayed it was something different. But as the voices drew nearer and wails filled the air, tears stung her eyes. *Not again!*

Bethany and Roderick jumped from their chairs just as Mrs. White and two other maids ran into the dining room.

"What has happened?" Roderick demanded.

"It is Anne." Mrs. White wrung her hands against her chest. "She was attacked last night." Beside her, the two other maids cried into their hands.

"The white wolf?" Bethany's whisper was greeted with nods.

"But Anne is not dead," Mrs. White added.

Hannah gasped and leaped out of her chair, knocking it over. All heads turned toward her. "She is alive?" She hurried toward the housekeeper. "Where is she? We must ask her what happened."

"Henry, the footman, found her. She was still breathing. He took her to the physician in town."

Roderick ran his fingers through his hair. "Good heavens! I must go to her at once."

Bethany passed her husband a heated glare before rolling her eyes. "Fine, go. While you are gone, Hannah and I have birthday plans to make." She gave Hannah a feigned smile.

Hannah was shocked at Bethany's lack of sympathy for Anne, but she nodded and said, "Yes, we do have to finish our plans." She gave Mrs. White a sympathetic smile. "Please keep us informed of Anne's condition, and let me know if there is anything I can do."

Mrs. White nodded. "I will." When the housekeeper turned back toward the door, Roderick hurried after her.

"I certainly hope Anne is going to be all right. Maybe she can tell us what happened and how the white wolf attacked her." Hannah shook her head. "It is still hard for me to believe the white wolf has killed anyone. He certainly could have killed me, but he didn't."

"Yes. That's quite amazing. Perhaps the creature detected your sweet demeanor and pure heart, so he had no inclination to kill you," Bethany said with a touch of sarcasm.

Hannah shrugged. "Perhaps."

As she walked beside Bethany toward the parlor, she counted the minutes until she could be with Morgan. Would he remember anything about Anne? Was it really the white wolf who attacked her, or the rabid dogs?

She and Bethany sat at the table and addressed the invitations to the birthday ball. For an hour, Bethany chattered on about nothing, and Hannah had to concentrate to keep a smile on her face. Finally, when she could scarcely bear the woman anymore, heavy footsteps echoed down the hall and into the parlor. Jonathan appeared at the door and stopped, his chest rising and falling quickly.

"Oh, there you are," he said.

"Yes, dear. What is it?" Bethany stood and walked to him.

"Did you hear about Anne?"

"Yes."

"I can't believe . . . It is amazing, don't you think?" Jonathan's face was pasty white.

Bethany patted his shoulder. "Yes, it is truly amazing Anne is still alive. But you must not worry. Roderick and Mrs. White are with her now." She pulled Jonathan to an empty chair next to Hannah. "Why don't you help Hannah? I'm certain she would love your company, and it will take your mind off Anne."

Hannah nodded. "Yes. Your company would be most welcome."

Jonathan's countenance relaxed as he sat next to her and looked into her eyes.

"Now there. Don't you feel better, Jonathan?" Bethany stroked his hair.

"Oh, yes, dear sister. Seeing Hannah always makes my day."

Bethany pulled away from Jonathan. "Well, since you two are so cozy, I hope you don't mind if I leave for a bit. I have a few errands to attend to this afternoon."

Hannah lifted a brow. Not even an hour ago, all Bethany could think about was making birthday plans. What mischief was she up to now?

"We shall be fine, Bethany. Go and enjoy yourself." Jonathan smiled. He covered Hannah's hand with his and squeezed. "You have been a godsend. Do you know that?"

"Thank you, Jonathan. You are too kind."

"No, you are the kind one." He lifted her hand to his mouth and brushed his lips across her knuckles.

Hannah smiled and casually pulled her hand away. She pushed her stack of invitations in front of him and retrieved the pile Bethany was addressing. "Here is the list," Hannah told him. "Mark off the name once you have addressed the invitation."

They labored over the invitations, mostly in silence, which gave Hannah time to think. Why had the white wolf attacked two of the people Morgan had been ready to dismiss a year ago? Was Mrs. White next? Maybe Bethany and Roderick? Was the witch responsible for everything bad that had happened at Thornton

Manor during the past year? What did the island have to do with Morgan's curse?

A pain throbbed in Hannah's forehead, and she rubbed at it.

"What is on your mind, my dear?" Jonathan touched her hand again.

Hannah snapped out of her thoughts and met his gaze. She smiled. "Too much to talk about, I fear."

He squeezed her fingers softly. "Please tell me. Speaking of your troubles can help, you know. I'm a good listener."

"Well . . ." She took a deep breath, stalling for time until she could think of something to say. "I'm . . . uh . . . I'm having a hard time feeling comfortable around Bethany."

Jonathan threw back his head and laughed. Hannah breathed a sigh of relief. Apparently, she had touched on a subject he would not mind discussing.

She grinned. "What is so humorous?"

Tears moistened his eyes when he met her stare. "Oh, my dear, Hannah! You are such a delight."

She arched a brow. "Thank you, but why do you say that?"

"Because most people I know are hesitant to say anything about Bethany, especially if it does not place her in the best light."

"Why do you suppose that is?"

He shrugged. "I have known her most of my life. She is older than me by five years, I believe, and I think of her as an older sister. Her family worked for my father when I was young, and their cottage was a short distance down the lane from our manor. They were very poor, but Bethany would always come with her mother and older sister when they cleaned the rooms. Bethany's father died when she was very young. He had been my father's groundskeeper. My father took pity on their family and kept her mother and older sister as our maids until Bethany was older. Soon her mother's frail body could not handle the labor, and she became bedridden. I can't recall what happened to the older sister, but she stopped working for us before that happened. Bethany had to provide for her and her mother after that. I don't recall exactly what she did, but she worked in town for many years, and we didn't see her as often."

Hannah leaned her elbows on the table and scooted closer. "What an interesting story. Do you know how she and Roderick started courting?"

Jonathan's face reddened. "Well, I do know Bethany had her eyes set on my other brother, Morgan, but he didn't want anything to do with her. He had just taken over the manor and lands with the death of our father, and he was not interested in falling in love. His heart was in making money." He shrugged. "So when Bethany could not make Morgan her husband, she set her mind upon Roderick."

"And how did she win him over?"

"Well, you know Roderick and how he enjoys . . . er . . . the company of women?"

Hannah tried not to laugh over Jonathan's discomfort. "Yes."

"One day while he was riding, he caught Bethany swimming in the water hole." Jonathan's face reddened again. "She was in her altogether," he whispered, then resumed a normal tone. "As it was, Roderick could not resist taking a swim with her. When Morgan caught them, he forced Roderick to marry her, since what they were doing was improper and would ruin her reputation."

Hannah smiled. "And Roderick accepted this without a fight?"

"I thought he wouldn't want to comply, but he did so."

"That's good. Maybe they were meant for each other after all."

Jonathan chuckled. "That's a different story, if you ask me."

"I suppose you're right." She laughed. "So how did she treat Morgan after she moved into the house as Roderick's wife?"

"I'm not certain. Not too long after that I went to Italy with my friends. That's when Morgan died." Jonathan's smile disappeared.

Hannah touched his hand. "I'm sorry to bring up such bad memories."

"They are not bad memories as much as they are regretful ones. I wish I had been here. I would have done everything I could to try to save Morgan from the fire. I do miss him terribly."

Why didn't he know Morgan was alive? Morgan had told her that his family was ashamed of his curse, which is why he hid in the East Wing. Apparently, Roderick and Bethany had chosen not to let Jonathan in on their little secret. Morgan's words echoed in her head: *Ghosts are much easier to believe than the truth.*

Now she understood why Jonathan was kept in the dark. His simple mind couldn't grasp the truth. Even she had a hard time understanding everything that went on in the Thornton household.

"Jonathan, will you tell me about your parents? I don't know much about your father and mother and how you boys were raised."

His face flushed, and he glanced down at the list on the table. "Morgan and Roderick have a different mother than I."

"Indeed? I didn't know your father remarried."

Jonathan shook his head. "He didn't. I am the result of a liaison my father had with one of the maids."

"Oh, dear." Hannah placed her fingers to her mouth, wishing she had said nothing. "I'm truly sorry I didn't know."

He met her gaze and took her hand in his. "There is nothing to be sorry about. It happened a long time ago. My father and brothers have treated me no differently."

"Is your mother still alive?"

"No. She died when I was young."

"Do you remember her?"

"Not much. Father kept her on as one of the servants, I do remember that. She took care of me while I was in my infancy, and from what I remember, she was a kind woman."

Hannah patted his hand. "I'm relieved to hear this."

From the corner of the room, the curtain moved. Her heart leaped, and she held her breath. Peeking around the curtain, Morgan smiled at her and motioned her to come to him. She knew it must be very important or he would not risk exposure.

Jonathan made the move to look over his shoulder, so Hannah pulled on his hand, bringing his attention back to her.

She smiled. "Do you mind terribly if we put off addressing these invitations for a bit? I didn't sleep well last night, and I would like to take a nap."

"I don't mind at all. You should have said something sooner."

"No. It was very enjoyable talking to you. I feel I know Bethany better now, thanks to you."

He cupped her face, his gaze dropping to her mouth. "Whenever you need to talk, let me know."

He leaned in and kissed her lips. After only a few seconds she pulled away. "Thank you, Jonathan. You are a gem." She winked, then stood.

As she walked out of the parlor, she tried to move slowly so Jonathan would not be suspicious. But when she reached the stairs, she lifted her gown to her ankles and sprinted up, then rushed to her room. Once inside, she locked the door and hastened back toward the hidden tunnel.

Just as she pulled back the curtain, Morgan's hand was there, grasping hers and pulling her through. She wrapped her arms around him and kissed him. He pulled her close.

"I missed you," she murmured.

"I have missed you, my darling." He pulled back and looked into her eyes. "I know I took a chance in the parlor, but I've found something that I must show you."

Thirteen

Hannah clutched Morgan's hand as he led her quickly through the dark tunnels, only a candle lighting their way. With very little light, the walls seemed to close in on her.

"What were you doing with Jonathan?" he asked.

"Addressing invitations to his masked birthday ball."

"Where was Bethany? Usually she watches him like a hen guards her chicks."

Hannah chuckled. "She made some excuse to leave the manor to run errands not too long before you came to get me. Roderick and Mrs. White went into town a few hours ago."

"Ah, so I have you all to myself for a while?" Morgan squeezed her hand.

Hannah giggled. "So it seems. Tell me, what did you find? I can't bear the anticipation any longer."

He looked at her, his grin widening. "You will have to wait, my love. But I can tell you something now. This does not have anything to do with the surprise, but I know you will want to hear it nonetheless."

He stopped and took both her hands. "While listening in on Beth and Roddy earlier today, I learned something about your maid."

"Francine?"

"Beth has done something with her—taken her some place—but your maid is alive."

Hannah sighed in relief. "But why would they take her? Is she all right?"

"My brother and sister-in-law enjoy playing with people's lives."

"But you don't know where they took Francine?"

"No. They didn't name a precise location, and I could not figure it out." Morgan cupped her face in his hand. "But we will. Beth and Roddy have a reason for everything they do, and it is usually a greedy one."

"I've learned that about them already."

Morgan turned back toward the path, and Hannah took quick steps to keep up with him.

"Nothing has ever been enough for Beth," he said. "She has always wanted more."

"Jonathan told me a little about her life. Apparently, she had set her sights on you at first."

Morgan glanced at Hannah over his shoulder. "That's true. The girl used to follow me when we were children. Every time I thought I had gotten rid of her, she would show up at the most unexpected moment."

Hannah laughed. "Well, if you were half as handsome then are you are now, it is no wonder she was taken with you."

He stopped short, causing her to bump into him. He turned and gathered her in his arms. "You think I'm handsome?"

"Yes, of course." Smiling, she swept her fingers through his hair. "Do you not notice me sighing every time I look at you?"

He pulled her closer, and his mouth covered hers in a slow, meaningful kiss. As she held his face and answered back, an overpowering, sweet feeling blossomed in her chest.

He pulled away, a smile on his lips. "Hannah, either you need spectacles or you lie extremely well."

She laughed and shook her head. "I'm certainly not lying. You are the most handsome man I have ever seen."

He stroked her cheek with two fingers. "I never thought I would hear those words again, especially after I was cursed."

She took his fingers from her face and kissed them, staring into his dark gaze. "Morgan, I'm . . ." Dare she tell him she was falling in love with him? No, she mustn't, for confessing would only make her heart ache that much more, knowing she couldn't have him. Unless and until his curse was lifted, they couldn't marry or live a normal life.

"Yes?" he urged.

"I just wanted to say that you make me very happy."

He pulled Hannah against him and buried his face in her neck. Tears filled her eyes as emotion clogged her throat. How could fate allow her to fall in love with such a wonderful man, not knowing if she could be with him for the rest of her life?

She grasped his hands and squeezed. "I can't go on like this, and neither can you. We must find the map, and soon!"

"Agreed." He kissed her once more before pulling her back through the tunnels toward his chambers. Once they entered, the bright lights made her squint. This was the first time she had seen his rooms lit up so lively, looking nothing at all like a dungeon.

"After we were almost caught by the witch," he began, "I noticed I had broken a couple of picture frames when I had accidentally kicked them over." He released Hannah's hand and knelt in front of the pictures, which were lined up side by side against the wall. "When I started putting them together, I realized they were not several different pictures, but one large picture that had been cut into many pieces. Each piece was framed separately."

Hannah knelt beside him. Once Morgan had placed the paintings flat on the floor and arranged them, she could see that together they formed the image of an entire island. She gasped. "Slumbering Giant!"

He nodded. "That was my conclusion. It does not resemble the island perfectly, but close enough. I also wondered why the painter would cut the painting into four smaller paintings, unless—"

"Unless he was trying to hide something?"

Morgan grinned. "Like the treasure map."

She clapped her hands and focused on the paintings again, her heart beating a wild rhythm. "Oh, Morgan . . . do you honestly believe?"

He stood and ran his fingers through his hair. "Amazing as it sounds, I actually do, Hannah. What if there was a treasure map, and that's why the painter gave these to your father? The painter had read your father's book, which explains that there is no treasure. But what if the painter knew differently?"

She rose and stood in front of Morgan, clasping his hands. "Oh, Morgan, if we can find the treasure, the witch will lift the curse."

"I can only pray."

Hannah tore away from him and grasped the first picture. "I will take this one, and you take the other. We will study them closely to see what we can find."

They sat together on his sofa as she concentrated on the painting. Occasionally, his arm would touch hers, reminding her how close they sat. She tried to concentrate on the painting, but she kept glancing at Morgan's profile, wanting to kiss him again. He was so handsome, his heart so kind and tender.

He was also cursed to shift into a beast.

Suddenly, she remembered about Anne. Did he know? "Morgan?"

"Yes?" he answered without looking at her.

"Did . . . did you hear about Anne?"

He lowered the painting to his lap and looked at her with wide eyes. "Besides that she is carrying my brother's baby? What else can there be?"

Suddenly, his face went pale, and Hannah knew he realized the white wolf had attacked the servant. Hannah wanted to wrap him in her arms and assure him everything would be all right. Instead, she placed her hand on his stiff one and squeezed. "But she was not killed."

"No?"

"She is in town under the care of the physician. Roderick and Mrs. White went into town earlier today to see how she is fairing."

Morgan set the painting on the floor, rested his elbows on his knees, and held his head in his hands. "Oh, Hannah. I know I shifted last night, but I really thought I didn't hurt anyone. Poor Anne!"

Leaning into him, she stroked his hair. "I know. It is not your fault."

"Why do I attack women I do not care for? True, I shift when I feel passion for a woman, and since you entered my life, I have been doing that a lot." He sat up and looked at her. "But why would I hurt anyone? Why would I kill? These women mean nothing to me."

"I wish I knew. But I still believe the white wolf does not kill. What if those rabid dogs are the culprits?"

Morgan frowned and shook his head. "I would love to believe you, but I don't dare. That's why you can't be in my presence at night when I shift." He wrapped his arms around her. "I don't know what I would do if I harmed you in any way. I would rather die than hurt you."

"You will not hurt me." She clutched his shoulders and held him tight. "Even when you were the white wolf, you cared for me."

"I wish I could remember." He rested his head in the crook of her neck. "I wish this nightmare would end, and that I could be the man I once was." His embrace tightened. "I want to be with you, my dearest Hannah, forever."

Her heart wrenched, and she bit back a sob. Right now it seemed like an impossible dream. "We will be together forever. I promise."

He caressed her cheek. "Hannah, I have to say this now, even though I'm certain it is too early, but I care deeply for you. I . . . I love you. You are the only woman I have ever felt this way about."

Tears of happiness filled her eyes. "Oh, Morgan, I love you too."

She fell into his embrace and they kissed tenderly. Morgan was the first to pull away. "As much as I don't want to let you go, I fear my brother might come looking for you, so you had better get back to your room."

She sighed, slipping her arms around his waist. "You are right, of course."

Arm in arm, Hannah and Morgan walked through the tunnels to the west side of the manor. When they reached her room, he looked inside first, then allowed her to enter. He kissed her one more time, then left her alone.

❦

Hannah paced the floor, thoughts whirling in her head. Morgan had allowed her to stay longer in his room, saying the witch would not interrupt them this time. How did he know that?

Maybe the witch was Bethany, since she had gone to town to run errands.

Then again, what if the witch was Anne? According to the Thorntons and the servants, when the white wolf attacked, he killed innocent women. But Anne was not innocent in the least. Come to think of it, neither was Sarah, since she had been carrying on a tryst with Roderick, too.

Hannah paused in thought. If Anne was the witch, why had the wolf attacked her? Perhaps she was trying to create a diversion and had only pretended to be attacked. Either way, Hannah could not mark Anne off her list of suspicious characters just yet.

What about Mrs. White? Out of everyone in this house, she seemed the least likely to want to hurt the Thorntons. In fact, she seemed to look out for the family and to truly care for them. The older woman had served them faithfully for years, and she even treated poor Jonathan with love and respect.

Yes, Hannah concluded, Bethany must be the witch. After all, she was a selfish, mean woman with a cold heart, and she had loved Morgan from the time she was a young girl. At first all the witch had wanted was his love, he had explained, but now she wanted the treasure map.

Now the question was, if Bethany and the witch were the same person, how could Hannah stop her? Grumbling, she walked to the vanity and picked up a brush. As she pulled it roughly through her hair, the bristles punished her scalp. She set the brush down, then sank in her chair and stared at her reflection in the mirror. Perhaps she would place some sleeping powder in Bethany's tea, so that Hannah and Morgan could spend some private time together. She chuckled at the thought.

She hurried downstairs, heading for the dining room. As she passed the drawing room, Bethany's voice rang through the stillness. Hannah turned and walked slowly into the room, trying to smile at her hostess.

"Good evening, Mrs. Thornton. I wondered if you had returned from your errands earlier today."

"I had a splendid time in town." Bethany grinned. "I purchased some new gowns, and some costumes for Jonathan's party."

Hannah moved closer. "While you were in town, did you drop in to the hospital to see how Anne is faring?"

"I didn't have time for that. Besides, Roderick and Mrs. White were with her."

"Have they returned? Is there any news of Anne's condition?"

"None yet." Bethany moved from her chair and strolled to the table in the far corner of the room. "I did buy you a gown, though."

"A—a gown?" Hannah blinked.

"Yes. You will need a gown for the masked ball." Bethany picked up a box and handed it to Hannah. "Last night, Jonathan and I were talking, and he asked if I would buy you this gown." Her smile widened. "I must say, he is quite smitten with you."

Hannah nodded and took the box. "Thank you, Mrs. Thornton. I appreciate your generosity."

"It is Jonathan whom you should thank, you know."

"I will when I see him next." She glanced out the door. "Will he be here for supper?"

"I'm quite certain he will." Bethany nodded toward the box. "Take a look at what Jonathan wants you to wear to the ball."

After sitting on the couch, Hannah opened the box. As she lifted the red silk gown, the daring bodice was what she noticed first. She stifled a gasp. Only ladies of ill repute wore such gowns.

"Jonathan and I thought you could go as a she-devil." Bethany laughed. "I thought it was a wonderful idea."

Hannah hated the costume, but she could not let anyone notice her consternation. Jonathan had been thinking of her, and she must appreciate his gesture. But why would he want her to wear such a revealing gown in front of everyone?

"It is a lovely gown—" Hannah smiled "—and I shall tell Jonathan when I see him."

Horace, the butler, walked in and handed Bethany a letter. She opened it and scanned the contents, then folded the paper.

"Thank you," Bethany said. "And when you leave, will you take this box and have it delivered to Hannah's room?"

"Yes, mistress."

As Horace left the drawing room, Bethany stood. "I believe it will just be us for dinner tonight, Miss Forester. Jonathan has been detained in town."

"Oh, I was not aware he went into town."

"Apparently he was worried about Anne."

"How sweet of him." Hannah surmised that at least Jonathan had a heart.

After they sat at the table and the servants brought in their food, Hannah could hardly bear the deafening silence, especially when it was accompanied by piercing glares from Bethany. Just as Hannah opened her mouth to speak, the mistress of the manor cleared her throat.

"You will never guess whom I saw in town today."

"I have no idea. Who?"

"Your uncle."

Hannah halted with the fork halfway to her mouth. "Uncle Timothy?"

"Yes. He asked about your welfare."

Hannah set the fork back on the plate without taking a bite. "Pray, what did you tell him?"

"I told him you were deliriously happy, as was Jonathan, and that your visit has brightened our lives."

"That was most kind of you. What did he say to that?"

"He was greatly relieved. He feared you would never find a man suited to your tastes."

Hannah nodded. Her uncle would say that, to be sure. "I'm quite certain he is delighted that Jonathan and I are getting along so well. Uncle Timothy would like nothing more to get rid of me."

Bethany sipped her wine glass and then set it back on the table. Leaning forward, she rested her elbows on the table. "Tell me, why is your uncle so determined to find you a husband? Truly, as you said before, it seems he does not want you back."

"My uncle was not very happy when I came to live with him after my father died."

"May I ask why?"

"Uncle Timothy could not tolerate children, and even though I was an adult when I entered his house, he still thought of me as a child. From the day I arrived, he treated me like a wayward child, punishing me severely for even the smallest things." Hannah took a gulp of her drink. "It is difficult to live somewhere you are not wanted."

Bethany sucked in a quick breath and placed her hand on her chest. "Oh, my poor dear. How awful for you."

Hannah knew the woman didn't care about her welfare, but she played along. "It was certainly hard to live with Uncle Timothy and all his rules. He would not allow me to have friends or attend parties. It was like he wanted me kept prisoner in his house." She sighed. "That's why I was so thrilled when you asked me to come here."

Bethany smiled and picked up her wine glass again. "And you may remain here as long as you like." She took a sip. "If Jonathan has anything to do with it, you'll be here forever."

Sadness washed over Hannah. She knew Jonathan was in love with her, and she didn't want to hurt him. How would he take the news when she told him she loved his brother?

Fourteen

Hannah beamed as she took a bite of poached egg the next morning. It was a good thing she was alone in the dining room, because she could not stop smiling. All night she had listened for the white wolf's howl, but she never heard it. She and Morgan had spent time together, kissing and confessing their feelings, so he should have shifted. But he had not.

She finished her meal and pushed away from the table. Just as she stood, Mrs. White walked into the room.

"You look happy this morning," the housekeeper remarked with a smile. "Did you have a good rest?"

"Yes, I did." Hannah approached her. "But how are you? I have not heard anything about Anne, and I'm very concerned about her."

"She has not yet awoken, but she is alive. The wolf nearly ripped out her throat, so the doctor fears she may never be able to speak again."

"Oh, dear! I'm relieved she is alive."

"As am I. She is a good friend."

Hannah clasped Mrs. White's hand and squeezed. "You are the good friend, staying by her side the way you did."

Tears formed in the housekeeper's eyes, and she blinked them away. "If you will excuse me, I must be on my way. There is still much to do before Jonathan's birthday ball. The days are just flying by, and I fear I shall run out of time."

As Hannah stepped into the hallway, the butler was walking towards her. "Horace, have you seen Master Jonathan? Is he still out riding this morning?"

"I believe so, Miss Forester. I have not seen him since last evening, but he usually rides in the morning."

"Thank you."

She hurried up the stairs to her bedroom and changed into a riding habit. Soon, she strolled outside toward the stables. The sun stood high in the sky without any threat of clouds. Not even a cool breeze disturbed her. Hannah reached the stable and asked a stable lad to saddle a mare for her. As she waited, she gazed across the field, then off to the side where the forest began. Shivers ran down her arms, and her heart clenched as she thought of her maid. Hopefully, Francine was indeed alive, as Morgan had suggested.

The stable boy brought the mare to Hannah and helped her mount. She urged the animal into a slow trot as she studied the landscape. During the night, the place seemed most dreary, but now with the bright sun warming her face, everything appeared welcoming and cheerful—except for the forest, of course.

She scanned the fields and hills for Jonathan, wondering where he rode every day. Urging her horse faster, she rode to the top of a hillside that overlooked the island. She stopped and stared through squinted eyes. According to Bethany and Roderick, nobody dared set foot on the cursed island.

Hannah turned away and headed back down the slope. A movement in a thicket of trees caught her attention. Her heart stilled for a moment as she tightened her fingers on the reins and slowed the horse. Someone in a black-hooded cape peeked out from behind a tree.

She sighed in relief. *Morgan!*

He motioned with his hand, inviting her closer. She guided the mare into the cover of the trees. Morgan tied the horse's reins to a thick branch and lifted Hannah from the saddle.

"What are you doing out here?" she asked before wrapping her arms around his neck.

He laughed and pulled her further into the shadows. "I missed you, and since you were not in the house, I thought to come outside and look for you."

Keeping her in his arms, he leaned against a large trunk. She pushed the hood from his head and ran her fingers through his hair. "Why are you not asleep?"

"How can I sleep with you on my mind?"

She sighed and rested her head against his chest. "I'm happy to know you think of me."

"Always." He kissed her head. "Did you notice anything different about last night?"

"Yes." Hannah raised her head and looked into his twinkling eyes. "You didn't shift."

"What do you think it means?"

"I don't know for certain, but . . ." She cupped his face in her hands. "You were cursed to shift when you feel passion for a woman, and in the past our embraces have caused you to shift. But last night you told me you were in love with me, so perhaps that protected you from shifting."

He groaned and kissed her lips briefly. "I do like the way you think, my love. I pray you are correct."

"I won't accept any other explanation. When I'm with you, I don't want to think about the real world. It is as if only you and I exist."

"I have never known anyone like you before." Morgan stroked her bottom lip with his thumb. "When you look at the world, you see the good in it. You are always hopeful."

"Not always, but I do see everything as a new adventure."

"So much like your father."

Hannah nodded. "That's where I learned it."

Morgan pulled away and grasped her hand. "Come. I want to show you something."

She followed him deeper into the wooded area, the trees becoming thicker the farther they walked. Soon, a small hut appeared, nearly hidden within the trees.

"What is this?"

"This cottage has been empty for several years. Since I inherited the manor, I have never used this place. In fact, nobody uses it. Strange, because I figured Roddy would have it for his love nest, but there are no signs of that."

Morgan opened the door and led her inside. Holding hands, they walked through the three rooms. The kitchen was barren, except for a chair, a table, and an old trunk. One room still held a wide bed. The small rug on the floor looked old and dusty, and the cupboards on the wall in the kitchen were laced with cobwebs. The dusty scent tickled Hannah's nose, and she sneezed.

"Clearly, no one has lived here in a while," she said as they moved back into the front room.

Suddenly, something Jonathan had said came back to her. "Is this where Bethany and her family lived while her mother and sister were working for your father?"

A scowl marred Morgan's handsome face. "Yes, this is where they lived. I swear, my father took in every tramp and freeloader he found." Morgan shook his head. "But that was a long time ago. Did Jonathan tell you about that?"

"Just a little."

Morgan took Hannah in his arms. "This is where I would like for us to meet in secret, if you don't mind. It is obvious the place has been ignored, so I don't think we will be discovered. I will clean it up, of course."

She laughed. "That's a wonderful idea."

He ran his finger along her chin, then lifted her face until she met his eyes. "I wish we didn't have to meet in secret."

"One day we won't need to hide."

"I pray you're right. It is torture for me not to tell the world how much you mean to me." Morgan bent his head and kissed her.

The kiss did not last long, and he broke away but kept her in his embrace. Hannah glanced around the room once more. It was hard to imagine Bethany and her family living here. Jonathan had told Hannah that Bethany's father died when she was young, so it was just Bethany, her mother, and her older sister.

Hannah raised her head and met Morgan's gaze. "Whatever happened to Bethany's older sister?" she asked.

"I don't know. Ethel probably ran away with some neighbor boy—or a servant. Both Bethany and Ethel were quite flirtatious and set their sights on wealthy men, though such men would not consider them for a wife."

"Why? Because of their upbringing, their station in life?"

"Yes, mainly, but there was also something odd about them, something that is hard to explain. I just remember feeling eerie every time Bethany gave me her 'come-hither' look."

"Did Ethel try to flirt with you?"

"No. She was older than me by quite a few years. And even if she had tried, I would have discouraged her attempts, just as I did Bethany's."

"I almost feel sorry for them, being raised poor and relying on others to make it from day to day."

"Do not pity them, Hannah. They learned their greediness from their mother. To this day I don't know why my father kept them as part of his staff. They were not loyal servants."

Hannah eyes kept drifting toward the trunk, and since curiosity always got the better of her, she pulled away from Morgan and moved to the trunk. She knelt in front of it and brushed the cobwebs away from the latch.

"What are you doing, my love?" Morgan stood behind her.

"I just want to see what is inside."

"I doubt there is anything in there at all."

"Possibly, but I simply must know." She pushed up the latch and lifted the lid.

Two aprons, a few writing feathers and some paper, and four books sat at the bottom of the trunk. Hannah picked up the closest book.

"What is it?" Morgan asked, moving to stand next to her.

"A diary."

"Here, let me see." He took it and opened the hard cover.

Hannah remained on the floor but tilted her head to watch him. His eyes narrowed, and a scowl furrowed his expression as he scanned the pages.

"To whom does the journal belong?" Hannah asked. "Bethany?"

"No. I thought it was hers, too, but it is not." He shook his head. "It is all very strange. The entries are from a woman, and she talks about her sister Bethany and her other sister, Ethel."

Hannah looked at Morgan. "There was a third sister?"

"I don't recall them having another sister."

"How strange indeed! Is there a name anywhere on the book?"

He flipped to the front again, then to the back. "Not that I can see."

"Read the last few entries. What does it say?"

He held the book up to the light pouring through the dirt-streaked window and read aloud.

> *I sit in misery, waiting for my child to be born. The heat suffocates me, and the pain in my belly and the cramping in my legs are nearly impossible to bear. But it is my heart that is most heavy with sadness and pain. He knows he is the father, yet he does not want to accept the fact.*

Hannah gasped. "Do you suppose she is one of Roderick's liaisons?"

Morgan chuckled. "That was my first thought as well, but the date on the page reads . . ." Suddenly, he clamped his mouth closed, and his face went pale.

Hannah jumped up beside him. "What is it?"

"This is the journal of Jonathan's mother."

A gasp sprang from Hannah's throat. "Bethany is Jonathan's aunt?"

"That's certainly the way it looks. But I don't know who the woman is. I don't remember anyone else but Bethany and Ethel living here with their mother."

"How very odd." Hannah peeked at the book in Morgan's hands. "She said that the baby's father didn't want to acknowledge Jonathan's existence, yet we know your father did."

"Yes, he did." Morgan met her stare. "But then again, maybe at first he didn't."

"True. I didn't think of that." She nodded toward the book. "What does the last entry say?"

He turned the page. "It is dated a week after Jonathan's birth."

I am an outcast now, and my life is ruined. He wants to raise our son without me. Most the staff knows, yet he is still acting as if this never happened—as if Jonathan just magically appeared in his life as his son. Jonathan does not deserve a father like that. I do not deserve to be treated in such a manner. Today, I vow that I will see that all the Thornton men—every one but my Jonathan—are destroyed. If it takes my entire lifetime, I will ensure that the Thornton men regret their actions.

Hannah covered her mouth with her hand. Morgan's gaze met hers, his eyes reflecting the same bewilderment.

"Morgan, you don't suppose Jonathan's mother is . . . the witch?" she ended in a whisper.

Slowly, he nodded. "That's exactly what I'm thinking."

Hannah glanced back at the other books in the trunk. The strange shapes on one book cover caught her attention, and she bent to pick it up. After dusting off the cover, she could read the title. *Witchcraft.*

She yelped and dropped the book. Morgan grasped her arm and pulled her away. "Let us leave this place," he said.

"Yes, please."

They hurried out of the cottage, and he closed the door tight behind them. He wrapped his arms around her and held her close. Almost immediately, she felt much calmer.

"Forgive me for taking you in there. If I had known—"

She stopped him. "It is all right, my darling. I know you didn't realize what was in there." She took a deep breath. "At least we know now why Bethany treats Jonathan the way she does. She probably knows he is her nephew."

"I agree." Morgan kissed Hannah's forehead.

She didn't voice her thoughts, but now—more than ever—she knew Bethany was the witch, especially since her sister was one.

"I suppose I shall have to find us another place to meet in secret," Morgan said apologetically.

"You must not worry. We shall find a way to be together. I know it."

"You're right." He pulled back slightly and looked into her eyes. "I just want you by my side every waking hour."

"We belong together. My father even knew it."

"Yes, he did." Morgan smiled and shook his head. "I don't think we were supposed to meet when your father wanted us to. I was a different man back then, and certainly wasn't ready for love."

Hannah nodded. "There is a time and purpose for everything."

"I agree, which is why I don't want to miss one moment of being with you."

As she kissed Morgan, tears of doubt collected in her eyes. Would they ever really be together? When he pulled away, she placed her face against his chest, not wanting him to see the moisture in her eyes.

"Hannah, my love?"

"Yes."

"Jonathan's birthday will be here shortly, and I think he is going to propose to you then."

She blinked quickly before looking up at Morgan. "Why do you think that?"

"Because, my dear, I overhear my family when they don't think anyone else is there."

"True." She frowned. "What am I going to do? I don't want Jonathan to think I love him, not when it is you who holds my heart. But if I tell him I don't love him that way, he will send me home. I can't return to my uncle's until we find the map."

Morgan sighed heavily and rested his forehead against hers. "I don't know, Hannah. Because of my youngest brother's feeble mind, it would be best if you don't lead him to think you will marry him. Yet at the same time, you must not give my family a reason to make you leave."

"Perhaps I shall avoid the subject all together. If it seems he is going to ask me, I'll do something to distract him."

Morgan chuckled. "It had better not be what you do to distract me."

Hannah wound her arms around his neck. "Of course not."

He kissed her thoroughly. "As much as I hate to leave you, I fear if I keep you from my family any longer, they will send out search parties."

She laughed and pulled away. "Yes, they will. I don't know why they insist on keeping an eye on me every minute of the day, but it is getting bothersome."

"Just remember not to be alone with Roderick."

A shiver ran through her as she remembered the middle Thornton brother's actions the other night. "Of course."

"I'm proud of the way you hold your own when you're with Bethany."

Hannah held Morgan's arm as they continued to walk. "I have discovered this about Bethany. I don't like her one bit, and I definitely can't trust her."

"No, you can't. You can't trust anyone in that house."

She squeezed Morgan's hand. "Except you."

"Yes, me . . . unless I become the wolf. Then I don't even trust myself."

Fifteen

Today was All Hallows' Eve—Jonathan's birthday. Hannah stood in front of the full-length mirror as Mrs. White helped her with the finishing touches of her costume. The dress's puffy sleeves tapered down to her elbows, and the square-neck bodice dipped too low, showing off quite enough skin, in Hannah's opinion. The waist fit her snugly, and then the skirt ballooned out with help from the hoops underneath. The deep, blood red silk was stunning, but the style of the gown was rather tasteless, she thought.

To add insult to injury, Mrs. White caked on more face powder, making her appear like a walking corpse. Hannah tried not to grimace as she stared at her reflection.

As Mrs. White ratted Hannah's wavy hair, Hannah sighed. She didn't enjoy looking like a harlot, but she had to play along with Jonathan and Bethany's plans for the evening.

"I must say, Miss Hannah, you are very pretty tonight," Mrs. White said. "Jonathan will be very pleased."

Forcing a smile, Hannah nodded to the servant. "I sincerely hope I don't stand out. I have never been to a masked ball before. Will others be dressed as vividly?"

"But of course." Mrs. White chuckled. "And I promise, you will not stand out. Mistress Thornton usually dresses above everyone. She will be the one standing out, I assure you."

"Splendid."

Mrs. White stepped to the small table in Hannah's bedchamber and picked up the black mask, which was complete with horns and trimmed with white beads. "Don't forget this."

"Thank you, Mrs. White. I don't know what I would have done without you."

The older servant beamed as she walked Hannah to the door. "Jonathan is especially looking forward to spending this special evening with you, Miss Forester."

Hannah's heart filled with dread. She fervently hoped he would not try to get her alone or—especially—attempt to ask her a serious question in front of his guests. She didn't know how she would answer without hurting his feelings. If he did propose to her, either in public or private, she would just have to think of a witty way to avoid a direct answer.

As she made her way down the grand staircase, the musicians were beginning to play. Roderick and Bethany stood by the front door and greeted guests, who were lined up outside. Just as Mrs. White had promised, Bethany stood out. The mistress of Thornton Manor wore a glittery, white silk gown that cascaded around her thin frame. Attached to the woman's back were fairy wings, and in her hand, a sparkling wand. Roderick stood beside Bethany, looking debonair in a pirate's costume, a large sword tied to his waist.

Hannah scanned the ballroom as she entered, looking for Jonathan. He stood with a group of people, each sipping a flute of champagne. When she saw his costume, she groaned. Now she knew why she was dressed as a she-devil. Jonathan was dressed as her companion—Satan himself. Even if she used the mask, the guests would assume Hannah was with him.

Before he could spot her, she turned and made her way through the throng of people to the other side of the room, glancing at masks and costumes on her way. She thought she recognized a few villagers, but she didn't know them well enough to stop and make conversation. Many men eyed her as she floated past them, but she didn't acknowledge their presence for fear they would ask her to dance. Then she realized if she did dance with them, she could avoid—as long as possible, anyway—dancing with Jonathan.

With firm decision in hand, she adjusted her mask, spun around, and hoped to catch some man's attention. Instead, she ran right into one. He grasped her arms and kept her from falling. "Oh, forgive me for not looking where I was going," she said, stepping back.

Hannah lifted her gaze to his face, most of which was hidden by a large, black mask trimmed with silver beads. A black scarf hid his hair color, and a black hat was tipped low on his forehead. His shirt, trousers, knee boots, and cape were black as well.

Something was familiar about him, but it was not until she caught his manly scent that she knew. *Morgan!*

She gasped and clutched his hands. "What are you doing here?" she whispered.

He smiled his beautiful, crooked smile. "I could not leave you alone in this den of wolves. Besides, nobody will recognize me."

"I did!"

"True, but you will be the only one, my dear. Nearly everyone thinks I'm dead."

Hannah glanced back to the entrance to the ballroom, but didn't see Roderick and Bethany. "Are you certain *they* will not know who you are?"

Morgan gently grasped Hannah's chin, turning her face until she looked at him. "No, I can't promise, but what will they do even if they notice me? Scream and run? I highly doubt it."

She chuckled and shook her head. "You are hopeless."

"Thank you, my dear." He took a step back and bowed formally. "Now we have that out of the way, may I have this next dance?"

With a smile, Hannah stepped into his arms, and he began spinning her around the dance floor. Soon, she realized how well they danced together, and she very nearly forgot they were not the only people in the room.

"Will you do me a favor?" Morgan asked after a few minutes, interrupting the magic.

"Anything."

"Don't allow Bethany to pick out any more of your dresses. This one is definitely not your style."

Hannah threw back her head and laughed. "I thought the same thing." She glanced over as much as she could of his costume. "And let me know next time you want to choose a costume, because I think we need to add a little color to your wardrobe."

His deep laugh caused tingles in her belly, and his kind smile warmed her heart. It was as if they had known each other much longer than a few weeks, and she no longer questioned why she fell in love with him so quickly. After all, she'd had her father's blessing on their courtship before she even met Morgan.

His eyes twinkled through his mask. "Hannah, do you know how much I love you?"

She sighed. "I hope as much as I love you."

Morgan pulled her as close as the dance would allow. Nothing more was spoken between them as they floated around the room, but his gaze told her all she needed to know.

When the music stopped, Hannah forced herself to stop smiling. She curtsied and placed her hand on Morgan's arm, and he escorted her off the dance floor.

"Would you like something refreshing to drink, my dear?" he asked.

"No." She quickly glanced around to make sure no one could overhear. "You must mingle with others. We don't want anyone getting suspicious."

"As you wish." He winked, then turned and left her side.

Once he started visiting with the guests, Hannah let out the big breath she had been holding. Morgan didn't seem worried about Bethany seeing him. If she was the witch, Hannah thought, surely she would recognize him.

"There you are."

Hannah gasped and swung around, almost spilling her punch. Jonathan's smile widened as he stared at her costume.

"Jonathan. You startled me." She forced a smile.

"I have been looking all over for you." He took her glass and set it down. "And now that I have found you, I want to dance with the prettiest girl here."

"Oh, what a flatterer you are. If you don't watch yourself, I will be swooning all night." She motioned toward his costume. "Does your boldness have anything to do with whom you represent tonight?"

"Not at all." He took her hand and led her toward the dance floor. "I'm trying to sweep you off your feet, if you have not noticed."

"Oh, so that's what you are doing." She looked at him mischievously. "You are such a devil."

He laughed and gathered her in the dance hold. "I adore your personality and how you make me laugh."

Jonathan's gaze darkened as he stared into her eyes. Panicked, she struggled to think of something to talk to him about. She took a quick glance around the ballroom and spotted Morgan dancing with another woman. He was looking at Hannah instead of the woman he danced with, and when he bumped into a nearby couple, Hannah tried in vain not to smile.

"Why are you so happy tonight?" Jonathan asked.

She snapped her attention back to him. "I—um, well, I can't help but chuckle over some of these costumes."

"Why so?"

"Probably because I know some of these people, and their costumes don't reflect upon their personalities." She nodded to the couple twirling beside them on her right. "That's Mr. Turney and his wife. I can't fathom why he chose to dress like Napoleon, when he is a man of God. And his wife—" Hannah peeked at the woman. "Why did Mrs. Turney adorn herself in peacock feathers when she is highly fearful of birds?"

Jonathan laughed heartily and squeezed her hand. "You are such a delight."

She hurried to comment on other people she knew, which made Jonathan laugh, hopefully keeping his thoughts from drifting anywhere near romance.

"What about Roddy and Bethany?" he said.

Hannah snorted. "Well, I suppose Roderick's costume suits him well in one way, because a pirate is a roguish character. But he is trying to look heroic, which you and I both know he is not. And Bethany . . ." Hannah paused. Jonathan may not know his true relationship to Bethany, but he did love her, so Hannah wanted to speak kindly. "I don't know if a fairy costume suits her, either."

A low, rumbling chuckle came from Jonathan's chest as he leaned his head closer. "If you ask me, *she,* not you, should have worn the she-devil gown."

His comment caught Hannah off guard, and she laughed exuberantly. Then, realizing she had attracted the attention of nearby guests, she closed her mouth. She and Jonathan smiled at each other in merriment.

After the dance, another man came to claim Hannah for the next song, and she quickly accepted his invitation.

Bethany stood in the corner of the room, clutching a goblet of wine as she stared at Hannah. The fury inside Bethany grew stronger by the minute. The gown she had picked for Hannah did exactly what Bethany expected—it made it obvious that Hannah was somehow attached to Jonathan. Yet men flocked around little Miss Forester and kept taking her to the dance floor. The girl had danced with Jonathan only twice!

When Hannah and Jonathan were together, Bethany waited to see any signs he had proposed, but none came. This was unacceptable. And she didn't like it that Hannah danced so many times with the man in black. Since the mask covered most of the stranger's face, Bethany had no idea who he was. She tried a few times to strike up conversation with him, but he would always move away from her and take a woman out on the dance floor. Right now the dark stranger danced with Hannah again. The young woman's eyes sparkled like diamonds, and obviously she could not stop smiling at him. If Bethany didn't know better, she would think Hannah had become smitten with this man.

As Bethany watched the pair, familiarity nudged at her conscience. She knew this man from somewhere.

"You do not appear to be enjoying yourself, my dear."

Roderick's voice snapped Bethany out of her thoughts. She glanced at her husband and rolled her eyes before returning her focus back on the Hannah and her dance partner.

"Not as I had expected to." Bethany sipped her wine glass. "How about you? Have you been able to charm any women tonight?"

Roderick chuckled. "Ah, my dear, why do you ask such a question? You are much happier if you are ignorant of my faults."

"Which means you have charmed a few women already this evening," his wife grumbled. "Just don't ruin the night for your brother. I happen to know he plans to propose to Hannah tonight."

"Indeed?" Roderick gulped down his brandy. "Why has he not done so yet?"

"Because it just so happens that other men find our dear, innocent Hannah very appealing this evening. Especially the one dancing with her now."

"And what exactly do you wish me to do?"

"Not a thing, Roddy, only because I know you would not lift a finger to help your brother find a wife."

When the music ended, Bethany shoved her nearly empty goblet in her husband's chest. He grabbed it before it spilled. "I, on the other hand," she continued, "*will* help Jonathan find a wife, even if it means taking out the competition."

Shoulders back and chin erect, she marched toward the muscular man guiding Hannah away from the dance floor. When the girl's eyes met Bethany's, they widened.

Bethany put on her practiced smile. "Are you two enjoying yourselves this evening?"

"Uh . . . of course, we are," Hannah answered hurriedly.

The man nodded.

Bethany pushed herself between them and sidled up to the man in black. "I must admit, sir, you have me intrigued."

"Why is that?"

"Because I don't know who you are."

Hannah released a laugh. "Oh, come now, Bethany. This is a masked ball, is it not? We are not supposed to know each other's identities until midnight."

"True, but still—" Bethany moved to stand very close to the stranger. "I would very much like to dance with you, if you don't mind."

The man shrugged and then offered his black-gloved hand. "Why should I mind? I enjoy dancing with lovely ladies." His attention moved back to Hannah. "Again, Miss Forester, it was a pleasure dancing with you."

Hannah curtsied. "And it was a delight being your partner."

The man met Bethany's stare again. "Shall we?"

"But of course."

She studied him as best she could, but since the dance was a country dance, she could not get close to him, and when she did, it was only for a moment. And with his mask hiding most of his face, she could see only his eyes and his lips. The way he carried himself seemed familiar, yet Bethany was still at a loss as to his identity.

"Pardon me, sir, but have we met before?" she finally asked.

"I don't believe so." He tilted his head as if studying her. "But then you are wearing a mask, so I can't be certain."

She laughed. "I would very much like to get to know you."

He shook his head. "Not until after midnight, remember?"

She pouted. "But I am the mistress of Thornton Manor. I can break the rules."

The corner of his mouth lifted in a lazy smile. "You are correct, although—" He leaned closer to her ear as he passed her. "I don't break the rules."

"Ah!" She swatted his shoulder playfully. "You are just wicked!"

He laughed softly, and she realized that perhaps she didn't know him after all. But clearly he was a very fine gentleman, and it would be torture to wait until midnight to see his face, to be sure.

As the dance ended, he gave a small bow. "It was a pleasure, mistress."

"Yes, it was." She smiled at him, entranced.

He didn't say another word as he walked her off the floor. Then he turned and moved away from her, weaving through the crowd. A few times she could not see him, so she had to move around other guests to see where he headed. In the corner of the room stood Hannah, and as the stranger passed her, he slowed and leaned into her.

Bethany knew the two of them shared some kind of secret. Even from a distance, she could see Hannah's face light up when she looked at the man in black.

Grumbling, Bethany moved to a wall to try to watch the mysterious stranger, but dancing couples kept blocking her line of sight. When had Hannah met this man? By the way they danced together and smiled at each other, Bethany could tell tonight was not their first meeting. Perhaps they had met here at the manor. The man was definitely not one of the staff, because none were so tall and muscular.

Recognition finally hit her like a tidal wave. *Morgan!* Anger boiled through her, and she clenched her fists. There was one way to find out if this was indeed her eldest brother-in-law.

Bethany spun around and marched out of the ballroom, glancing at the servants as she passed by. She didn't want them to suspect anything as she made her way toward the back of the house, looking for one person in particular. When one of the servants peeked her head out of the room, then quickly closed the door, Bethany cursed and marched toward the door. She didn't knock, but pushed open the door and walked into the small room. The servant jumped and scurried toward the bed.

"I thought I told you to stay hidden!" Bethany snapped.

The servant shrugged. "You did, but I just had to see how the party was fairing."

"The party is not fairing at all! *He* is here!"

The servant shook her head. "He, who?"

"Morgan, that's who!"

The other woman's eyes widened, and she gasped. "He is here?"

"Yes, you imbecile. I danced with him. Not only that—" she took a step closer "—he is with Hannah!"

"What? That cannot be."

"Oh, yes, it can. All you have to do is watch the two of them together. Hannah knows about him—I would stake my life on it."

Frowning, the other woman folded her arms and shook her head. "I'm very disappointed. Hannah was different from the other women. I wanted her to marry Jonathan."

"I'm quite certain she would have if she had not met Morgan. He is a charmer, no matter what kind of beast he is underneath."

The servant sighed. "I will take care of it."

"If you don't, I will! And I can assure you, my way will not be pleasant."

The other woman arched an eyebrow. "Are you threatening me?"

Bethany rolled her eyes. "You do as I tell you, and I will do your bidding. We have an agreement."

"Not to worry, Beth. I will take care of Morgan."

Bethany laughed haughtily. "Obviously, your way of taking care of him is not working."

"What do you suppose we do about it, then?"

Closing her eyes, Bethany rubbed her chin. "I think I know a way." She looked back at the servant. "For months now, we have tried to get Morgan to give us the treasure map. It appears the only way to find the treasure is to take the girl to the island. I know she knows where the treasure is buried. She will tell us where it is."

The servant chuckled. "And what if she doesn't?"

Bethany grinned and rubbed her hands together. "Oh, she will. She is in love with Morgan, and if we threaten to kill him, she will sing like a lark."

❦

That was too close! Bethany had asked Morgan to dance—how forward of that woman. Did she suspect that Hannah knew the stranger? It frightened Hannah nearly to death to think Mrs. Thornton might discover they had been seeing each other—and falling in love.

Fifteen minutes. Hannah wrung her hands. As he had walked past her, Morgan had whispered to her to meet her in his room in fifteen minutes. Time had stopped, it seemed, because she wanted to go there now. But leaving right now would cause suspicion, especially if Bethany noticed, and that was something Hannah could ill afford to have happen.

When another gentleman asked her to dance, she accepted, since it would take at least a few more minutes of her time. Yet when the dance ended, she still had ten minutes left. Slowly, she wandered out of the ballroom and toward the buffet table. She picked up a cream tart and nibbled on it as she continued to move away from the crowd. The stairs were in view. If only she could reach them without being noticed. Perhaps she should use the servants' stairs instead.

By the time she reached the servants' stairs, she had finished eating her tart. As she placed her hand on the railing, someone behind her grasped her arm.

"Miss Forester, where are you going? Master Jonathan's party is that way." Mrs. White motioned her head toward the other side of the manor.

Hannah's heart knocked crazily against her ribs. "Not to worry, Mrs. White. I need to freshen up just a bit. I will not be a moment, I assure you."

Mrs. White nodded. "Beg pardon, but Mistress Bethany is looking for you. I suggest you see what she needs before leaving to refresh yourself. You know how upset that woman gets if things don't go her way." The grimace on the older woman's face let Hannah know she didn't like Bethany either.

"Where is she?"

Mrs. White pointed down the hall. "That way, Miss Forester."

Hannah smiled. "Thank you."

Even though she didn't want to speak to Bethany, she definitely didn't want the mistress to suspect her of sneaking out of the party on purpose.

She left the servants' quarters and walked down an empty hallway. Mrs. White had pointed in this direction, yet Hannah didn't think Bethany would meet her here. "Mrs. Thornton? Are you there?"

Just as she passed a room, someone stepped out and collided with her. A pair of hands clutched Hannah's shoulders, and before she had time to catch her balance, she was pulled into the dark room. The door slammed behind her.

Moonlight spilled through a small slit in the curtains, barely outlining the other person. At first, Hannah didn't recognize her, but then the shape of her face and her body became noticeable. Wild hair framed her head, instead of the bun and servant's cap Hannah had always seen her in.

Hannah gasped as a cold chill ran through her. "What are you doing here? I thought . . . I thought—"

"You thought wrong." The witch tilted back her head and cackled.

Her fingers still dug into Hannah's shoulders, and Hannah felt as if the long fingernails had punctured the material of her gown. Fright consumed her, and she could barely breathe.

"What do you w–w–want with me?"

"You and I are going somewhere."

"Wh–where?"

The witch tsked and shook her head. "No questions now, my sweet. You will know soon enough. And, if you are a good girl and do not give me any trouble, I will allow you to live."

Hannah's whole body shook, but she nodded and followed. The witch led her back through the servants' quarters and out of the manor. Hannah prayed Mrs. White would spot her, or that *someone* would see her, but everyone was inside.

The witch pushed her toward the forest—the same way Francine had gone. Tears stung Hannah's eyes, and she blinked to clear her vision. In her heart, she prayed Morgan would find her. He was her only hope.

Sixteen

Morgan grumbled as he walked out of his bedchambers, buttoning his shirt. He should not have danced with Bethany, but he knew she would've been even more curious if he had refused her. She had studied him carefully during their dance, and he was grateful they had not danced a close dance such as a waltz.

As he turned the corner, he tripped over two of the paintings he had been studying the past couple of days. They fell over and he reached down to stand them aright, but something on the back of one painting drew his attention. A corner was pulled up slightly, and he realized the painting had a false back.

He grabbed a candle and set it on the floor next to the painting, then carefully began peeling the paper off the back of the painting. There was some kind of drawing on the back of the canvas, and someone had obviously gone to great pains to hide it. Morgan took the next painting and found a thin layer of extra paper on that one, too. He removed it, then moved on to the next painting. Soon, he sat on the floor and flipped all five paintings over, side by side. He gasped.

The map! Nervous excitement shot through him as he paced across his room. Where was Hannah? He checked the clock and found she was over ten minutes late to meet him. Something was wrong.

He went to the tunnel where she usually entered, but saw no sign of her, so he hurried to another hidden tunnel. As he passed each room on his way to the ballroom, he peeked in the mirror window, but didn't see her. By the time he reached the ballroom, his heart raced with worry.

Roddy stood with a group of women, drinking spirits. By the way his brother slurred his words and wobbled from side to side, Morgan could tell he was already intoxicated. But where was Bethany? For that matter, where was Jonathan?

Fear pricked the back of Morgan's neck. Moving quickly, he followed the secret tunnels to every room, peering inside just in case Jonathan had taken Hannah into one against her will. When Morgan reached his old bedroom, he saw Jonathan sitting on the edge of the bed, his arms wrapped around his middle as he rocked back and forth, mumbling. Morgan moved closer to the false mirror, trying to hear his brother better.

Jonathan's eyes were swollen and red, brimming with tears. "Oh, please help me," he muttered. "Morgan, I know you are a ghost, but I need your help. I can't do this on my own."

Morgan's heart twisted in agony for his brother.

"I have known for a while how cruel Bethany is to others, but why?" Jonathan sobbed and wiped his eyes. "I thought she loved me and wanted what was best for me."

What has Bethany done this time? Morgan wondered.

For several moments, Jonathan stared at the wall as if in a daze, but soon his face flushed with anger. He jumped to his feet. "But this time . . . this time Bethany has gone too far. They took Hannah, and they plan to kill her. I cannot allow them to do that!"

Morgan pushed against the secret door and rushed inside the room. Jonathan jumped when he saw his brother.

"M–M–Morgan?"

Morgan reached out to touch him, but Jonathan quickly retreated, his eyes growing wider by the second. "Jonathan, it is me. I'm not a ghost."

Jonathan shook his head. "But you d–died in the f–fire."

"No, Brother. There was no fire. Roderick and Bethany made up that story to keep me hidden in the East Wing."

Jonathan rubbed his eyes with shaky fingers. "That can't be true. They would not do that."

Morgan arched an eyebrow. "You know our brother and his deceiving wife as well as I. Can you stand there and tell me they didn't do this to me?"

Jonathan looked his brother up and down, and then his focus rested on Morgan's scarred visage. "What happened to your face? Where have you been all this time?"

"Jonathan, there is no time for me to explain everything. I need to know where Hannah is, and I need to know now."

Anger crossed his brother's features once more. "They took her to the island. I heard them talking when they didn't know I was there. They—they are going to kill Hannah after she shows them where the gold is buried."

"Who is going to kill her?"

"Bethany and Anne."

"Anne? But she's in the hospital, barely alive."

Jonathan shook his head. "No. That's what they wanted everyone to believe, but it isn't true."

Cursing, Morgan grabbed his brother's arm. "I have to go save Hannah."

"I'll go with you." Jonathan squared his shoulders.

"No, you need to stay here and take care of your guests. And keep a glass of spirits in Roddy's hand at all times so he does not try to stop me."

Jonathan's eyes widened. "Roddy knows?"

"Oh, yes." Morgan squeezed his youngest brother's shoulder. "Jonathan, that's how you can best help me. Will you do that for me?"

He smiled. "Yes, Morgan." He stepped closer and threw his arms around Morgan's shoulders. "I'm so happy you're alive!"

Morgan embraced him and then stepped back. "If I don't leave now, I just may meet my own Maker tonight after all. Say a prayer for Hannah and me, that we will get through this night alive."

"I will."

Morgan rushed back through the hidden tunnel toward his sanctuary. He needed weapons. He just didn't know if the rifles he had would kill a witch . . . or two.

❦

I can't believe this is happening! Hannah thought as she, Bethany, and Anne were rowed to the island. It was almost as if she was watching a play—a dreadfully frightening play—at the theater she and her father used to attend. Yet as the island grew closer and closer, Hannah knew this was real, and that her life was in grave danger. As soon as she showed Bethany and Anne where the treasure was hidden, or admitted she had no idea where it was, they would kill her.

She scrambled to remember the story her father had written about the Slumbering Giant. Although she didn't believe a treasure of gold and silver existed on the island, she must make Bethany and Anne think she knew where it was. Hannah's only hope was to stall them until Morgan rescued her—if he figured out where they had taken her.

When the boat hit the small dock on the island, it came to a sudden stop. Hannah jerked forward and nearly fell into Bethany.

Hannah's hands were tied together, making it hard to climb out of the dinghy. Once her feet touched the wooden planks, Anne grasped her by the arm and pulled her forward. The night wind nipped at Hannah's cheeks and arms, but fear itself had numbed her more than the cold, damp air.

Soon, they approached a dark cave. Bethany lit a lantern before leading the way inside. Up ahead, another light shone, growing brighter as they walked toward it. The narrow tunnel of the cave opened into a wide space. Several women, dirty beyond recognition, stood near the walls with picks and shovels.

Hannah stopped and gasped. "What—what is going on here?"

Bethany stood in front of her and planted her hands on her slender hips. "These women are trying to find the gold and silver. They have been at it for nigh on a year, and they still have not found a trace. That's how I know the curse is real. None of them is the pure-hearted woman who will lift the curse."

Hannah stared at Bethany. "And you think *I* am that person?"

"Yes, we do," Anne answered for her as she moved next to Bethany and untied Hannah's wrists.

Once the ropes dropped to the ground, she rubbed the raw skin where the ropes had been.

"Mademoiselle Hannah!"

Hannah looked toward the voice as a frantic young woman broke away from a guard and ran toward her.

"Francine!" Hannah pushed past the two witches and met her maid, throwing her arms around her. "I'm so glad you are safe."

Francine sobbed against her shoulder, and Hannah stroked her maid's hair. "Shh. No need to fret. I'm here now."

Another woman darted away from a guard and ran toward her. Hannah blinked in surprise. "Amelia?"

Crying, Amelia Hartley wrapped her arms around Hannah as well. "Oh, Hannah. I prayed someone would come rescue us."

"Rescue?" Bethany snipped as she pulled the sobbing women apart. "You think Hannah is here to rescue you all? Think again!" She pointed back to the wall of the cave. "Now get back to your post, or I will have my guards make an example of both of you in front of everyone."

Hannah nodded to her friends. "Do as she says."

Still crying, Amelia and Francine turned and walked back to their posts.

Hannah's heart wrenched, but she faced her captors with a stony expression. "Will you kindly tell me what is going on here? I think I have a right to know, especially if you are going to kill me after I lead you to the treasure."

Bethany glared at Anne and then at Hannah again. "I suppose we can let you in on our little secret. You see—" she stepped closer "—Anne and I are determined to get the gold and silver. We've done all we can to find it, but we have been unsuccessful."

"That's where you come in," Anne continued. "There is a curse on the island, and only a lovely women who is pure in heart will be able to lift it." She motioned to the many women scattered around the cave. "One by one, we brought these women to the manor under the pretense that Jonathan wanted to court them. When each of them succumbed to Roderick's charms, we knew she was not the one who could lift the curse. That's why we brought them here—to dig until someone finds our treasure."

"And that's why I was invited?" Hannah aimed her question at Bethany.

"But of course." Mrs. Thornton grinned.

Hannah looked back at Anne. "And who are you? How did you and Bethany become partners in this despicable venture?"

The two other women glanced at each other and giggled.

"Oh, my dear Miss Forester," Bethany began. "Forgive me, but let me introduce you to my sister Ethel."

"You are Ethel?" Hannah shook her head. "But why didn't Morgan recognize you?"

Ethel shrugged. "Nobody but my sister recognized me. You see, my sister and I have a very special talents."

"Yes, I know," Hannah said. "You are witches."

Ethel hitched a breath. "My dear sister, I thought you said Miss Forester would not suspect us."

Bethany glared at Ethel. "You imbecile. She has been secretly meeting with Morgan. That's how she knows."

"Morgan didn't tell me who the witch was," Hannah said. "I figured it out on my own." She looked at Ethel. "So, your special talent is to change your appearance so you appear prettier than you really are?"

Ethel growled and clutched Hannah's arms. "I will have you know that many men worship me now. My *talent* has gotten me this far, and it will eventually get me everything I want."

Although the woman's fingers dug painfully into Hannah's arms, she didn't cry out. "And what is Bethany's talent?"

Mrs. Thornton threw back her head and laughed. "I can make men love me."

Ethel snickered. "Beth has not yet perfected her talent."

Bethany huffed and planted her hands on her hips. "It is good enough."

"Why, then, is Roderick not in love with you any longer?"

Bethany rolled her eyes. "Because I tired of him, so I lifted the spell."

Not thinking, Hannah chuckled and said, "Indeed? If your spell works with other men, then why couldn't you get Morgan to love you?"

Hatred burned in the depths of Bethany's gaze. She yanked a lock of Hannah's hair, making her yelp.

"I think it is time we stopped chatting. Tell us where the gold is."

The pain in Hannah's scalp brought tears to her eyes. "Fine. I just have one more question."

"Question-and-answer time is over, dearie," Ethel snapped.

Hannah ignored her. "I just want to know which one of you put the spell on Morgan to make him shift into a wolf."

The sisters looked at each other and laughed. "You will have to figure that out for yourself." Bethany pushed Hannah ahead of them. "Now start walking, and you had better take us where we want to go."

Hannah needed to pretend to know where she was going, but that would be difficult, since she had never been to the island before. She could not recall the layout of the island from the paintings in Morgan's room, or even the drawing of the island that her father had added to his book. When the sisters found out she knew nothing, they would kill her.

Behind Hannah, Bethany and Ethel whispered back and forth. It was hard to believe they were sisters, especially since Hannah knew Anne—Ethel—was having an affair with Roderick.

At that thought, Hannah stopped dead in her tracks. She spun around and met Bethany's angry stare. "There is another thing that puzzles me."

Bethany sighed impatiently and folded her arms. "What now? I'm tired of your tricks, Miss Forester."

Hannah lifted her chin. "If you want my help, then you will have to indulge my curiosity."

"Fine. What do you want to know?"

"If you two are such loving and devoted sisters, why is Ethel sleeping with your husband?"

Bethany hissed and turned to Ethel. "What? You are having an affair with my husband?"

The color disappeared from Ethel's face, and she looked at Hannah and then back at Bethany. "Of course not. That's utterly ridiculous."

"It is?" Hannah said to Ethel. "Jonathan and I saw you and Roderick kissing behind the house the first day I was here. Not only that, but once while I was with Morgan, we overheard your conversation with Roderick while the two of you were hiding in Morgan's old bedchambers."

"What?" Bethany's voice turned shrill. She shoved at Ethel's shoulder. "What were you and Roddy doing in Morgan's bedroom?"

"Nothing. Nothing at all. Hannah is lying."

Feeling victorious, Hannah folded her arms and shot a knowing glance at Ethel. "Does that mean you lied to Roderick and are not carrying his child?"

Bethany screeched and wrapped her fingers around Ethel's throat. "How dare you!"

"She is lying, I tell you," Ethel rasped as she tried to peel Bethany's fingers off her neck.

"No, she is not! I know my husband was sneaking around with one of the maids, but I had no idea it was you. I thought it was Sarah!"

Hannah shrugged. "He was having an affair with her as well."

"Let . . . me . . . go." Ethel wheezed. "I . . . can . . . explain."

"Explain?" Bethany roared. "I think not, *sister.* You always thought you were better than me. You always wanted what I had, and you hated me because I married a Thornton and you could not. You always thought you were the better witch. Well, not any longer. I shall *not* let you win this time."

Mrs. Thornton pushed her sister against the cave wall and continued choking her. Hannah had to stop her! If Ethel had put the curse on Morgan, and she died now, he would always shift into a wolf.

With a sob, Hannah lunged for the struggling women, trying to pull Bethany away. "Let her go!"

"No. I want her out of my life forever!"

"But Morgan's spell—she has to lift the curse."

"She didn't curse him, you fool," Bethany shouted, shoving Hannah away with her elbow.

Hannah stumbled back and fell over her long gown. Tears filled her eyes as she watched Ethel's eyes close in death.

Seventeen

Morgan had not been on the island since he was a boy, but as he made his way through the thick trees and underbrush, memories returned of the trails he had discovered. Soon, he followed a pathway that appeared to have been used recently—and frequently. It led to a tunnel in the side of a cliff, and he hurried through the tunnel. When the light at the end of the tunnel grew, he slowed and carefully approached.

Women filled a large cave, each wielding a shovel or pick axe. Four burly men with whips and pistols watched over the operation, pushing the women to dig faster.

Morgan flattened himself against the wall of the tunnel. If he went barging into the cave, the guards would certainly shoot at him and try to stop him from rescuing Hannah. They might even hurt her, and he could not allow that. There must be another way. He rubbed his forehead and groaned.

Just then, the sounds of digging halted, and Morgan dared peek inside once again. There was some kind of commotion in one of the side tunnels, because the guards walked away from their posts to head in that direction. The women stopped their work and watched in interest.

Morgan made his move and sneaked into the cave. When a few of the ladies saw him, he lifted a finger to his lips, urging the women to keep quiet. They nodded and quickly passed the word to the others.

Morgan nearly stumbled over a shovel lying on the ground. But just as he stepped around it, an idea struck. He lifted the shovel and motioned for the women to do the same with theirs. Not saying a word, he made actions with his hands, trying to show them what to do. The guards must be taken out first.

Soundless excitement grew from one woman to the next as their faces lit up. They followed Morgan toward the guards, who had stopped at the tunnel entrance and seemed to be discussing whether or not they should leave their posts. Morgan sneaked up behind the closest guard, then lifted his shovel and brought it down hard on the man's head. A *crack* echoed in the cave, and the man fell in a motionless heap.

The three other guards spun around, each grabbing at his pistol. Before Morgan could get to the men, the women swarmed around the men and whacked their heads with the shovels. Within seconds, all the guards lay still.

Cheerful voices rose in victory, but Morgan hushed the women again. "It's still not over." He pointed to the tunnel, from which other voices could still be heard. "Stay here."

Hannah's maid, Francine, touched him on the shoulder. "Monsieur, we want to help."

"Not this time, my dear. These women are very dangerous, and this is something I must do alone." He squeezed her hand. "But go with the other ladies and leave this place. Now!"

Tears streaked down the women's faces as they embraced each other, and then they quietly hurried out of the cave.

Tightening his grip on the shovel, Morgan proceeded down the tunnel. The voices grew louder by the second, and when three women came into view, his heart burst with relief. Hannah was alive.

Bethany held a woman against the wall by the neck, and when she released her, the woman fell to the ground, clearly dead. Morgan flattened against the tunnel wall again.

Sighing heavily, Bethany brushed her hands together. Then she turned and looked down at Hannah, who sat in the dirt with her knees pulled against her chest. Tears pooled in her eyes, and the look on her face nearly broke Morgan's heart.

Bethany shrugged. "Told you I would win."

"I had no doubt," Hannah said quietly.

"Ethel liked to think she was the better sister, but I am."

"Obviously."

Bethany grasped Hannah's arm and pulled her up. "Now, where were we?" She tilted her head, studying Hannah. "Oh, yes. You were going to show me where the treasure is located."

A tear fell from Hannah's eye as she shook her head. "Why, Bethany?"

"What do you mean, why?"

"Why are you doing this? You are wealthy already. You are married to a Thornton, just as you have always wanted. So why go through all of this?"

"My mother always told me I was too dim-witted to make it through life and marry out of my class. We were always poor. I decided many years ago I would not have this kind of life. I want to be the richest person in the world, and having all the gold and silver here in these caves will get me that." She frowned. "And just because I am married to a Thornton does not mean I am happy."

"You still want Morgan, don't you?" Hannah asked.

Morgan held his breath.

"Yes, I do." Bethany raised her chin stubbornly.

"Even if he does not want you?"

"He *will* want me. Once I get the treasure, another curse will be put upon him so he will love only me."

Bile rose in Morgan's throat. He could not let that happen.

"But Bethany," Hannah said, "don't you want a man who will love you without being forced to?"

Morgan's sister-in-law scowled. "Of course I do, you idiot, but powerful men have never wanted me. Believe me, I have tried to seduce them without my magic, but it does not work." She growled and grasped Hannah's arm again. "Enough of this! Show me the treasure."

Hannah shook her head. "I don't know anything about the treasure. My father didn't find a single evidence of it in his research. Bringing me here was a waste of your time."

"Forgive me, but I don't believe you." Bethany tightened her grip, making Hannah whimper. "Your father knew something, I just know it. I could see it in his eyes and hear it in his voice."

"What do you mean by that? You never met my father."

"Oh, yes, I did—before I killed him."

Hannah felt fury surge through her, an anger like she had never known. She screamed and began hitting, clawing, and kicking at Bethany. Although the woman tried to fight back, Hannah overpowered her. Morgan pulled out his pistol, preparing for the moment when he would need it.

"How could you?" Hannah sobbed, plowing her fists into Bethany. "He did nothing to you! Nothing at all!"

A loud growl sprang from Bethany's throat, and she pushed Hannah off her. Hannah landed on her back, and Bethany jumped on her and grabbed Hannah's neck.

"I will do whatever I want to get the treasure."

Hannah cried out as she tried to peel the woman's fingers away from her throat.

Morgan rushed from his hiding spot and pointed the pistol at Bethany. "Release her now!"

Bethany gasped and did as she was told. Using his foot, Morgan pushed her off Hannah, who scrambled to her feet and clung to his side. Protectively, he wrapped his arm around her, still keeping a steady aim on his sister-in-law.

"May God forgive me, but I cannot have you hurting the woman I love."

The blood left Bethany's face as she stared at him and slowly stood. Her gaze darted between him and Hannah, but then something behind them caught her attention and she smiled victoriously.

"Think again, dear Morgan."

Before he had time to look behind him, two arms wrapped around him like bands of steel. Hannah cried out and fell to the ground.

As Morgan struggled, he glanced over his shoulder. One of the guards had gained consciousness and now had him in a death grip. Bethany laughed and yanked the gun out of Morgan's fingers, then pointed it at Hannah.

"What a surprising turn of events, is it not?" Bethany snickered. "Now, I know one of you can tell me where the map is—or better yet, where the gold and silver are hidden. You have three minutes to speak, or Morgan's lady love is going to end up just like her father."

Morgan met Hannah's frightened gaze. "Bethany, I know where the treasure is," he said.

His sister-in-law produced a self-confident smile. "Splendid. Morris, loosen your hold so Morgan can take us to the treasure." She glared at Morgan. "And if you do anything to trick me, I will kill the woman who means so much to you."

Just as Bethany's henchman released Morgan's arms, another voice sounded from the other side of the tunnel.

"No!"

Before anyone had time to react, Jonathan ran out of the shadows and hit Bethany over the head with a shovel. She fell to the ground without a sound.

Hannah screamed and covered her face. The guard left Morgan and ran to Bethany, lifting her and holding her against him as he let out a mournful wail. Jonathan ran to Hannah and knelt beside her, taking her in his arms protectively.

Morgan jumped for the pistol that had fallen by Bethany's side. He cocked it and aimed it at Morris. "Now you will do as I say!"

Morris jerked his head toward Morgan. A growl-like sound escaped the man's throat as he lunged forward. Morgan pulled the trigger. The gunshot pierced the tunnel, echoing all around them. The guard clutched his bloody chest and sank beside Bethany.

Hannah pushed Jonathan off her and glared at him. "Why did you kill Bethany? Now the curse will never be lifted."

"No need to fear, my dear." Morgan pulled her up beside him. She threw her arms around his shoulders and buried her tears in his chest.

Morgan met his brother's puzzled stare. "Let us leave this place. We will explain everything when we return home."

He tightened his arm around Hannah and led the way back toward the open cave, Jonathan following behind with hurried steps. Just as they reached the cave, a woman jumped out in front of them, seemingly out of nowhere.

❦

Hannah lifted her head and gasped in recognition. Standing in front of them in a sheer white gown, Mrs. White grinned triumphantly. No longer was the housekeeper's hair wound in a bun and covered with a servant's cap. Instead, her long, brown hair hung down her back and over her shoulders.

Morgan stiffened as he pushed Hannah behind him. "Leave them alone," he said to Mrs. White. "It is me you want, not them."

Hannah's heart sank. Would this nightmare ever end?

Mrs. White tsked and shook her head. She slithered up to Morgan, standing scandalously close to him. She drew a long-nailed finger across his scars. "My dear, brave, man. You can't save them. Only I can."

"I know where the treasure is located," Morgan said tightly. "I will tell you where it is, but you can't hurt them. And you must release me from this spell."

Hannah hitched a breath. *Impossible!*

The housekeeper laughed eerily, waving her hands in the air. Immediately, Morgan's body rose from the ground and then slammed against the cave wall. Jonathan pulled Hannah to him as if trying to shelter her from the awful sight.

Morgan groaned and struggled to stand, holding his ribs. Hatred glowed in his eyes as he stared at Mrs. White.

"Have you not learned your lesson yet?" the witch asked him. "You do not control me. I control you!" She scowled. "And do you really think I plan to harm Jonathan? It is Hannah I am after."

"Why?" Jonathan asked angrily. "Why are you doing this, Mrs. White? Why have you become this . . . this . . . thing!"

A different expression crossed the other woman's face as she stepped up to Jonathan. Lovingly, she caressed his cheek. "My dear boy. I was never able to control your father. But I will control his sons, especially *my* son."

Hannah gasped. "You're his mother?"

Mrs. White grimaced. "You are very intelligent, Miss Forester." She looked back at Jonathan. "Yes, I'm his mother.

Right after Jonathan was born, I was able to act as his nanny, but soon Thomas didn't want me around *his* son, and he told me to leave. I knew I had to do something. That was when I started studying witchcraft. Not too long after that, I knew what I must do in order to raise my son."

"That certainly explains a lot of things," Morgan said as he limped toward the housekeeper. "But it doesn't explain why you cursed me. Why do you want to control me?"

Mrs. White tossed an evil glare at Morgan. "Because I was supposed to be mistress of Thornton Manor. Your father was supposed to marry me! When my daughter Bethany could not win you for her husband, I decided to charm you myself. But after I overheard you dictating those letters of dismissal that day, I knew I hadn't made you love me after all. That's why I cursed you."

"Bethany is your daughter?" Hannah asked. "But I read your journal, and you referred to Bethany as a sister."

"We are sisters—sisters in the craft."

"But why do you want the treasure?" Morgan interrupted. "In the last few months you have come to me asking for a treasure map you say Peter Forester gave me. Why?"

"Because my daughter put a hex over Jonathan." Mrs. White turned sad eyes to her son. "My poor son is not in his right mind. Bethany knew I controlled you, Morgan, and she wanted the gold and silver. She told me that she wouldn't lift the spell on Jonathan unless I forced Morgan to produce the treasure map."

Hannah sighed. Now everything made sense. But poor Jonathan would have this spell on him forever, since Bethany had died before lifting it. Hannah feared his older brother would have the same fate.

"Mrs. White, will you tell me one thing?"

"My, aren't you a curious young woman," the witch replied.

"Did Morgan truly kill all those women when he was the white wolf?"

Chuckling, the housekeeper folded her arms. "What do you think?"

Hannah squared her shoulders. "I think you lied to him all this time. I don't believe Morgan killed anyone—especially *innocent* women."

"You are correct, Miss Forester."

Hannah met Morgan's wide-eyed stare.

"Then who killed Sarah?" Jonathan asked.

"Bethany did, my dear son. She caught the maid having an affair with Roderick. In fact, the few women who actually died have done so at Bethany's hand, not Morgan's. Bethany made it look like the wolf was the culprit. And unfortunately, Bethany is not alive to kill one more woman." She stepped closer to Hannah and yanked her away from Jonathan. "I'm sorry, my sweet son, but Hannah is not the woman you must marry. She knows too much. Not only that, but your brother is in love with her, and she returns his love." The housekeeper shook her head. "I can't have that. The woman you marry must have a simple mind like yours, and she must love you completely."

Tears formed in Jonathan's eyes at he looked at his eldest brother. "You . . . love her?"

Frowning, Morgan nodded. "I didn't want to, but I fell in love with her almost upon our first meeting. How could I not? She was the first person to see inside of me and love me regardless of my scars."

Mrs. White stared at Jonathan as if she could control him with her gaze. "Now, Son, return to the manor," she said slowly. "I don't want you to witness this."

As if in a daze, Jonathan nodded, turned, and walked out of the cave. Hannah choked on a sob.

Once Jonathan was out of sight, Mrs. White tightened her grip on Hannah's arms. "Miss Forester, I have little need of you now."

"Harm her and you will die!" Morgan shouted.

"I think not." The housekeeper raised her hand toward Morgan, and he flew back against the wall.

This time when he struggled to stand, he could not. It was if an invisible force kept him on the ground. Hannah cried out and tried to lunge toward him, but Mrs. White was stronger, and Hannah could not escape the woman's grasp.

"I'm disappointed that you could not love Jonathan, Miss Forester. He would have made you very happy, I am sure." She wrapped her fingers around Hannah's neck, just as Bethany had done, but the mother's hands were far more powerful.

Tears coursed down Hannah's face. Although she fought to release the woman's hold, she could not. Slowly, the energy left her body, and she became a limp rag in the housekeeper's hands. Hannah's lungs burned as she struggled for breath. *Morgan, never forget I loved you!*

A gunshot echoed through the cave, and Mrs. White fell to the ground. Freed, Hannah dropped beside her, gasping for breath. Blood poured out from a bullet hole in the housekeeper's head, her sightless eyes staring up into the cavern.

"Hannah."

Morgan's weak voice brought her around. He fell beside her and gathered her in his embrace.

"Morgan, why did you kill her?" She cried into his chest. "Now your curse will be with you forever."

"Oh, Hannah, my love." He kissed her forehead. "It doesn't matter. I would rather be a wolf every night for the rest of my life than live without you. If Mrs. White had killed you, I would've died inside as well."

He kissed her wet eyes, then moved his mouth to her lips. Hannah hugged him close and kissed him, grateful they were both alive. He was right. It didn't matter if he shifted into a wolf at night; they loved each other and would be together. Her heart rejoiced with the knowledge that he had not killed anyone.

With a weary sigh, he stood and pulled her up with him. "Let's return to the manor. Poor Jonathan needs to know what has transpired, if he even remembers being here at all. And" —Morgan bent and kissed Hannah again— "I want to hold you tonight and tell you how much I love you. You will never leave my arms again."

❦⸭ᑕᏕ

It was some time before Morgan and Hannah could be alone together. Once they reached the manor, all the women from the island were waiting for them, along with the constable. Some of the guests from the masked ball still lingered, eager to hear the news. Hannah held on to Morgan's arm as he told the constable what had happened.

Jonathan stood back and watched with a forlorn expression. Hannah wished she could say something to console him, but she feared her words would do no good. She hoped someday he would forgive her for loving Morgan instead, and for deceiving Jonathan in her purpose for coming to the manor in the first place.

After everyone finally left, they found Roderick on the couch, deep in an inebriated sleep. Morgan shrugged and told Hannah they would leave him there.

Francine was in Hannah's room, eager to return to her duties, but Hannah hugged the maid and sent her to her own room to rest.

Now Hannah sat in front of the fireplace after a refreshing bath. She combed her wet hair, allowing the heat from the fire to dry the wavy locks. Though she was relieved the ordeal was over, she still worried about the man she loved. She had no doubt they would marry and that he would resume his role as master of the manor, but in the back of her mind, she feared the townsfolk would kill him one night when he shifted into the wolf.

Footsteps in the corner of the room made her jump. She turned just in time to see Morgan step through the hidden door in the wall. She smiled and held out her hands. He grasped them and raised her to her feet before wrapping his arms around her.

"You know you don't have to sneak around any longer," she said with a smile.

He chuckled. "It is a habit. Forgive me."

"Of course, my love." She kissed him quickly, then pulled away. "Shall we adjourn to the sofa? I fear my limbs are still very weak from tonight's torture."

"As are mine."

He led her to the sofa, where they collapsed in each other's arms. Hannah laid her head on his chest and sighed contentedly.

He kissed the top of her head. "Have you noticed anything different tonight?"

She lifted her face and looked into his eyes. "What?"

"This house. Can you not feel a change? It is as if the evil has disappeared, and dark clouds of gloom are no longer hanging over the place. I'm certain tomorrow morning we shall walk outside and it will look different as well."

"You are probably right, but I fear I'm too exhausted to notice much of anything right now."

Morgan frowned. "Then I should leave and let you rest."

"No." She snuggled closer. "Please don't go. I want you to stay with me tonight. We can sleep like this on the sofa, wrapped in each other's arms, with the fireplace to keep us warm."

"Hmm . . ." He pulled her closer. "I do like the way you think."

She closed her eyes. "In the morning we can talk about when we will get married."

He laughed softly. "If I had my way, we would get married tomorrow."

"Well, if you can talk someone into performing the ceremony, I shall be quite content with becoming your wife tomorrow."

"Excellent." He kissed her head. "But now let's rest. I don't think I can keep my eyes open any longer."

Hannah was already drifting off to sleep, dreaming of her wedding day, and hoping Morgan would not shift on their wedding night.

Eighteen

Warmth and comfort surrounded Hannah, and she wanted to keep sleeping. But the stirring of the person beside her caused her body to awaken. When her mind became alert, she realized she still lay in Morgan's arms. He trailed soft kisses over her face, her eyes, her nose, then down her cheeks to her mouth.

Moaning softly, she wrapped her arms around his neck and kissed him.

"Hannah, my sweet," he muttered against her lips.

"Yes?"

"I didn't shift last night."

She chuckled. "Of course not, silly. You were too exhausted."

She cupped his face and stroked her fingers across his cheeks. Gasping, she pulled away and blinked open her eyes.

"What is it my dear?" he asked with a smile.

Not believing what she was seeing, she ran her fingertips over his face again.

"Your scars are gone."

"What?" He sat up straight and felt his face. "I can't believe it." He jumped off the sofa and ran to the full-length mirror that stood in the corner of the room.

Hannah moved off the sofa and followed him. He stared dumbfounded at his reflection as he touched his cheek.

"They are gone," he whispered. "I look . . . different. Almost the way I used to before the curse."

"You do look different, but you were always very handsome to me."

He turned and took her in his arms again. "If my scars are gone, could that mean the curse is gone?"

She covered her mouth, her eyes widening at the realization. "Oh, Morgan." She dropped her hand. "It very well could be! Mrs. White lied to you about killing innocent women as the wolf, so she may well have lied to you about the curse itself. She wanted to control you, and by making you believe that if she died the curse would stay with you, she kept you from killing her."

"I do feel different, my dearest Hannah. I feel as if a great burden has been lifted from my shoulders." He laughed joyfully and spun her around. "This is an amazing day indeed."

He captured her mouth in an electrifying kiss that left her knees weak. But a knock on the door quickly ended their embrace.

She smoothed her wrinkled gown, hoping nobody would notice she had slept in it, and went to the door. When she opened it, Francine stood there, wearing the worried expression Hannah knew so well. "What is wrong, Francine?"

"It is Monsieur Jonathan. Something is wrong with him. He is in his room, and he is not doing well, mademoiselle."

Morgan cursed and rushed past Hannah and Francine, taking long strides toward Jonathan's bedchamber. Hannah and her maid hurried after him.

Two servants stood outside Jonathan's room, frowning. When they saw Morgan, their eyes widened in surprise. He said nothing to them but continued into the room. Roderick sat on the edge of the bed, holding Jonathan's hand. A physician stood nearby, folding up his stethoscope and placing it in his black bag.

"What is wrong with him?" Morgan demanded.

Roderick jumped up, his red-rimmed, glassy eyes nearly bulging out of his head as he stared at Morgan. "What are *you* doing here?" He scrunched his forehead. "And why do you look so . . . different?"

"Because I'm no longer cursed," Morgan snapped, moving past him to stand near Jonathan. Morgan met the doctor's stare. "What is wrong with my brother?"

"He has had a terrible fever. He has been mumbling incoherently all morning long. He is not conscious, I'm afraid."

Morgan sat on the edge of the bed and tenderly pushed the strands of hair from his brother's forehead. Hannah knelt beside Morgan and caressed Jonathan's arm. The young man's chest rose and fell erratically, and every few seconds his body jerked violently.

Morgan looked up at the doctor again. "Is he dying?"

"I don't know. His heartbeat sounds good, but his fever is high. I have examined him thoroughly, yet I can't find what is causing it."

Morgan leaned closer to his brother. "Jonathan, it is I, Morgan. Please open your eyes and speak to me."

Fitfully, Jonathan tossed his head on the pillow and mumbled again.

"Jonathan, talk to me, please. I'm here, and I will never leave you again."

Within seconds, the young man's breathing slowed, and his writhing soon ceased. Hannah held her breath, praying Jonathan would survive the ailment, whatever it was.

Slowly, his eyes fluttered open. Behind Morgan, Roderick gasped, but Hannah didn't look at him.

"That's it, Jonathan," Morgan encouraged. "Keep waking up. Come back to us."

"M–Morgan?"

"Yes, it is I."

Jonathan's eyes darted around the room from Hannah, to Roderick, to the doctor, and then back to Morgan. "Where am I?"

"In your bed," Morgan answered.

Confusion creased Jonathan's brow. "Why am I not in Italy?"

"Jonathan," Morgan said, "you came back from Italy a year ago."

"No, I didn't." Jonathan met Hannah's gaze. "Who are you?"

At a loss for words, she looked from him to Morgan. Her heart hammered in her chest as she feared for Jonathan's state of mind.

"She is my fiancée," Morgan replied.

Jonathan smiled. "See what I miss when I'm away?" He took hold of Morgan's hand and squeezed. "Congratulations. I'm happy for you."

Morgan glanced at Hannah and winked.

The doctor moved closer. "If you all will leave, I will examine him once more."

Morgan nodded, took Hannah's hand, and led her from the room. Roderick followed.

Once the door was closed, Roderick grumbled. "What is going on around here? Why can't he remember this past year?"

"Because he has been under a spell, you imbecile," Morgan supplied, glaring at his brother. "Your wife hexed him. Now that she and her witch family are dead, the spells we were all under are gone as well."

Roderick raked his fingers through his hair. "I was under a spell, too?"

"Yes, I suppose you were, although I believe stupidity was not part of it." Morgan shook his head. "From this day forth, all rights to the manor and the estate will be turned over to me. If you don't like the way I run things, you are more than welcome to leave—posthaste, in fact. I don't want you interfering with Jonathan's recovery. He will probably never remember this past year, and I for one, want to keep it that way."

Roderick nodded, his shoulders slumping before he turned and walked away.

"As for you," Morgan said, pulling Hannah into his arms, "I will find a preacher to marry us today. I want us to forget this ordeal and become acquainted with each other as normal people do."

Smiling, she stroked the side of his face where the scars had been. "I always thought of you as normal, my wonderful man. That will never change. Our love will only grow stronger from this day forward."

"You are correct about that, my dear."

"And from now on" —she paused to kiss him— "there will be no secrets between us."

Morgan tilted his head. "Speaking of secrets, I do have one more, but the only reason I have not told you is because there was no time."

"What is that?" she asked warily.

"I found the treasure map."

"Indeed?"

"It was on the back of the paintings. Although your father believed there was no treasure, the drawings behind the paintings say differently. In fact, if you like, we can go to the island and find our treasure."

She shook her head. "You are the only treasure I need, my love."

Morgan pulled her in for a kiss, one that left her breathless.

She smiled and closed her eyes. *Look, my dearest father, you got your wish. I'm finally happy and in love.*

About the Author

Since Marie Higgins was a little girl playing Barbies with her sister, Stacey, she has loved the adventure of making up romantic stories. Marie was only eighteen years old when she wrote her first skit, which won a Funniest Skit award. A little later in life, after she'd married and had children, Marie wrote Church road shows that were judged Funniest and Best Written. From there, she branched out to write full-length novels based on her dreams. (Yes, she says, her dreams really are that silly, and she's like that in real life.)

Marie has been married for twenty-five years to a wonderful man. Together, they have three loving daughters and several beautiful grandchildren. Marie works full time for the state of Utah, where she has lived her entire life. She plans to keep writing, because the characters in her head won't shut up. But her husband smiles and pretends this is normal.

Secrets after Dark is Marie's fourth novel with Walnut Springs Press. Marie enjoys hearing from her readers and may be contacted at mariehiggins84302@yahoo.com. Please visit her blog, http://mariehiggins84302.blogspot.com.

Whoever said the quest for love wasn't comical never met Charlene Randall. Charley is looking for a man who wants to start a family, a man who will take her to the temple. Problem is, she has never dated a man for longer than three months. When she reads an internet article called "Ten Ways to Win Your Man," she decides to try it on her new coworker, Maxwell Harrington. Max was her crush in high school, but the superstar sports anchorman doesn't even remember her.

Enter ladies' man Damien Giovianni, Charley's handsome neighbor, who agrees to help her win Max over. What follows is a hilarious tale of mishaps and misunderstandings where Charley learns that what she really needs may be right in front of her.

When Summer Bennett returns to Richfield after a five-year stint at her aunt's finishing school, she discovers a lot has changed. Her father has suffered a crippling injury, and Summer is desperate to get the money to pay for surgery that could allow him to walk again. She hears of a reward offered for the capture of a cunning gang of bank robbers, and her years of etiquette training fall by the dusty roadside.

What Summer doesn't count on in her quest to capture the bandits is the competition from her family's longtime friend, Jesse Slade. Now a deputy marshal and local hero, Jesse keeps thwarting Summer's plans, just like he did when she wore pigtails. She would like nothing more than to use Jesse's head for a slingshot target, but soon Summer finds her aim shifting from his head to his heart. Problem is, Jesse is engaged to her sister Violet.

For seven years, little Summer Bennett was the burr under Jesse's saddle. Now he feels a different irritation as Summer is always on his mind—whether he wants her to be or not. But Summer's father expects him to marry Violet, and he won't let him down. So why does Jesse find himself encouraging Summer's attentions, and why do sparks fly every time they are together?

When a woman claiming to be a ghost from 1912 appears in Nick Marshal's office and begs for help in solving her murder, he thinks he has lost his mind. A scandal that rocked Hollywood almost destroyed his law practice, so he doesn't need any more fireworks as he rebuilds his life. Still, he is intrigued by Abigail Carlisle's plea, and he needs clients, even if this one insists she's dead. The more secrets Nick uncovers, the deeper he falls for the beautiful ghost.

Abigail believes Nick is her heart's true desire, but how can happily-ever-after happen when she's already dead? The more time she spends with him, the more real she becomes, until Nick can finally touch her.

In a strange turn of events, Nick is suddenly whisked back to 1912, two weeks before Abby's murder, but she doesn't remember him. When he attempts to win her over so he can save her from a tragic destiny, Abby thinks Nick is courting her for her inheritance. But even if he can rescue her and make her trust him again, how can they be together forever?

Praise for *Winning Mr. Wrong*

Warning! Warning! Warning! This is a "chick flick" in book form. For those of you who are allergic to fun and clean chick flicks, find another read. For those of us who love clean chick flicks, this is a must read.—Karen Hamiliton

Light and fluffy—the way a good romantic comedy should be.
—Alison Palmer

It's been a long time since I've read a book that made me really laugh . . . While my heart had a soft spot for the characters who were trying their best to find love, the quirky little mishaps mingled within the story tickled my funny bone.—Christine Bryant

I highly recommend this book to anyone who needs a quick, lighthearted read that will make you laugh out loud. I think you'll enjoy it just as much as I did.—Tristi Pinkston, author of the Secret Sisters Mystery series

This was such a fun book! It kept me smiling and laughing throughout. For the first time in quite a while I stayed up late reading a book I didn't want to put down. . . . Just reading the title you know Charley's trying to win the wrong man through the help of the ridiculous Internet article. And yes the "right man" is so amazingly perfect he couldn't exist in real life, let alone live next door. But that's what makes this such a fun book.—Inspired Kathy

This was just too adorable not to love.—Heather

Marie Higgins has captured humor and romance in this delightful book. From start to finish one cannot wait to read what happens next with Charley and her love life. Laughter really is the best medicine for love!—Stacey

Praise for *Heart of a Hero*

I loved the unpredictable plot. The banter was priceless, making me smile and at times laugh out loud. I have a short attention span so the quick pace of adventure mingled with romance was just what the doctor ordered to kick me out of my humdrum week. By far my favorite thing about Heart of a Hero *was how much my* Wuthering Heights, *pirate adventure, sword-fighting addict of a daughter loved it. I've never seen her so alive about a book.So cheers to those who daydream on paper and double cheers to Marie Higgins for doing it well!*—Sheryl Johnson

Really great historical romance with a sassy heroine and a pesky hero. —Danyelle Ferguson

With many twists and turns in the plot of Heart of a Hero, *there is never a dull moment. For action, fun and frolic, romance and downright old-fashioned values, this book will not disappoint you.*—Coleen Bay

Sometimes you need a good clean romance novel to escape to! —Melissa

Loved Summer—she's spunky, sassy, and a lot of fun.—Brenda

This book has got adventure and romance that will keep you interested until the very end.—Leaffrog03

Praise for *Hearts through Time*

If you like time travel like I do with a beautiful female ghost from the past trying to solve her murder from 100 years ago, you'll love this romantic, suspense tale.—Teri

What do you get when you take a high-profile lawyer and an attractive ghost who has been waiting for just the right "solicitor" to come along for almost a hundred years? You get a romantic encounter filled with suspense and intrigue!— Theresa

I really loved the mystery aspect. . . . The author is quite skilled at drawing out the anticipation of how it's all going to end, and that alone makes it a book worth having. So, if you're looking for an entertaining afternoon read, Hearts through Time *is the novel for you.*—Julie

Squeaky clean, fun adventure in both the present and the past. Once the mystery starts to unfold, you can't close this book until you get your Happily Ever After.—Brenda

Hearts through Time *would definitely be a good one to add to the summer reading list or it would be great for anyone who just needs to escape the stresses of life and relax with a good book.*—Kay

I was taken with this book immediately. The cover is absolutely perfect for this book and so beautiful. I love romance, mystery, murders, time travel, haunting, and ghosts. Who could ask for more? . . . Once started, it was hard to put it down. I carried it all over the house with me and read it every chance I had. I recommend it as an excellent book. —Mary